D0104937

"We could have a midnight swim."

Nora leaned forward also and gave Liz's hand a squeeze, then held it. "I'd love to. But I can't leave them alone."

"No." Liz squeezed Nora's hand back. "I know. Of course you can't."

"Maybe sometime I can get Patty to stay with them for a couple of hours at night. Sometime before you go back. I'd like that."

"I'd like it, too." Liz said, stroking Nora's hand.

And then they both leaned forward a little more, till their faces were close together, and they kissed.

Visit

Bella Books

at

BellaBooks.com

or call our toll-free number
1-800-729-4992

BY
NANCY GARDEN

Bella
BOOKS
2002

Copyright© 2002 by Nancy Garden

Bella Books, Inc.
P.O. Box 10543
Tallahassee, FL 32302

All rights reserved. No part of this book may be reproduced or transmitted in any form or by any means, electronic or mechanical, including photocopying, without permission in writing from the publisher.

Printed in the United States of America on acid-free paper
First Edition
Second Printing March 2004

Cover designer: Bonnie Liss (Phoenix Graphics)

ISBN 1-931513-20-1

For Sandy, *my sine qua non*

And with thanks to Detective Nancy Iosue of the Carlisle, Massachusetts, Police Department, who advised me about procedural matters. Any errors are mine, not hers.

I

One

It was dim in the kitchen. The sun slanted through the window over the dark sink, picking up dust motes, but Nora Tillot did not allow herself to dwell for long on the joy of their dancing. As her hand curled around the green pump handle, sending a stream of cold water into the pitted aluminum kettle and then into the oversized iron pot, her motions were that of an old woman, slow, careful, deliberate. But at forty, Nora was hardly old, though her face was lined and her dark blond hair, caught up in a severe bun, showed streaks of gray.

She bent to pat the small black and white cat that was curling himself around her ankles, purring, and filled his dish with kibble from the box beside the sink. "There, Thomas," she said absently, "sweet kitty." She knelt in front of the iron cookstove to open the oven, and blew on the glowing coals till they flared. "Careful," she could remember her father saying authoritatively around the panatela clamped between his teeth. "Careful. You'll singe your hair."

Back then, her usual rejoinder on days when she felt defiant had been, "What about you with your infernal cigars?" But no one smoked any more in the old farmhouse whose clapboards were rotting and whose walls sagged inward, not Corinne, Nora's invalid mother, and certainly not her eighty-five-year-old father, semi-bedridden for years with what the doctor called "hypochondria, depression, and God knows what." Ralph Tillot was a disappointed, penny-pinching man who had never managed to make much of himself, despite the "friends in high places" of whom he had often bragged, sometimes at the expense of his one or two actual friends.

Nora lifted the kettle and the pot onto the stove, after opening two of its "burners" — holes that would be called burners, anyway, on a modern stove like the one Louise Brice, who took Nora to the grocery store on Fridays and to church on Sundays, kept saying Nora should buy despite her father's objections. "And electricity and plumbing and a telephone," Mrs. Brice said almost every week, chipping away at Nora's resolve to keep peace with her parents. "At least a telephone. It's not safe, dear, you alone in this firetrap of a house with two old people. What if your mother has another stroke?"

"Then I'll do what I did before," Nora had said doggedly last time. "Run to the neighbors' and call from there."

"That's a half-mile run," Louise Brice said dryly, "to the Lorens' house, and you're no athlete."

Nora turned back to the sink, smiling briefly at the memory as she let the cat out. She'd long since stopped explaining to Mrs. Brice and to the minister, the Reverend Charles Hastings, that the way she and her parents lived was, after all, not unlike the way many people had lived as recently as eighty or so years earlier, and certainly the way her father's forebears had lived when they'd built the house in the late

4

eighteenth century. People had managed then, so why not now? That was one of her father's arguments, and Nora, when she was challenged, borrowed it defensively, though when she let herself, she longed for electricity, a refrigerator instead of an ice box on the back stoop, an indoor bathroom instead of an outhouse, a furnace, a modern stove, a telephone.

Oh, especially a telephone, she thought, moving the pile of galley proofs — Nora proofread for pin money — away from the rusty canister under the window and spooning loose tea into the everyday brown pot. Mrs. Brice is right about that. And young Patty Monahan — Nora smiled to herself once more — who sat with her parents while Nora was at church or out shopping, had widened her eyes in obvious shock the first time she'd come, clearly more startled at the absence of a phone than at the lack of electricity and running water.

But Ralph wouldn't hear of it.

After her solitary cup of tea, sipped slowly at the scarred pine table opposite the sink while she watched the sun rise wearily over the woods that edged the back field, Nora enveloped her slender body in a huge coverall apron made of plain unbleached muslin, which she'd found was best for the bathing ritual. That involved pans and pitchers and basins of water, carried to her parents' bedsides along with sponges, washcloths ("flannels," Mama had called them before her stroke, as in English books), plus soap (pink geranium for Mama, tan sandalwood for Father), and towels. At least this task, the most odious of all, usually came early in the day.

Grimly, Nora smoothed down the apron, knotted it around her waist, and ladeled hot water from the steaming pot into a white enamel basin, then added cold via a saucepan carried from the sink pump. Draping a clean white towel and a blue "flannel" over her arm, and carefully balancing the basin plus the bowl into which she'd poured her father's shaving water, Nora went into Ralph's room off one end of the kitchen. Corinne's was off the opposite end, so both rooms were able to absorb some of the heat from the cookstove. Even in winter

5

Nora rarely lit its potbellied companion, isolated in the largely unused parlor; life in the Tillot household had always centered around the kitchen, and had done so almost exclusively since Nora's parents had entered old age.

"Morning, Father," Nora said cheerfully. "Want the urinal before your bath?"

Ralph Tillot, so far a lump under the threadbare green blanket and patched patchwork quilt (although it was warm for late May in Clarkston, Rhode Island), grunted noncommittally, so Nora unhooked the curved plastic bottle from the headboard and handed it to him.

"Umm," he grunted, taking it and sliding it under the covers.

"You're welcome," Nora said, and went to the window, pulling up the yellowing shade. It snapped out of her hand and flapped, making a whirring noise.

"Jesus Christ almighty," her father bellowed, holding the used urinal out to her. "Watch what you're doing, can't you?"

"Sorry," Nora said evenly. "It slipped right out of my hand."

"Well, watch that this doesn't slip, too," he growled, shoving the urinal at her. "No, wait," he said as she took it and turned away. "Any blood in it?"

"Blood?" Nora asked, surprised; this was a new worry.

"You heard me; blood. It's painful," he whined.

"What is?" Nora peered down the spout. She couldn't really see, but the urine seemed its normal early-morning color.

"Pissing."

"I'm sorry, Father." She stroked his arm briefly. "Want me to tell Dr. Cantor?"

Her father pulled himself up to a sitting position. "Is there blood?"

"Not that I can see."

"Well, let's keep an eye on it. Go ahead and dump it."

"I'll just put it here" — Nora hooked it over the back of a

6

chair — "till I finish your bath. Otherwise the water'll get cold."

Her father said something that sounded like "Erumph," so Nora, taking that for assent, unbuttoned his pajama top (he wore no bottoms), and slowly sponged him. He lay quietly, unmoving, as she passed the warm, dampened cloth over his flaccid body, till she told him to turn. The sheets were dry, thank God (he often wet the bed), so if she was careful she wouldn't have to change them or have the argument they frequently had about his wearing Depends at night, as did his eighty-two-year-old wife.

After she'd dried and powdered him, she shaved him, then laid out underwear, shirt, and pants. But he waved them away as he frequently did these days. "Not yet," he said, making kissing motions with his mouth. "Maybe later. You're a good girl, Nora. A nice girl. You take good care of your old father. I love you."

"I love you, too," she said automatically, grateful that all signs pointed to its being a calm day, at least as far as Ralph was concerned. "I'll bathe Mama and then I'll get your breakfast. Think about what you'd like."

"Just toast," he said as he always did. "And coffee."

"Coming right up," she said cheerfully. "After Mama's bath."

Giving him a little wave, she went back to the kitchen, dumped his bath and shaving water, and poured fresh for her mother. Too late, she remembered the urinal, so she poured her mother's water into the pot again and returned for the urinal.

"I feel dizzy," Ralph whined when she'd emptied and rinsed it, and brought it back.

So, she thought, it's not going to be a calm day after all. "Shall I get you a pill?" she asked. Dr. Cantor, a tall, mournful-looking man who had been the Tillots' doctor for as long as Nora could remember, had prescribed Dramamine for his dizzy spells. "Could be inactivity, could be a tumor, could be Parkinson's, could be an ear problem," he'd told her months earlier when the spells had started, his thin lips set in an exasperated line. "But since he won't go to the hospital for tests, we'll never know. At least the Dramamine won't hurt him."

"Yes, a pill," Ralph said, so Nora fetched the Dramamine and water, plus a flexible straw since he no longer was sitting.

"It's cold in here," he complained, after swallowing.

"I'll get you another blanket." Wearily, she fetched one from the chest in the hall.

Several demands later — window open, pillows rearranged, window shut, chair out of position, another bout with the urinal — she was finally able to go to her mother's room.

Corinne Tillot, a diminutive figure in a faded granny gown sprigged with roses, was snoring. Nora put one hand on her shoulder, patting it lightly. "Mama," she said softly. "Mama, bath time. It's a beautiful day," she went on, hoping she was right; it had seemed so, anyway, the little she'd seen of it.

"Goo' morn' — uh — dearie." Corinne opened a red-rimmed rheumy eye. Her voice seemed clear, though her speech, affected by the stroke she'd had three years earlier, was slurred and fuzzy.

"Father's had his bath." Cheerfully, Nora stripped off the covers and unbuttoned her mother's nightgown. "And Thomas is out." She removed the nightgown and the adult diaper her mother wore under it.

"Tom-ass?" A frown furrowed Corinne's forehead, deepening its wrinkles.

"You remember Thomas." Nora wet the flannel and wrung it out, applying soap. "The cat. He's chasing grasshoppers, I imagine."

"Izzat — all right?" Corinne asked anxiously.

"Yes, Mama, it's all right." Nora gently sponged her

8

mother's frail body, the shriveled pendulous breasts, the protruding belly.

"Nora, Nora," her mother cried, looking down at herself in alarm. "I haven't anything on!"

"It's all right, Mama. It's just you and me. No one's here to see."

"But I'm cold!" Corinne wailed, tears pooling in her eyes. "I'm cold!" She reached up, curling her good arm around Nora's neck in a scissors grip, burying her head in Nora's collar.

Damn, Nora thought, pulling the sheet up. "I'm sorry, Mama. You'll be all toasty warm in a moment. There." She added the blanket. "Better?"

Her mother nodded and closed her eyes.

Nora waited. When her mother was breathing evenly, she continued the bath, lifting the sheet and blanket a little at a time, and sponging her mother's body under it.

Then, quietly, she glided into the kitchen to make breakfast.

TWO

The motel coffee shop was grim, hardly deserving the name. Small formica-topped tables were set at angles to one another on a green linoleum floor that had seen better days. Once-colorful plastic chairs, rose and tan mostly, with a couple of dingy yellow ones thrown in, surrounded them, but they, along with the dusty plastic flowers on each table, failed to brighten the room. Fat glass coffee pots, one topped with brown plastic, the other with orange, steamed on a two-burner hotplate alongside baskets of hard-edged muffins, individual-serving-sized cold cereals, and overdone bagels. Smaller baskets held packets of sugar, Equal, and Sweet-and-Lo, along with plastic soufflé cups of half-and-half and envelopes of Cremora.

Liz Hardy tossed her jacket over one of the yellow chairs and poured coffee from the brown-topped pot into a chipped white mug. Well, she thought, doubtfully scanning the offered food and plopping a muffin — corn? "plain"? — onto a paper plate, what did you expect? You didn't exactly choose a five-star-er, kiddo!

Still, the bed had been comfortable enough, though she'd felt startled all over again at waking up without Megan beside her. Why, she'd wondered, for she had left Megan three months earlier; surely she should be used to her absence by now! Then she'd realized this was the first time she'd stayed in a motel without her. Not that they'd stayed in many motels in the seven years they'd been together, but a few — enough, I guess, Liz mused, to make it feel strange to be in one without her now.

She sat down, but the coffee was weak and the muffin she'd chosen was dry and tasteless, as if it were at least yesterday's, if not last week's. There didn't seem to be any butter, nor did there seem to be anyone to ask. "Shit," Liz muttered, fighting off an unexpected wave of grief and self-pity. She crushed the muffin in her fist and was hurling it into the trash can near the coffee pots when a man reeled sleepily into the room, heading for the counter. The muffin went in, but only because the man, grinning, ducked. "Two points," he said, lurching toward her, holding out his hand. "Mind if I join you?"

"Oh, stuff it," Liz barked, shoving her chair back and scuffling noisily to her feet.

Back in her dismal motel room she stood for a moment, fists clenched, in front of the window. The sun was already making the cars in the parking lot cast shadows on the asphalt, still damp here and there with last night's rain. Poor guy, she thought; it's not his fault I'm in a lousy mood.

Late the day before on the phone with Jeff, her brother, she had cried, and he'd said, "Don't go, Liz; don't do this. It's too soon," and she'd said, "If you don't want the house, I don't either. Too many memories."

"You mean memories of Megan," he'd said. "I wish she'd take you back."

"Well, she won't. Would you go back to someone who ditched you?" Megan was already with someone else anyway; she decided not to remind Jeff of that.

"No," Jeff had admitted, "but don't go to the house now, okay?"

The "house" was a cabin, really, a summer retreat Jeff and Liz had grown up in year after year, fishing and rowing and roaming the woods, playing cowboys and astronauts and spies. Even as adults, they'd visited it every summer, till five years ago when their mother had died of breast cancer. After that, their father had been too sad to go back, and when he'd died, recently, of a heart attack, Liz and Jeff had tentatively made plans to put the cabin on the market and split the money when it sold. But before it could be shown, Liz knew, it would need cleaning, and, now that school was almost out (Liz taught biology and physiology in a private school in Manhattan) and now that Megan was gone, she'd decided she might as well tackle that job and also actually meet the real estate agent she'd contacted by phone and e-mail. She'd taken the Thursday and Friday before the long Memorial Day weekend off from school so she could get started. And she'd left as planned despite Jeff's reservations, stopping overnight at the motel to avoid having to face five years' worth of dust and mouse leavings in the rain and the dark.

"I wish I could come and help," Jeff had said on the phone when she'd made it clear that she was going through with her plans.

"I wish you could, too." But she knew he couldn't. He'd

12

already taken two weeks when their father died, and she knew he wouldn't want to be away again from Susan, his wife, and Gus, their two-year-old son.

Liz turned away from the window and dabbed fiercely at the tears that had sprung to her eyes. She wheeled decisively, picked up her suitcase and backpack, and strode out through the lobby to her rental car.

A few minutes later, driving the speed limit on the highway toward Providence with the windows open and the wind blowing through her short dark brown hair, she felt better. I can do this, she told herself. I really, truly can do this. She had already learned in the three months since she'd left Megan that it was risky to think too much about the future, to worry about spending the rest of her life alone, or about turning into "a dried-up old schoolteacher," a hackneyed phrase one of her colleagues liked to use. When Dad had died, Megan had called, all sympathy and warmth, and Liz had wanted to ask her to come back. But Megan was already with Janey by then, had moved in with her a scant six weeks after the night when Liz had said, as kindly as possible, "Meggie, it's not working; it's just not working with us."

What I meant, Liz thought now, forcing her mind to jump beyond the memory of Megan's astonished tears, was that I couldn't do it, couldn't let myself be one-half of a permanent couple.

"Couldn't let yourself take the risk," Jeff had said when she'd told him. "You have to take risks, Lizzie, in love. Susan taught me that. It's like that song, you know, that Bette Midler song, 'The Rose.' "

Liz had played the song and denied that she fit any of its lines, but now, as the car crossed into Rhode Island and a

13

sudden traffic pocket roared and whirred around her, she found she was grateful that she had to concentrate on staying alive instead of on the memories that crowded her mind.

But once she was through the city and driving more slowly on suburban streets that soon thinned and gave way to narrow country roads and sleepy, ill-kept towns, the memories crowded back. It didn't seem as if five years had passed since she'd driven out to the lakeside cabin. No one's ever believed in paint in this state, she thought fondly, passing familiar shabby houses and smiling at old landmarks: Genovese's Bakery, Blue Seal Feeds, The New York Department Store, the white clapboard church with the stone front, Casey's Pharmacy and Drug . . .

And Bob's Tackle Shop, where she and Dad and Jeffie had pored for hours over lures and flies, next to Acme Sporting Goods, where they'd bought baseballs and where Dad had bought her a fielder's mitt — and then, outside of town, the rutted dirt road leading to the farm where the crazy people lived without electricity or running water — and at last, the hill . . .

There was a sudden crunching sound and the car bumped rhythmically on one side as if one wheel had turned square, the unmistakable sound of a flat.

"Damn!"

Liz pulled onto the shoulder. The road was deserted and she knew it was miles to the nearest service station that offered more than gas and candy bars. Sighing, she got out. Yes, it was the right front tire, but that's okay, she told herself; there's got to be a spare, you know how to change a tire, just get the damn jack and stuff out of the trunk.

But although there was a full-sized spare, there was no jack, no tire iron, no wrenches, no tools of any kind, and she kicked herself "three ways to Sunday," as her father had often said, for not checking before she'd driven the car away from the rental place.

14

The old farm, she thought; the crazy people will have a jack. Farm people always have tools.

Besides — she slung her backpack over her shoulder — maybe it's just a rumor that they don't have electricity or water.

God, she thought, as she trudged back to the farm's road, I hope they haven't died or moved away or anything like that!

THREE

The knock at the door was louder the second time.

"What's that?" Ralph bellowed from his room.

Nora, in the kitchen putting the finishing touches on lunch, wiped her hands wearily on her apron, then took it off and draped it over a chair. "Someone's at the door, I think."

"Don't answer it."

"Why on earth not?" Nora said, rolling her eyes. Lately she'd been doing that, indulging in little childish expressions of disgust or anger.

"Because you never know who it might be. Some jerk, wanting money."

Nora stuck her head into her father's room. "Don't be silly. It's probably Mrs. Brice or Mr. Hastings."

"Or the doctor," her father said suspiciously, swinging his legs clumsily over the side of the bed. "Did you call him? Your mother's worse, isn't she?"

"No, Father, no," Nora crooned, going into the room as the knock came again, a volley this time, increasingly determined. She bent, lifting his legs up and attempting to swing them back.

Her father kicked her, hard. "Don't do that!" he shouted, struggling to his feet while she stepped back, shocked, rubbing her jaw where his foot had caught her. He'd never done that before.

"Ouch," she said deliberately, accusingly. "That hurt."

"Well, get out of my way. Someone's got to protect this place." Reeling, her father stood, the pajama bottoms she'd put on him after his bath slipping below his waist, barely covering his groin.

Suppressing a desire to laugh, Nora hiked them up. "Coming!" she called as the knocks sounded again. She attempted to slide out the doorway, but Ralph gripped her shoulder. His gait was slow, shuffling, worse, she realized, than the last time he'd walked unaided. When had that been? Three weeks ago, maybe, when the drugstore boy had come and Father was sure the pharmacist had overcharged for his and Corinne's medicine.

Nora put her left arm around his waist and held his near shoulder with her right hand. Shuffling and reeling, they moved slowly to the dark front hall and the door, which was now silent. "The person probably left," Nora said, accusingly again.

"Good riddance," Ralph grumbled. "I told you not to answer it."

Nora opened the door. Pale gray light illuminated the hall, falling on a blue and white porcelain bowl and showing the scratches in the dark finish of the table on which it stood. A small woman stood outside, half turned away as if she had, indeed, begun to leave. Her hair, dark brown and windblown,

17

was a mass of short curls that capped her head and her face was pleasant enough, though obviously stressed.

"Sorry to bother you," the woman said, looking as if she was trying not to stare. What a picture we must make, Nora thought, Father and I! "My car had a flat out on the main road. I remembered your house was here and I wondered if I could borrow a jack. It's a rental car; there isn't one in it."

"Why, I — a what?" Nora sputtered.

"What's your name?" Ralph asked belligerently. "You're not from around here, are you?"

"Liz Hardy," the woman answered pleasantly. "Elizabeth. No, I'm not really *from* around here, but my family has a cabin on Yellowfin Lake. I was just going out there when . . ."

"I know those cabins. Summer people." Ralph studied Liz suspiciously; Nora turned away in embarrassment. "It's not summer yet."

"No," Liz said; she sounded tired. "Not quite. But my father died recently and I want to clean up the cabin so I can sell it. I've taken a little time off from work to do that. Look, I'm really sorry to intrude. If you do have a jack . . ."

"Might, might not. As you can see, I'm ill. Can't change your tire. You'd better go to the gas station."

"That's okay, I don't need help. I can change it myself. But if you don't have a jack, maybe I could call a neighbor, see if someone else nearby has one?"

Nora finally recovered enough to speak. "We don't have a phone." She stepped between Liz and her father; the woman looked harmless enough; nice, even. "But there's an old car in the barn. I'm not absolutely sure what a jack looks like, though."

Liz quickly hid her astonishment. "It's sort of an accordion-pleated pump for lifting part of a car up so you can change a tire," she explained. "Metal. Most cars come with them. They usually come with sort of wrench things, too, for removing the nuts." Her eyes turned mirthful, and Nora could see that she was suppressing a laugh.

Nora herself felt inclined to giggle, then wondered if she should have felt angry instead. *Removing the nuts,* she thought; if she's spent summers here, she'll know the rumors.

Ralph growled stormily. "Dunno if there's a jack in that old car. Nora, go with her to look. Stay with her," he added, barely under his breath. He gripped the edge of the door, turning. "Dizzy. Have to lie down."

"I'll help you, Father." Quickly, Nora tightened her hold on his arm. "Barn's out back," she said over her shoulder to Liz. "You can't miss it, as they say. I'll be out in a minute."

"Thanks," Liz called, watching as Nora steered her father down the hall. Odd pair, she thought; poor woman, wonder why she stays with him. But maybe she doesn't; maybe she just comes in to help. Then, shrugging, she went out and followed the house's perimeter to the back yard, examining it as she went. The walls sagged inward, the little remaining paint was peeling off the worn clapboards, and there were signs of rot around the windows. She must be my age, Liz thought, that woman. Or older. Not to know what a jack is, living in the country! Maybe she's not very bright.

Or not very worldly, if she's stuck living here with the old man.

The barn sagged also, its once-red boards warped and collapsing into each other. There was no door, just an opening edged with a few rusty hinges. A small black and white cat, lying on its side in the sun, scrambled to its feet as Liz approached, arching its back as if afraid or angry.

"Nice puss," Liz said quietly. "It's okay. I won't hurt you." She knelt and held out her hand.

The cat crept closer, sniffing, then rubbed against her.

"Good, you've met Thomas." The woman approached and squatted next to Liz, her fading housedress bunched between her knees. "He doesn't get much company." She smiled, her weary face becoming almost attractive. It's her eyes, Liz thought as Nora held out her hand. They were blue with green flecks, friendly and sad.

19

"I'm Nora Tillot," Nora said. "That was my father inside. He's — well, he's a lot of things."

Liz, smiling back, took the offered hand; it was rough and workworn, with a crack across one knuckle and nails cut straight across; nurse's nails. "I could see that." She smiled.

"He's also very old-fashioned. Crusty. Suspicious." She stood; Thomas curled around her legs. "Well, you want the car. Here."

She led Liz into the shadowy barn; it smelled of well-rotted manure, stale hay, and mildew.

"It's back here near the tractor. I doubt that it runs. No one's used it for twenty-five years."

Next to a rusty John Deere was an ancient Ford sedan, its black paint surprisingly intact.

"Someone took good care of it, though," Liz said, running her hand over the car's side.

"Yes, Father was quite fanatic about it. Even long ago when he used it for work and to take my mother and me for Sunday drives, he always kept it inside, and he polished it a lot."

"More than the tractor, I see."

"Oh, that. He was never much of a farmer. He wanted to be, but he was really a salesman. Farming was just a dream."

"But everyone called this 'the old Tillot farm,' " Liz said. "When I was little.

"Yes, I know they did. That was nice of them, I guess. I think they also said the crazies lived here."

"That, too." Liz smiled again. "But you don't seem crazy."

"No." Nora walked rapidly to the rear of the car. "Might the jack be in the trunk?"

"Probably."

Nora opened the trunk. It was empty except for something wrapped in what looked like an old towel. "Could this be it?"

"It could. Let's see. May I?"

"Yes. I'm really not sure what I'm looking for."

"You don't drive, then?" Liz unwrapped the lumpy package, revealing a jack, a tire iron, and a tool set. Perfect. "Perfect," she said aloud.

"No. Father doesn't approve of women driving."

Liz paused, her hand on the tools. "But how . . . ?"

"How do we manage? We do, that's all. People are kind."

"You live here, then?"

"Yes."

"Wow! It must be hard, without a car, I mean. And without a phone. Grocery shopping, doctors, emergencies."

"A woman from church helps. So does a girl from the village. The doctor and a visiting nurse come here. The only bad time was my mother's stroke. I had to run to the neighbors'. And if you know the, um, the area, you know that's not very near."

"Yes. It must be at least half a mile to the next house." More words crowded Liz's mind, but she bit them back. "You've been very kind. Thank you." She shifted the tools, rewrapping them and balancing the package on her hip. "Could I ask one more favor?"

"Of course."

"Could I just use the bathroom before I go? I know it's an intrusion, letting a stranger use something so private, but . . ."

Nora looked amused, even mischievous. "Oh, ours isn't very private. It's just to the left of the barn. You can't miss it. A little red house with a . . ."

". . . half moon cut in the door?" Liz laughed.

"Right."

"I'll be back in a second, then." Liz set the tools down in the trunk again.

Nora watched her go, watched the smooth way she walked, confident and slender inside her close-fitting blue jeans and her aqua polo shirt, obviously comfortable in her body, as Nora was not in hers, and self-possessed, too, holding some of herself back. Dignified, Nora decided; that's it, and able to move about in the world, changing tires. She's nice, she

21

thought with a pang. Friendly and nice. She'd make a good friend, maybe.

And she's pretty.

Thomas mewed and jumped up into the trunk. "Careful!" Nora picked him up and snuggled her cheek against his silky fur. "You don't want to get shut up in there."

"That's the nicest outhouse I ever was in," Liz said a few minutes later, coming back into the barn. "All the ones I've been in before smelled."

"It's the lime," Nora said. "You did . . . ?"

Liz nodded. "Yes. I saw the little box and shovel and when I looked in the box, I realized what it was for." She chuckled. "Some dim memory or other that I can't place. Maybe my grandfather's house. Or maybe the cabin, when Jeff — that's my brother — and I were really little. There was a while when we didn't have plumbing either."

"It must be nice to have a brother."

"It is. We were always pretty close. We fought, but not as much as most kids. Are you an only?"

"An only? Oh, an only child? Yes."

"So you live here" — Liz looked back toward the house — "without a phone or a car or indoor plumbing, taking care of your elderly father."

"And mother," Nora said.

"And mother." Liz found she was shaking her head and stopped, not wanting to seem rude. "I admire you," she said. That's true, she thought, but pity's true, too.

"It's not so bad. People lived this way eighty years ago," she added automatically, "so why not now?"

"That sounds as if you've said it before."

"I have," Nora admitted. "Many times."

"It must get annoying, having to defend your way of living."

"My father's way," Nora said carefully. "Mama and I, well, we'd choose something different."

"You would?"

22

Nora hesitated; she'd never said it aloud, despite thinking it with increasing frequency. "Sometimes," she said carefully, "I imagine what it would be like to have just one of the things we don't have. Some days I think of plumbing and every time I pump water or go to the outhouse or heat water for washing, I imagine having shiny chrome faucets that send out streams of hot or cold water. Other times, but this is harder, I imagine what it would be like to have electricity." Nora stopped; her game must seem silly.

"It must be awful, not having that. Everything's electrical."

"Yes. But when there's a bad storm and Mrs. Brice — she's the lady who takes me to the store and to church — when Mrs. Brice tells me there's been a power failure, I realize how well off we really are. I don't have to change anything I do. So you see in a way my father's right: it's better without all the modern conveniences. And I like the quiet, the simplicity, I guess you could call it. The world outside, the little I know of it, seems too busy sometimes. Too full of *things,* too." Nora brushed a wisp of graying hair off her forehead.

"You are a truly amazing person," Liz said.

Nora regarded her, her head cocked to one side, a slight smile playing about her lips. "Am I?" she asked softly.

"Yes. Yes, you are."

For a moment they looked at each other, and Liz felt as if the blue-green eyes that gravely held her own were considering her, examining her; probing, even.

"Well . . ." Liz turned toward the trunk, breaking the somewhat discomfiting connection. "I'd better be going. I'll bring the tools back when I'm done."

"No hurry," said Nora. "You must be anxious to get to your cabin. I don't need them, obviously." She cuddled Thomas, still in her arms, then put him down.

Liz hesitated; maybe she should hold onto them for a while. The road to the cabin was bound to be in bad shape, and the spare hadn't looked exactly new. "Thank you," she said finally. "I could drop them off on my way back Monday night or even Sunday; I may leave then. And maybe there's a jack at the cabin that I can take for the trip back in case another of those tires goes. We've got tons of old stuff in the shed, stuff we thought we might need. You know how it is."

"Oh, yes," Nora said emphatically. "Indeed I do. Keep the tools as long as you like, forever if you want." She held out her hand. "It was nice meeting you," she said formally. "I'm glad we could help."

"Nice meeting you, too." Liz lifted the bundle of tools, uncomfortable at being equally formal. "And thank you."

They stood awkwardly facing each other.

"Well." Liz turned, feeling she was breaking the connection again. "See you!"

"Right," Nora answered. "See you." She echoed Liz awkwardly, as if she'd never used the expression.

But she waved as Liz rounded the corner of the house. Then she picked up her cat and went inside.

FOUR

Liz felt her throat tighten as she turned down the dirt driveway that snaked through the woods toward the cabin for more than a quarter of a mile. She had changed the tire without difficulty and driven to a proper service station, where she'd had the puncture patched. Then, deciding not to count on there being a jack at the cabin after all, she'd bought a cheap one at the village hardware store along with the necessary tools.

I will not cry, she said to herself now, ducking instinctively but unnecessarily as the car's roof slapped low-hanging branches and bounced in and out of ruts. I will not.

But she did anyway, a little, when she saw the old sign fastened to the big white pine where the drive curved as it approached the cabin. The words PINEY HAVEN, carved deeply into the wood by her father, were still legible, though the black paint that she and Jeff, tongues protruding between teeth and foreheads scowling in concentration, had painstakingly taken turns laying into the gouged-out letters, had largely worn away. Moss flaked onto Liz's fingers from the edges of the sign when she gave in to an overwhelming impulse to get out of the car and touch it. Then, giving in to an even stronger impulse, she unhooked the sign from its nails.

"Hello!"

Liz turned, startled and angry; trespassers already?

"Yes?" she said curtly as a snappily dressed middle-aged woman, her dyed blonde hair carefully coiffed, appeared around the curve. "May I help you? This is private property, you know."

The woman gave Liz a sympathetic, lipsticked smile. "Yes, I do know. I was about to say the same to you. I'm Georgia Foley, the real estate agent handling this property. That sign belongs to the owner; you need to put it back. You are . . . ?"

"The owner. Elizabeth Hardy," Liz told her with a certain relish.

The woman clapped a well-manicured hand to her head. "Oh, my God! Open mouth, insert foot, right?" She stuck her hand out. "Of course! Can you forgive me, Elizabeth?"

"Liz." Liz smiled thinly as she shook Georgia Foley's hand; it was very soft, the opposite of Nora's, she found herself thinking. "Sure. I didn't tell you exactly when I was coming. But what . . . ?"

"I thought if I was going to handle the property I should take a look at it. You'll be glad to know I already have an interested buyer! And I was curious to see at least the grounds before you came. What a lovely spot!" Georgia scanned the dense woods as if she were surveying a vast plain. "The lake fairly sparkles! I wish I'd brought my bathing suit. Of course the house does need work; I wanted to check that as well, since you said it hasn't been used in a while."

"Five years," Liz said. "Since the summer before my mother died."

"Oh, dear, I'm sorry. Have you not been here since? I mean, if so, then it must be difficult."

"It *is* difficult." Liz wished she could make herself stop sounding stiff, but really, this woman was so impossibly silly it was hard to avoid. "But I might as well show you the inside, since we're both here." She strode to her car and opened the passenger door. "Hop in."

Georgia hesitated. "Oh, but there's no need," she said. "I mean it's only a few steps!"

Liz shrugged, then smiled again, still holding the door.

Georgia glanced at her, and then, her manner almost frightened, got in. "I do like that sign," she said when Liz settled beside her and turned the key in the ignition. "Original but recognizable. I mean, most people would have called it Pine Haven, you know? 'Piney' is a nice touch, I think. I hope I'll be able to persuade you to leave the sign here for a while; I think it'll help sell the place. It provides a nice rustic flavor."

"I doubt it," Liz said, gritting her teeth.

"That it's a rustic touch? Well, the name, I mean, and the wood and all."

"I doubt I'll leave it here." Liz rounded the curve and pulled the car up behind Georgia's, which was a red Dodge convertible. Why am I not surprised at what she drives, she thought.

Aloud, she said stiffly, "My mother thought of the name. My father carved the sign and my brother and I painted it. He was six and I was eight. So I think I'll be taking it with me. There may be other things I'll take as well." She opened her door.

"Why, yes, of course!" Georgia scrambled out. "Sentimental value; I do understand. And it is your place, after all, isn't it, till I sell it."

If you sell it, Liz thought, but did not say. As they walked, her eyes went to the roof, where she could see several loose shingles among the large moss islands that were trimmed with twigs and one or two medium-sized branches.

"Yes, I'm afraid the roof may need a little work, beyond cleaning it up," Georgia said, following her gaze. "The, er, siding, too."

Liz nodded. The brown stain on the board-and-batten outer walls could use renewing and some of the battens had pulled out; there were probably rusty nail holes.

"I can't decide," Georgia said as they went up the field-stone path to the granite slab that formed the front stoop, "if it would be better to leave these stones as is or scrub the moss off. What do you think?"

"Leave them as is," Liz said gruffly. "In fact" — she turned, her key already poised to open the door — "I'd like to be the one to decide what to leave and what to change."

"Yes, of course." Georgia cast her eyes down, subdued. "I didn't mean . . ."

"Ms. Foley," Liz began, "I . . ."

"Georgia, please. And I *am* sorry. I know this must be hard for you. Why don't I leave and come back another time? Will you be in town for a few days?"

"Yes," Liz said, but she realized she wanted to get showing the house to Georgia over with as soon as possible. "I will. But you might as well come in now, since you're here. I'll be staying on afterward by myself, though. I could call you later to discuss repairs."

"Certainly. But, oh, dear, I do feel I'm intruding!"

"And," Liz made herself admit magnanimously, "I feel I've been rude." She forced a smile. "Let's start again, shall we?" She held out her hand. "Hi. I'm Liz Hardy. It's so nice to meet you, to put a face to the voice on the phone."

"Ditto, ditto!" Georgia seized Liz's hand heartily, with more strength this time, and pumped it vigorously. "What a charming place this is! I just know someone's going to love it and snatch it right up. In fact, as I said, someone's already interested, a nice man, a teacher like you, as it happens."

Liz gave her what she hoped was a dazzling smile and unlocked the front door.

The odor of five years' worth of dust, mouse droppings, and cobwebs assailed her nostrils, shot through with the unmistakable stench of decaying animal flesh. Liz, with a quick glance at the stained yellowish linoleum on the kitchen floor (for the "front" door opened into the kitchen), went rapidly through to the living room/dining room and without thinking turned to the fieldstone fireplace, for that was where the bodies usually were. Squirrels came down the chimney and then couldn't get out again. Sometimes they chewed at the windowsills and died there, but this one hadn't; she spotted the limp body immediately, near several small skeletons that were nestled in what was left of their rotting gray fur.

"I'll just clean these up," she said, brushing back past Georgia into the kitchen, where she took the metal dustpan and its cobwebby black brush from their hook behind the door along with a plastic bag (later she was surprised there still were some) from the squeaky drawer under one end of the sink counter. Stooping, she swept up the squirrel leavings. It was only after she'd put the bag outside that she noticed Georgia hadn't moved and that there was a look of frozen horror on her face.

"It's all right," Liz said, suddenly sorry for her. "After spending every summer here as a kid I'm kind of used to country messes. My dad used to pay me and my brother a quarter for each mouse body and fifty cents for each squirrel every spring when we opened up. Well," she went on, throwing her arms expansively out from her sides, surprised to find that cleaning up the squirrel bodies had cheered her, "this is it!"

Georgia swallowed hard, as if fighting nausea, and moved quickly to the bank of windows that lined the wall facing the lake. "What a marvelous view!"

"Yes, isn't it? Although it needs clearing, a bit." Every year she and Dad, and later Jeff as well, had snipped and pruned and trimmed while Mom watched from inside the house, directing them, warning them not to cut too much, battling good-naturedly with Dad's desire to have a clear, unobstructed view to the lake. Mom wanted the cabin to remain "nestled in the trees," as she put it, "camouflaged by them. Our own tree house." That had been Dad's suggestion for a name: The Tree House. But Liz and Jeff had held out for Mom's suggestion of Piney Haven, and Dad had agreed, saying that way, if he carved the sign and Liz and Jeff did the painting, they'd each have had a share in it.

"There are three more rooms off this one," Liz said, turning abruptly away from the windows and opening the doors that led off the big central room where she'd spent the rainy summer days of her childhood, building castles and railroad stations with the blocks that were still in their box in the corner by the fireplace, drawing or coloring, working endless picture puzzles, playing Monopoly with Jeff, and reading all of Nancy Drew and every baseball book she could find in the small library in the village. "They're small, but there are a couple of rooms upstairs as well. I guess the house would be good for a fairly big family or for people who have a lot of guests. Or maybe for someone who wants a small playroom and a downstairs study or computer room or something."

Nodding palely, Georgia peered into each of the three rooms, Liz's room, Jeff's, and the guest room, while Liz made mental notes of the acorn shells on the window sills and bureaus, the mouse droppings on the yellowed newspapers that covered the bare mattresses, the grime and cobwebs clinging to the brightly painted chairs. Mom had decorated most of the cabin's simple wooden furniture, painting one

30

downstairs room's yellow, another's blue, and the third one's green.

"Charming furniture," said Georgia, and Liz, sad again and aching for her parents, replied simply, "Thank you. Come on upstairs. Watch your head as we go up. The ceiling's low on the landing."

The two rooms above were larger. A ceramic vase that Jeff had made in middle school, still sporting a dusty bouquet of faded dried flowers, graced the large lavender bureau in their parents' room. And in the other room, Dad's huge desk, stripped at the end of the last summer they were there of the papers and books with which it had usually been strewn, sat regally in its place under the window — which, Liz saw, had somehow cracked open. A large water stain discolored the wall nearby. Liz tugged the window closed, trying not to picture her father slumped at his desk back in New York, ten blocks from her own apartment, where she'd found him after his heart attack.

"It's a shame about that stain," Georgia said softly.

"Yes. The window needs fixing."

"I know a good carpenter." Georgia rummaged in her large handbag. She held out a card. "Here."

"Thank you," Liz said, pocketing it. "I guess I may need one." But she'd already decided to tackle the window herself.

"And of course," Georgia went on as Liz led her to the bathroom, "you can add the cost of any repairs to your asking price. Nice big bathroom," she said approvingly, looking in. "I do so like a sunny one. That makes all the difference, sometimes. Clients are fussy about kitchens and baths especially, you know. And what a quaint tub!"

"Yes, isn't it?" Liz remembered their deciding, the summer before Mom's cancer diagnosis, to redo the bath. Mom insisted on buying an old-fashioned tub. "With claw feet," she'd said, "like a big friendly hippo one can bathe in."

"Hippos don't have claw feet," Jeff had said, and Mom had

31

winked at Liz, saying, "My hippos do." The hand-painted sign, "MOM'S HIPPO," still hung over the tub. Georgia looked at it curiously, but didn't mention it.

"Well, that's about it," Liz said briskly. "I'd offer you coffee or something but I doubt there's any here. And if there is, it'll be five years old. Besides, even though I've had the pump re-installed, the water's not on yet."

"That's all right." Georgia started down the stairs. "You'll be turning the water on soon, though, won't you, if you're staying here? And cleaning? Or having someone clean? I can recommend someone." She fished in her bag again, but Liz stopped her.

"No, that's okay. I'd just as soon see to that myself."

Georgia nodded. "Maybe you could leave the water on after you leave, so it'll be on when I come back with clients? People want to see the oddest things. In summer camps especially." They were at the foot of the stairs now. "Is the phone working?" she asked. "I'll just give my office a call if it is, tell them I'm on my way. I've got a showing in about half an hour. I forgot my cell phone, stupidly."

Without reason or warning, Liz felt overwhelmed with sadness. "It should be," she managed to answer. "I called the phone company from New York and asked to have it turned on." She went to the wall phone in the kitchen, lifted it, then handed it to Georgia. "Yes."

While Georgia was chirping into the phone, Liz went into the living room and leaned her head against the cold stone of the fireplace. "Mom," she whispered. "Dad. How can I sell our Piney Haven?"

FIVE

Noontime rain sluiced past the kitchen window and spattered on the sill, splashing drops against the glass. It was dark enough for a lamp, and Nora, reading poetry earlier — she was taking a correspondence course in writing it — had huddled close to the kerosene lamp, but had blown it out when she'd finished making lunch and before she'd helped her parents to the table. "Waste of good kerosene," her father would have barked if he'd seen that she'd lit a lamp during the day; the light wasn't worth his anger.

Now his soup bowl was nearly empty; as soon as she'd seen the rain, Nora had thought clam chowder would be a good idea for lunch. That was one of Ralph's favorites as long as it wasn't tomato-based, and he'd slurped it eagerly, ignoring the milky liquid that dribbled down his chin, while Nora spooned chowder carefully into her mother's mouth. Corinne seemed vague today, more so than usual, and although she often wanted to feed herself, today she sat slumped docilely in her wheelchair, both arms instead of just the one hanging uselessly by her side.

"You've got dribbles," Nora said to her father when he'd taken the last spoonful.

Grunting, he dabbed ineffectively at his chin.

"No, down more," she told him, and then, laughing, took the napkin from him and mopped up the mess. Quickly finishing her own chowder, she took the bowls to the sink and removed the shopping list from its place on the bulletin board over the table.

"Let me see that," her father said.

She handed it to him and he peered at it in the dim light while she pumped water into the bowls. Corinne began humming tunelessly.

"What're you singing, Mama?" Nora asked fondly, returning to the table. " 'Alice Blue Gown' " or 'Down By the Old Mill Stream'?" Both were songs Nora knew Ralph had often sung to her; lately, Corinne had been reminiscing about the early days of their marriage. She and Ralph had both been in their forties when they'd met and married, but according to Corinne, Ralph had courted her as ardently as any twenty-year-old. He was still affectionate to her, inadvertently reminding Nora that he'd often been loving and fun to be with when she herself had been a small child, before whatever disappointment, fear, or anger that had changed him had taken over. Nora had always meant to ask her mother if she knew what had embittered him, but hadn't wanted to open old wounds, if wounds there were. And now, of course, it was too late.

" 'Millstream'," Corinne mumbled with a crooked smile that sent a slow string of spittle down her chin.

34

" 'Down by the old mill stream,' " Nora sang softly, carefully wiping her mother's mouth, " 'where I first met you . . .' "

" 'With your eyes of blue,' " Ralph joined in noisily, " 'dressed in gingham too . . .' " Here he reached out, smiling, toward his wife, whose hands, however, were still at her sides. He patted the table in front of her instead, keeping time. " 'It was there I knew, that you loved me true . . .' "

They all three sang the rest of the song, more or less lustily, and after the last line, Ralph, with a rare burst of his former spark, grinned mischievously as he used to do and added under his breath, "Without a shirt."

Nora laughed.

But Ralph turned back to the shopping list. "Don't need butter, do we?" he asked.

"I'm afraid we do," Nora told him. "We've only got a quarter of a pound left."

"Let me see."

"Father!"

"Daughter! Let me see."

Sighing, Nora went outside to the back stoop against whose far edge the rain was splashing down off the roof and making puddles in front of the adjacent woodshed; she took the butter out of the ice box.

Ralph eyed it suspiciously when she handed it to him. "You didn't take some out of the package, did you, to fool me?"

"No, Father, of course not."

"All right. But we don't need so much meat. You have three things down here. Hamburger. Chicken. Lamb. We don't need all that. We're not made of money, you know."

"Mrs. Brice told me there are sales this week," Nora said evenly. "I thought we should take advantage of them."

"A sale is never an excuse to buy what you don't need. Meat doesn't keep that long. You know that."

Nora sat down at the table again. "Father, Mrs. Brice has

offered to let me use part of her freezer. That way I can take advantage of sales and freeze meat to use later. It'll save money in the long run. I could even freeze vegetables from the garden."

"What's wrong with canning? Your mother canned for years. Louise Brice is an interfering old bitch."

Nora swallowed her temper with difficulty. "Freezing's quicker and the food tastes better," she said quietly.

"Ha! And Mrs. Brice will want some of what you freeze to pay for the use of the freezer."

"No, she won't, Father. She even said she wouldn't."

"Nothing's free in this life, Nora. You're old enough to know that. She'll want something."

"The more food that's in a freezer, she says, the better it works. It uses less electricity because it stays colder. So we'd be doing her a favor."

"No. I won't be beholden to anyone. It's bad enough she has to take you to the store and to church."

"If you'd let me drive," Norah retorted, noticing that Corinne's eyes and head were swaying from one of them to the other, "she wouldn't have to."

"Driving's not for women," Ralph said illogically.

"Plenty of women drive. Patty Monahan drives and she's only eighteen, still just a girl. In fact, I'm probably the only woman my age who doesn't."

A moan from Corinne stopped both of them. "Don't," she pleaded. "Don't."

Nora got up and hugged her. "I'm sorry, Mama. We both are. Aren't we, Father?" She glared at him.

He grunted, then said, "Just because that woman who was here yesterday about the tire — just because she drives doesn't mean you have to. Look what happened to her any- way."

Nora laughed, hard. She knew she was on the edge of

losing control, but she let the laugh go anyway. "Men have flat tires, too, Father."

"Men don't let tires get to that point."

"I imagine any tire can go flat if you run over something. A nail, glass . . ."

"Men have the right things in their cars."

"She had a rented car."

"What do you care, Nora? She's nothing to you. Is she?"

"Of course not," Nora said. "I never saw her before in my life, and I'll probably never see her again."

"Did she return the jack?"

Nora stared at him. "No." To her surprise, she felt a smile spread over her face. "No, as a matter of fact, I told her not to hurry to return it."

"Hah! Probably three states away from here by now. We'll kiss that jack goodbye." He wagged his finger at her. "It doesn't pay to lend things. You can't trust people these days. There's the front door again. Don't answer it."

But Nora was already up. "It'll be Mrs. Brice," she said, "with the nurse."

"Look out the window to make sure. It might be that woman again."

Nora turned, hands on hips. "Oh? Does that mean you don't want the jack if she brings it back?"

"It means I don't want strangers here. If it's her, don't answer. If she's brought the jack, she'll leave it in the yard."

I may go mad, Nora thought as she went to the door. I may scream soon. I may just walk out of here and never come back.

But I can't leave Mama.

She did not look out the window, and she opened the door to Louise Brice, a stout church-going woman wearing a sensible black raincoat, and Ms. Sarah Cassidy, Visiting Nurse, in a dark blue dress covered with a yellow poncho, over which

37

tumbled quantities of wavy red hair that spewed out from under a wide-brimmed yellow sou'wester. She carried a small black bag.

"Hello, Nora, dear," Louise Brice said brightly. "Isn't this rain something?" She wiped her plastic-overshoe-clad feet on the worn sisal doormat, leaving streaks of mud from, Nora realized, what was left of the washed-out front path.

"Come on in out of it," said Nora, "while I get my coat. Hi, Sarah."

"How are they today?" Sarah Cassidy shucked off her poncho and sou'wester and held them uncertainly with two fingers while, dog-like, she shook out her hair. "Where . . . ?"

"Oh, anywhere," said Nora feigning a gaiety she didn't feel. "What are front halls for if not for rain and mud?" She hung Sarah's things on the rack beside the hall table.

"There's plenty of both," said Louise, opening and flapping her raincoat. That action stretched the jacket of her new-looking light green suit across her ample bosom, threatening the grasp of several buttons. She untied the clear plastic kerchief that covered her limply curled gray hair and shook it vigorously over the doormat before hanging it and her coat next to Sarah's. "But April showers bring May flowers."

"Of course," Sarah whispered to Nora as all three women went through to the kitchen, and Nora handed Sarah a towel for her hair, "it's already May. Thanks." Sarah shook out the towel, then rubbed her hair briskly before bundling it into a net that she took out of her pocket. "Any change?"

"Not really," Nora whispered back; they were still in the doorway. "Father's argumentative and Mama's a bit vaguer than usual, but I don't think there's anything special wrong. We had a visitor yesterday; maybe that tired them, although Mama didn't see her."

"A visitor?" Louise asked with interest as she moved into the room. Smiling at Ralph and Corinne, she raised her voice several decibels and caroled, "Hello, all, how are we today? Was it a nice visitor, the one you had yesterday?"

"Some woman had car trouble," Ralph grumbled. "I think my blood pressure's gone up." He held his arm out to Sarah.

"We'll just see." As Sarah whipped out her equipment, she looked toward Corinne, who hadn't acknowledged her presence; she seemed asleep. "Hello, Mrs. Tillot," she shouted. "How are you today?" She wrapped the cuff around Ralph's arm, pumped it, and applied the stethoscope. "I hear you had a visitor yesterday."

"How can you hear through that thing if everyone's yelling?" Ralph said, shouting himself. "Let's have a little quiet."

Nora had already taken her raincoat off its hook by the back door and picked up the list. "I'll be back in a couple of hours," she announced to no one in particular.

"Hadn't you better wait to see what my pressure is?" Ralph whined. "I think it's probably high."

"Your pressure's fine." Sarah unfastened the cuff; Louise nodded and glanced significantly at Nora as if she'd suspected as much. "Now your turn, dear," Sarah said to Corinne.

Corinne blinked. "Do I know you? You look famished, but . . ."

"Familiar, I think you mean." Sarah patted Corinne's shoulder. "Yes, you know me. I'm Sarah, your nurse."

"Sarah *Cassidy*," Louise confirmed, bending closer. "You remember. Moira Cassidy's girl, Moira had that wonderful bakery on Main Street."

But Corinne was frowning. "Sarah. Sarah, Sarah," she murmured, then brightened. "What a nice name!" As if with a huge effort, she lifted her good arm and held a limp hand out in Sarah's general direction. "How do you do? I'm Corinne Parker."

Nora turned from buttoning her raincoat, startled; Parker was her mother's maiden name.

"Is this your house, dear?" Corinne asked Sarah.

"Sweetheart," Ralph said, leaning toward her, "you're Corinne Tillot now."

"No, Mrs. Tillot, it's your house." Sarah listened through the stethoscope for a moment while Nora, now worried, watched; Louise put a stubby, protective hand on Nora's arm. Absently, Nora noticed a chip in the dark red polish on Louise's thumbnail.

"Pressure's a bit low," Sarah murmured to Nora and Ralph. "But I think she'll be okay. Has she been disoriented all day?"

"Not like this." Nora knelt beside her mother. "Mama?" she said. "Hi. How do you feel?"

Corinne blinked again. "Why, I feel fine, dear. How are you? Hello, Sarah, Louise. What a rainy day, isn't it?"

Ralph smiled and Louise said, "My goodness, yes. Nice weather for ducks."

Nora laughed with relief and hugged her mother. "I'm just going out with Mrs. Brice to do the shopping. Okay?"

"Of course, dear. Have a nice time. Buy yourself a treat. You deserve one, doesn't she, Louise?"

"She certainly does."

"Your mother might have had a tiny TIA," Sarah said *sotto voce* to Nora, following her and Louise into the front hall. "But I think she's come out of it fine. I'll keep a close eye on her, don't worry, and I'll call Dr. Cantor from my car phone after I've observed her a bit longer. It's possible he'll want to see her or prescribe something, but I think her regular medication should still be okay. She's been having it regularly, yes?"

"Yes," Nora said. "But I wish Father would let us take her to the hospital when she has these spells," she added wistfully.

"So do I," Sarah said. "But" — she patted Nora's arm — "we know he won't, and that's that. Besides, I really do think she'll be fine."

"When you girls have finished your tea party," Ralph bellowed from the kitchen, "maybe one of you would deign to get me my pills. My heart's been racing; I didn't sleep a wink last night."

Sarah grinned at Nora. "He's in top form," she said. "Off with you. Don't drown!"

SIX

Rain pelted against the windows and wind made catspaws on the lake, but still Liz lay in bed, though it was well into morning. She'd bought some groceries the night before after turning on the water in the cabin, and then cooked herself a quick supper of bacon, eggs, and toast. She'd stripped the newspapers off her parents' bed, made it, swept the floor, and, trying not to think, crawled under the covers. But she'd gotten up several times, sleepless, to make cocoa, to read, to look for suddenly remembered books, games, puzzles. She wasn't sure but what she'd finally slept a little; certainly she'd heard the rain start. And now it was coming down harder than when last she'd noticed.

I've got to do something, she thought, getting out of bed stiffly and stretching. I've got to decide.

She struggled into jeans and a turtleneck, then went downstairs into the gray morning, thinking, All my childhood is here, all my roots, my beginnings. She ran her fingers over the surface of the table in front of the sofa, over the sofa's corduroy cover, over its worn wooden arms, remembering lying there for most of one summer after she'd had her appendix out, lying there reading, watching television, watching the sunlight on the lake and longing to be outside.

But it had been good then, too, she remembered, with Jeff running in every few hours to tell her what he'd been doing and what he'd discovered in the woods, bringing her rocks, flowers, worms, once a blinking toad they'd named Hortense and decided was a witch — a good witch — in disguise. Mom and Dad had read to her, played games with her; Mom tried to teach her to knit. Liz almost laughed, remembering her crooked edges and Mom's kind laughter when she said, "Well, Lizzie, maybe you haven't found your true calling." That was when Dad had given her an X-acto knife and a hunk of balsa wood; then, when she felt stronger, a gouge and a flat piece of pine. Mom had laughed again, sweeping up shavings and crumbs of wood, and saying, "Well, Lizzie, I guess maybe now you *have* found your calling!"

And then she'd gotten much better and had been allowed to go outside; no swimming or rowing yet, but she could walk in the woods and sit outside when the mosquitoes weren't too bad, and later she was allowed to fish from the dock as long as Jeff agreed to land anything she caught.

Liz walked through the cabin room by room, memories crowding her; she saved her room for last. Once there, she rolled the mouse droppings up in the newspaper and lay down on her bare mattress, remembering lying there with Megan when they'd first been lovers. They'd come to Piney Haven alone early one spring and it had rained as it was raining now.

Liz closed her eyes, hearing the drops' insistent pounding on the cabin roof, remembering Megan's softness, Megan's hands on her body, hers on Megan's. And yet there'd always been a barrier; she'd felt something closing up in her when Megan touched her, though it was pleasurable and comforting, and though it aroused her to touch Megan. "You have to give *yourself* in love," Jeff had said once, "you have to *be* there, Lizzie" — and she, who had always been considered generous and compassionate, knew he was right about her; he was the only person who could see through her, who seemed to know her secret better than she did. He'd recognized it before she had, anyway.

"It scared me, Meggie," Liz whispered. "It scares me still."

She sat up, rubbing her eyes; she hadn't realized she'd nearly wept.

The rain had slowed to a steady patter, and the room was cold. She should build a fire, make coffee, eat something, start cleaning.

She glanced at her watch; it was nearly ten. No wonder my stomach's grumbling, she thought, and made herself pancakes from a mix, and coffee. She'd forgotten syrup, but there was a half-full box of cinnamon, and she'd bought sugar, so, thinking again of Jeff, she slathered the pancakes with butter and when it had melted, sprinkled on cinnamon-sugar. Biting into the crunchiness, she thought, I could call Jeff. In a couple of hours, I could call Jeff.

Energetic now, Liz finished her coffee, rinsed her dishes, and scrubbed and polished the kitchen till noon, when, suddenly finding the heavy kettle in which her mother had made jam from the blueberries she and Jeff and their father had picked, her eyes filled with tears and she stood, paralyzed, sobbing, by the sink.

Jeff, she thought again, when the paroxysm had passed. It would be nine o'clock in California; she'd have to call him at work and go through his secretary. But that was all right; he'd never minded that.

44

He answered himself.

"Secretary goofing off?" Liz said, closing her eyes in unexpected relief at hearing his voice. She could almost pretend he was with her, that their parents were in the next room or outside, or shopping and due home any minute.

"Hey, Lizzie," Jeff said jovially. "Yeah, she's not in yet. There's a lot of traffic, some tie-up on the freeway, as usual. What's up? Have you been to the cabin?"

"I'm there now." Her voice caught in her throat.

"Oh, wow! You okay?"

"Yes." She hesitated. "Well, not quite. It's weird, Jeffie. It's like — I don't know. It's like it's the shell of me, of us; you know? And Mom and Dad are all around me, Mom especially."

There was a pause. Then: "Yeah. Yeah, I can imagine. And you can't sell it, babe, right?"

"Right. At least not yet," she said relieved again and understanding that was what had gnawed at her last night, keeping her from sleeping, and had enervated her this morning till she'd started cleaning. "I guess I feel I'd be violating it somehow, if I let other people have it. The real estate agent was here when I arrived, snooping. It was awful seeing her looking the place over like a cat waiting to pounce." Liz felt herself shiver. "It's like we'd be selling Mom and Dad, Jeff. And us as kids. Me and Megan, too, a little, our beginning, anyway."

"So no sale at all, huh?"

"Not now. If it's okay with you. Maybe in a year or so. Unless you really need the money."

"Don't worry about that. It's okay."

"Are you sure you and Susan don't need it? With Gus and all?"

"No, we're fine."

"Then if it's okay with you, I'd like to call off the real estate creep and clean the place up and — and maybe spend the summer here alone," she added, surprising herself, realizing she could actually do that, there would be nothing to stop her. She could sublet her apartment, buy a car with the money she'd been saving for she was never sure what, and spend a quiet summer figuring things out, recovering from leaving Megan and trying to understand the flaw that had made her run from her; she could try to put herself back together again.

She heard Jeff's voice, muffled, saying something away from the phone.

"Hey, babe," he said into it a moment later. "I've got to go. My secretary's here now and I've got some stupid meeting. Go ahead and do what you want, though. It's okay."

"You're really, truly sure? About the money?"

"Yeah, I'm sure. And you know what? I'm kind of glad the old place'll still be in the family. Maybe we'll come for a visit, me and Sue and the kid, this summer. How about that? Maybe Gus could get to like the old place, too, who knows? It's so great for kids." His voice softened. "I remember, too."

"That'd be fine," Liz said, smiling. "That'd be fine. Only maybe toward the end of the summer? Give me a little time?"

"Sure, sis. End of summer. Hey, we'll talk later, okay?"

"Okay. 'Bye, Jeffie. And thanks. You're a prince."

"Yeah, right. Tell that to my clients! Love you!"

"Love you, too," Liz whispered after he'd hung up.

I wonder if you're the only person I'll ever really love, she mused as she replaced the receiver.

SEVEN

The rain had stopped by the next morning, and the lake was still, with no ripples breaking its surface. Liz made herself coffee and took a mug of it down to the dock, where she sat, an old flannel shirt over the long t-shirt in which she'd slept; she dangled her legs over the edge of the dock, drinking her coffee and watching the lake steam as the sun climbed higher. As it rose, a gentle breeze sent tiny catspaws scudding over the water; a fish jumped, two darning needles danced — courting, Liz thought — among the lily pads, and a hawk flew low overhead, then turned abruptly and dropped aggressively into the reeds to her left. Bird voices — wrens, thrushes, some kind of warbler — trilled and called. There was one in particular that Liz couldn't identify, whose notes cascaded up and down and across its non-human scales; it made Liz smile. She'd forgotten what it was like to wake up with "the lake folk" as Dad had called them whenever he'd joined her.

She could almost feel him with her now, sitting quietly beside her as he so often had, and for a while she was able to bask in good memories of him instead of guilt at his having died alone and horror at imagining what he must have gone through when his heart had given out. The loss still ached, but less sharply than before, here in the place they had both loved above all others. She felt less rootless, too, less abandoned here than in the city where the shock of his death, so soon after Megan had moved out, had made her feel insubstantial, adrift in a world that had lost its meaning.

Piney Haven had already begun to anchor her again, and she stretched, congratulating herself for her decision. She could heal, she felt sure, if she woke here every summer morning to long, quiet days with nothing to do but read, swim, row, fish, repair the cabin, and perhaps even try to restore the gardens Mom had made at the edge of the woods. Mom would like that, she thought. There'd been a perennial garden, a cutting garden, and a vegetable garden with a small herb bed. The weedy, overgrown perennial garden might be the place to start. She'd have to do some reading; for all her knowledge of biology, Liz was weak in botany, and by the time gardening had begun to interest her, she was already living in the city.

Piney Haven is so empty now, she thought, the garden bringing back an unexpected wave of sadness. She stood to shake it off, and stretched. So empty.

Later, after washing windows and making a list of which ones needed repairing, she made herself a lunch of tunafish salad on an English muffin. Afterward, she took inventory in the tumbledown toolshed at the edge of the cabin's clearing, and then, as she set off in the car to buy putty and glazing

48

points, she remembered the jack. But after her stop at the hardware store, she found herself driving back roads, retracing childhood Sunday rides instead of going to the Tillots' farm. When she passed her parents' favorite vegetable stand, she spotted a plump late middle-aged woman and recognized Clara Davis, who owned and ran it with her husband, Harry. Clara was applying a fresh coat of white paint to the stand's neat clapboard walls.

Grinning, Liz pulled into the gravel parking lot and climbed out of the car just as Clara looked up.

"Liz Hardy, my word!" she shouted jubilantly, her wrinkled, weatherbeaten face one huge smile. "Look, Harry, it's the Hardy girl," she called to her husband, who was just coming slowly around the edge of the stand, leaning heavily, Liz was startled to see, on a cane.

"Mrs. Davis, how nice to see you again." Liz took Clara's outstretched hands. "You're looking well."

"And you, too, dearie," Clara said as Harry reached them. His blue eyes looked a little vague, but he nodded at Liz and touched his hand to his head as if tipping a hat. "What brings you here?" Clara asked. Before Liz had a chance to answer, she went on. "I was so sorry to hear about your father, dear. What a fine man he was! We've missed you, all of you, these years since your sweet mother died. What has it been, five, six years? So sad, losing her. And how's your brother? Is he here with you?"

"No, but he's thinking of coming. He's married now, living in California. And he has a little boy." Liz pulled her wallet out of her back pocket and extracted a picture of Gus, a chubby, smiling, blue-eyed baby. "He's bigger now, of course."

"Oh, my. Looks just like Jeff, don't you think, Harry?" she shouted.

Harry nodded; Liz remembered that he was hard of hearing and stubborn about getting a hearing aid. He didn't seem to be wearing one now.

"Getting ready to open, are you?" Liz said.

"Yes. Though we had such a strange winter, we're not at all sure how we'll do. Lettuce is coming along, though; we'll start selling it next weekend, I think. And the peas don't look bad."

"I'm thinking of restoring my mother's old perennial garden, " Liz told them. "So I might be bothering you with questions."

"Oh, no bother, dear, no bother. We'll be glad to help. Your mother would have loved that, you restoring her garden. She loved all her gardens, she did, especially the perennial one, remember, Harry? Why, for a few years we even bought flowers from her, annuals along with the perennials, and sold them, she grew so many. The customers loved them. We could do that again, dear, if you want."

"Why, sure," Liz said. "If I can get it going. I didn't remember Mom did that."

"It was years ago, dear, when you were just a wee one." Clara paused, looking at Liz a moment as if considering whether to say something else. Then, shyly, she said, "But I heard you were selling the cabin?"

"We were going to, Jeff and I, but we've decided to hold on to it at least for a while. I think I'll be staying here this summer. I'm still a teacher, you know, so I get summers off."

Clara seized Liz's hands again. "Oh, my, that'd be wonderful! We'll have to have you for dinner, then, and of course we're just down the road so if you ever need anything, you can just shout." She paused again, with the same expression, hesitant but curious. "But surely there's a young man or two, a pretty girl like you?"

"No, Mrs. Davis, there isn't." Liz tried not to mind the assumption. "I'm fancy free."

Clara squeezed her hands, then let them go. "We'll just have to see what we can do about that." She winked at Harry, who looked startled, then puzzled, but finally chuckled. "There's one or two nice hardworking fellows around here."

"That's kind of you, Mrs. Davis, but I'm not in the market right now."

"Oh-oh. I'm sorry. Broken heart?"

Well, why not, Liz thought. "You might say that," she told her. "I've just split up with someone and I need to be by myself for a while."

"I'm sure he didn't deserve you, dear. Don't stay alone too long, though; that's no way to heal, I always say!"

The phone rang inside the white frame farmhouse.

"There's your phone," Liz said hastily, giving each Davis a hug, surprised again at Harry's frailty. "And I should be going. I'll see you in a few weeks, when I come back for the summer."

By the time she'd finished driving to all her old haunts and treating herself to an ice cream cone at Harmony's, where she and Jeff had always argued over which was better, butter pecan or peppermint royale, it was late afternoon and Liz had no inclination to stop at the Tillots' farm. What a depressing place, she thought, turning deliberately away from the farm road; that poor woman, stuck there with two old people and no electricity! I'd have left long ago.

Maybe she enjoys it, though; maybe she's some kind of masochist or one of those do-good types, a martyr to duty.

But Liz had to admit that Nora really didn't look the part.

Back at the cabin, Liz baked a huge potato, cooked herself a steak, and ate them, plus a salad, at the table overlooking the lake. She sat there for a long time, sipping red wine and watching the sun set, then took her wine out to the dock and, wrapped in a thick sweater, watched the moon and the stars rise and listened to soft night sounds till she felt sleepy enough to go to bed.

This is the life, she thought as she dropped off, the life I want.

But toward morning she dreamed uneasily of Megan and woke aching and covered in sweat.

The cabin seemed full of ghosts again the next morning: Megan, her parents, she and Jeff as children. Liz felt too restless and too sad to go back out to the dock, so after a quick breakfast of toast, coffee, and an orange, she set about pulling things — dishes, pots, cleaning supplies, books, games, knick-knacks, clothes too old to wear anyplace but at the cabin — out of cupboards and closets and off shelves, sorting, re-arranging, and throwing away. By noon, there was nothing she hadn't touched, but the ghosts were worse than before, especially when she handled the clothes and found an old green suede jacket of her father's and a matching one of her mother's, the latter with a broken zipper. Liz, blinking back tears, slipped her mother's jacket on. It fit perfectly, and she returned both jackets to the closet, though she doubted that Jeff would want their father's or that she'd ever replace the zipper or actually wear her mother's.

Maybe I shouldn't stay here after all, she thought later, nursing a beer at the table and looking out over the lake. Maybe I should go back to the city tonight instead of tomorrow. Think it over some more, staying here this summer.

Maybe I really can't take the memories. Or so much solitude.

Restlessly, she got up and took her beer outside, surveying the overgrown perennial garden, where a few bright green mounds showed among the decaying fallen leaves and pine needles. Intrigued, she knelt, pulling off the mulch and study-ing the emerging plants. Then she went back into the cabin,

52

found a pad and a pencil and, outside again, started sketching them.

When she finally stopped, stiff and damp from kneeling, she realized more than an hour had passed. So, she thought, going back inside, maybe I can deal with solitude after all. And the memories, if I lose myself in stuff like that. She'd felt as close to her mother, drawing her reviving plants, as she had to her father on the dock in the early morning. It was as if the ache of being reminded of them by the static cabin and its contents receded temporarily when she was outside and gave way to a nearly comfortable nostalgia.

If being here doesn't work, she thought later, packing to return to the city, I can always leave.

And go where, you jerk? Not back to the apartment if you sublet it. And if you don't sublet it, you won't be able to afford to come here. So you'll have to burn your bridges, kiddo, at least for the summer.

Feeling trapped, she opened the car's trunk to toss in her suitcase — and groaned, seeing the borrowed jack wrapped up in its towel with the other tools.

EIGHT

After knocking at the Tillots' door and getting no response, Liz went around back and spotted Nora kneeling in the large garden, with Thomas stretched out in the fading sun on a bare patch beside her.

"Hello," Liz called, approaching slowly, not wanting to frighten her. "It's Liz Hardy again. I've brought back your tools. Thanks so much for them."

Nora scrambled to her feet, wiping her hands on the enormous apron that covered her faded housedress. "Thank you," she said. "For bringing them back. I was just weeding."

Liz nodded. A neat row of young lettuces marched along the edge of the garden where Nora had been working, and new pea vines rose against a firm, straight trellis. A row of something with large leaves and red stems grew between two lettuce rows.

"Radishes," Nora said, nodding at them. "I don't know why I grow them. My parents hate them, but I love them. Sometimes I even cook them in a cream sauce for a private treat. And they grow really fast."

Nora seemed more relaxed this time, happy even, not like a masochist or a martyr at all. There was a smudge of dirt on her face that Liz found herself wanting to wipe away. "Maybe," Liz said impulsively, "you can give me lessons this summer. I've decided to stay in the cabin and fix up my mother's old garden."

Good grief, she thought, astonished; why on earth did I say that, especially since I already more or less asked Mrs. Davis?

"I'd love to," Nora replied. "That would be nice. But weren't you going to sell the cabin?"

"Yes. But I decided against it, at least for now." She paused. "Too many memories."

Nora nodded sympathetically. "I don't think I could ever sell this place," she said, "although I dream about it sometimes."

"You do?" Liz was surprised. Despite the fantasies about refrigerators and plumbing that she'd voiced earlier, Nora seemed too settled, especially now outside in her garden, to think about leaving. Liz could see her fixing the place up, perhaps, but not leaving it.

"Oh, yes. Silly dreams. But only when I'm tired."

"That must be pretty often," Liz said. "I mean," she went on, flustered, afraid of being rude, "yours must be a pretty hard life."

"As I said, it's how people lived not so long ago. And I do like the peacefulness of it, the solitude. But then when I get the Sunday papers — a woman from church takes me to get

55

them after the service — and I read casual references to things like computers and see ads for appliances and TVs, I realize how much free time most people must have. Oceans of time. Then I guess I do get a little envious."

Liz grinned. "We should have oceans of time," she said, watching Thomas, who had stood up and was intently stalking a butterfly. "But most of us don't. I guess we don't know how to use the leisure all that helpful stuff has given us. It seems ridiculous, but there we are."

"I think people use the time they have," Nora said, also watching Thomas. "People don't like being completely idle, at least most don't. So they find things to do in whatever time they have."

"Lots of people waste time, though. The mothers of some of my students spend hours watching soaps, for instance."

"Soaps?"

"Soap operas. On TV."

Nora nodded uncertainly, and Liz realized she'd probably never seen one.

"They're like little dramas," she explained. "Continuing stories. Each day there's a new episode."

"That must be nice," Nora said. "I remember now. I've read about them. They must be like novels. Serial stories."

"Well, sort of. But most of the stories are dumb. Lots of sex, lots of complicated relationships, very melodramatic. If they were books, they'd be considered trashy by anyone who's really into literature."

"Are you?" Nora asked. Thomas batted at the butterfly and missed.

"Am I what?"

"Into literature?"

"I suppose so. I don't have much time for reading, though."

"I like Jane Austen," Nora said. "And Emily Dickinson, and Henry James. More than modern books. I sometimes get best sellers when they come in to the library, though. Mrs.

Brice, that's the church lady, gets them for me. But I don't think most of them are very good."

"No," Liz replied uncomfortably, "I guess not." She hadn't read Jane Austen or Emily Dickinson since school, and she'd never read Henry James. You're outclassed, kiddo, she said to herself, amused, by someone who's never seen a computer or watched TV. How about that?

"Would you like to come in? I made some lemonade earlier, for my mother. Or we could have tea."

Liz looked at her watch. "I'd love to, but I think I'd better get going. It's a long drive to New York."

"Won't it be dark when you get there?" Nora asked, concern spreading over her features.

"Maybe," Liz said, amused again. "Depends on how many stops I make. But that's okay. I actually like driving in the dark."

Nora shuddered. "I'd be afraid," she said. "Not of the dark itself; I'm used to that. Of the city in the dark. But I suppose there are lots of lights."

"Yes. There are. Well . . ." Liz held out the bundle of tools. "Here's your jack and stuff. Thanks again for helping me out."

Awkwardly, Nora took the package. "You're welcome. Um, stop by when you come back. If you want. You know. In the summer."

"Sure," Liz said easily, sure that she wouldn't, then not sure. "That'd be fine. Okay, then. See you."

"Yes." Nora smiled. "See you," she added, more comfortably than she'd said it when Liz had left with the jack.

Nora watched Liz go, and realized only after the car had disappeared that she was still holding the tools. "I wonder if she'll come back," she said out loud to Thomas, who had given up on the butterfly and was scratching his neck. "Do you think so, puss?" She put the tools on the ground and picked Thomas up, cuddling him next to her cheek, but he squirmed and leapt down.

Unaccountably, tears sprang to Nora's eyes. She stood

there for a moment, uncertain what to do next, then returned the tools to the barn and ripped the few remaining weeds away from her lettuce rows.

She's halfway to New York now, Nora thought later, beating eggs for supper. She'd made a roast for Sunday noon dinner, putting it in the oven before church and asking Patty, who as usual had sat with her parents while she was out, to make sure that it didn't burn and that the oven temperature stayed constant. Halfway to New York.

What's Liz Hardy's life like, Nora wondered, grating cheese into the eggs. Parties, cocktails, the theater, movies? Or does she go home every night to an empty house? No, an apartment, it would be, in New York City. Wouldn't it? Maybe she lives with a man, her boyfriend. She doesn't seem to be married. Or maybe she lives with women, with roommates. Career girls, isn't that the term? Does she have a job? But she said she'd be here for the summer. Maybe she's rich and doesn't need to work. A socialite. Or maybe she's a teacher. Yes, that could be it; that way she'd have the summer off to come here . . .

"Nora!"

Nora put down the grater. "Yes, Father? What is it?"

"I have to piss."

"I'll be right there."

"Hurry up, will you?"

Nora wiped her hands on her apron, a different, smaller one from the one she'd worn for gardening, then went into Ralph's room and gave him the urinal, although they both knew he was perfectly capable of getting it himself from its spot hanging off the headboard of his bed.

After a minute he handed it back to her, not very full, from under the covers. "Empty it," he ordered unnecessarily.

Swallowing the impulse to say "Empty it, *please*," as one would to a rude child, she took the urinal to the outhouse.

"That woman was here again," Ralph said when she returned. "Wasn't she?"

"What woman?" Nora asked, although of course she knew. "Mrs. Brice was here taking me to church and bringing me back, as usual. And Patty Monahan was here as usual, too, taking care of you and Mama and the roast while I was gone."

"I don't mean them. It's cold in here. Close the window."

Nora closed the window.

"I mean that stranger woman. The one with the car trouble. What did she want?"

"She was returning the tools she borrowed."

Ralph grunted. "She shouldn't have taken them in the first place!"

"I told you I let her take them. We don't need them."

"You're naive, Nora. She probably didn't have a flat tire. She was probably casing the joint. Took the tools on purpose so she could come back."

"*What?*"

"You heard me. That's how thieves operate. She could have a boyfriend who's planning to rob us, once she's told him where the doors are and had a good look at the locks."

"That's ridiculous!"

Ralph struggled to a sitting position. "You'll laugh out of the other side of your face if they steal us blind! I see those papers you get on Sundays. I know about the crime rate. Don't you let that woman in if she comes back. Don't talk to anyone who comes. Just come inside if you're outdoors. Do you hear me?"

"I hear you," Nora answered, leaving, "but I don't believe you," she added under her breath when she was back in the kitchen.

"Nora!" That was Corinne, her thin voice snaking across the room.

Nora sighed. "Yes, Mama, coming." She poked her head in her mother's doorway. "What is it?"

Corinne seemed startled. "Why, I've forgotten, dearie. Maybe . . ." She frowned, looking dangerously close to tears. "Oh, what's wrong with me? Why can't I remember?"

Nora went all the way into the room and put her arms around her. "Maybe you just wanted to say hello, sweetie," she said.

Corinne looked up at her, blue eyes swimming. "Hello," she said, her soft face breaking into a wan smile. "Maybe that was it." She patted Nora's hand. "Is it very expansive?"

"Very what?"

"Expansive. Staying here. Do we pay a lot of money?"

"Oh, expensive, you mean," Nora said, then regretted it: *Don't correct her,* Dr. Cantor had said, *unless you really have to; it'll disturb her more.* But everyone — Nora, Louise Brice, Sara Cassidy, Ralph — frequently forgot, as they had the other day when she'd had that TIA and thought she was still Corinne Parker. Thank goodness Sarah had said Dr. Cantor had come and checked her over, and that he thought it was no more worrisome than the other little ones she'd had.

"No, it's not expensive," Nora told her mother. "We don't have to pay anything."

But she was worried now, anyway. What now, she thought. Where does she think she is?

"We don't? How nice of them. The Smithsons. How are they?"

Nora racked her brain, then dimly remembered: the Smithsons had owned the house briefly after the deaths of her father's eccentric parents, who'd sold it to them. Ralph had bought it back when he and Corinne had married, steadfastly refusing, as he said his own father had, to put in electricity and plumbing. "Got to stay true to history," her grandfather apparently used to say when Ralph was a boy. "And keep the taxes low." Ralph still quoted him when anyone dared suggest "improvements."

The Smithsons had never actually lived in the house, having bought it with the intention of modernizing it when they could afford to. But they'd lost the money they'd invested for that purpose, and were delighted when Ralph had agreed to take it back, or so Ralph had always said.

"The Smithsons are fine," Nora said, though they'd been dead for at least twenty years, both of them. "And guess what? They've let Father buy the house. So now we own it and don't have to pay anything. Isn't that wonderful?"

"Oh, yes," Corinne said sleepily, relaxing in Nora's arms; Nora laid her back against the pillows. "Very nice." Corinne closed her eyes, then opened them. "I'm hungry," she said plaintively.

"I'm just starting supper. Lovely eggs and cheese. It'll be ready soon. I'll get you up in a few minutes, okay? And then we'll sit at the table and eat it, and then I'll read aloud for a while. Would you like that?"

"Yes, dearie." Corinne seemed contented now. "Very nice. You're such a good girl, Nora," she added, suddenly lucid again. "And it's so hard for you. You do know how grateful we are, Father and I, don't you?"

Nora bent and kissed her mother's soft cheek. "Yes," she said, "I know."

II

NINE

It was stifling inside the little white clapboard church with the stone front. Mid-June sun burst through the stained glass windows, making hot multicolored splotches on the maroon carpet that ran down the center aisle and between the white, oak-trimmed pews. The day lilies and irises on the altar, a cheerful yellow and blue crazy quilt at the beginning of the service, had by now, as sweaty, shiny-faced ushers passed the collection plates, become a limp and faded blanket.

"Poor Charles Hastings," Louise Brice whispered to Nora after the service as they made their way with the rest of the congregation to just outside the vestibule, where the minister stood manfully shaking hands and thanking people for liking his sermon. His wife, Marie, who had always reminded Nora of a kindly giraffe, stood off to one side, her straw hat slightly askew, in earnest conversation with the choir director. She was a thin but rawboned woman, with a florid face and knobby features. They were an odd-looking pair, the Hastingses, for Charles was much shorter than Marie, and despite his plump cheeks and thick neck, had a slight but strong-looking build, a runner's body incongruously topped with a decidedly indoor face.

Nora didn't know if she'd liked the sermon or not; she'd been daydreaming, planning the rest of her garden. Could she get away with putting the second crop of beans along the back fence for another year? Or should she rotate them with the pickling cucumbers, which had been on the side fence the summer before?

"That cassock must be dreadfully hot, Charles," Louise said when they reached the minister, whose face was streaming sweat. Her own pink features, islands in folds of damp flesh, were shiny with exuded oil that had long since absorbed their liberal ration of powder. "I imagine you'll be glad to get it off."

"Oh, I'm used to it, Louise, I'm used to it. And how have your parents been this week?" he asked, turning to Nora and clasping her moist hand with his own.

"Father's been the same as always, thank you, Mr. Hastings," Nora said primly. "But my mother's going down-hill, I'm afraid. She's lucid less and less of the time."

A concerned frown creased Charles's forehead and narrowed his otherwise large eyes; he fumbled under his cassock, withdrawing a monogrammed handkerchief with which he delicately blotted his brow. "I am so sorry, my dear. Mrs. Hastings and I will stop in this week, shall we?"

"That would be lovely." Nora forced a smile and out of the corner of her eye saw Louise nodding vigorous approval. But Nora hated those ministerial visits, full of friendly advice and demanding careful preparations. "Come for tea, perhaps Wednesday?" she asked dutifully, knowing the visit was inevitable. When the Hastingses decided to do something, it was as good as done. Putting it off till Wednesday, she calculated, would give her time to make sure the parlor was aired and dusted and would perhaps allow the heat wave to break before she had to make cookies or a cake or whatever she decided to give them. Thank goodness it was easy enough to keep the dining room off the parlor closed even when the parlor was being used; at least she wouldn't have to dust and air both rooms.

The heat wave hadn't broken by Wednesday, and Nora had spent Tuesday scrubbing and cleaning, though she'd wanted to plant the beans, which she'd decided to rotate with the cucumbers after all. But of course in this heat, with no rain, that would be foolish, she told herself, momentarily longing for running water, an outside faucet, and a hose.

Wednesday morning she baked, in between answering her father's calls; he'd seemed unusually demanding after she'd helped him dress, though Corinne slept serenely. Nora had moved her mother's bed closer to her window in the hope of catching any stray breeze, and had dressed her in her gauziest nightgown, though she'd been tempted to try to convince her to stay nude after her bath till the company was due to arrive.

Just when the cookies were nearly done, Ralph called again and Nora swore softly under her breath as she went to the door of his room — where she stopped, horrified, for he was lying on the floor, eyes closed, his limbs flailing about helplessly — like a downed elephant, Nora thought. She suppressed a giggle even as she rushed to him, worried, and knelt by his side.

"Father, what happened?" she cried, and he said, not opening his eyes, "What the hell does it look like, girl? I fell getting off this damn bed. If you'd come when I called the first time

67

this would never have happened, but no, you had to be pottering around the kitchen making stuff for that ridiculous minister and his wife. God damn it, help me up!"

Nora closed her eyes with relief at his outburst. "Are you hurt?" she asked, opening them, layering her voice with an attempt at serious concern.

"Probably. Everything aches." He groaned, watching her carefully. "Are you going to help me or am I going to have to die here?"

Nora put her hands under his shoulders and tugged, but he was too heavy, a dead weight. She could smell the cookies burning.

"Father, you're going to have to help me. I'm not strong enough to lift you. Try to sit up."

He made a feeble attempt and then fell back, groaning again. But that morning he had sat up, unaided, in bed when Nora went in to rouse him for breakfast, and he hadn't seemed impaired physically despite all his demands.

"Try again, Father, please. You sat up this morning."

"This morning," he said angrily, "I hadn't fallen. Oh! My back!"

"Does it hurt? I'm sorry. Where?"

"My back, I said, damn it!"

"I meant where on your back does it hurt?" she asked patiently.

"All over. I'm afraid something's broken, Nora."

"Maybe strained, Father, or twisted; I'm sure it does hurt. But you were moving your arms and legs and head before" — again she stifled a giggle — "so I doubt that it's broken."

The burnt smell escalated, then died away. There was probably nothing left of the cookies.

"I think you'd better go for the doctor," Ralph moaned, closing his eyes.

"But Mr. and Mrs. Hastings; the cookies . . ."

"Damn the cookies and damn the Hastingses! Aren't I

more important? Let me have the urinal." He fumbled at his trousers.

Nora got the urinal and held it for him. "I don't think you have to go," she said after about three minutes. "Maybe the shock of falling, you know? Sometimes I feel I have to go, too, when something like that happens."

"I do have to go," he whined. "And my back hurts. And" — he looked at her reproachfully — " 'it is sharper than a serpent's tongue to have a thankless child'."

"Father," she said tiredly, "Mr. and Mrs. Hastings will be here any minute. The cookies have burned. You are obviously not seriously hurt. You could help me get yourself up, but you won't. I can't get you up alone. I think the best thing for me to do is to leave you here until the Hastingses come, and then Mr. Hastings can help me get you back onto your bed or into a chair. Meanwhile, I'm going to go back to the kitchen, start the water for the tea, and cut some bread for cinnamon toast. The cookies are cinders by now."

Ralph's eyes filled with tears. "I'm such a burden to you," he moaned, seizing her hand. "You're a good girl, Nora. You'll see. You'll miss me when I'm gone. I feel it won't be long, dear. I feel so weak. I'm dizzy. I think I might have banged my head. Don't bother getting the doctor. Just stay with me, sweetheart."

She studied him doubtfully. Could he really have hurt himself seriously? One other time when he'd fallen and she'd had to leave him for some reason (her mother had called, she thought), he'd gotten himself up by the time she returned to him. But this time, in her annoyance over the cookies and the impending ministerial visit, had she misjudged him?

He squeezed her hand. "It's nice sitting here with you," he said dreamily. "You're a good girl, Nora. I know it's hard for you, seeing your old father so sick and weak. You work hard, taking care of your old parents." He opened his eyes and smiled. "How's your mother today?"

69

"Sleepy," Nora said. Then craftily, she asked, "Would you like to go and see her?"

For a second he moved, lifting himself to a partial sitting position. Then, watching her face, he exclaimed, "Oh, ow! No, I can't." And he sank back down.

The hell you can't, she thought. And then, mercifully, there came a knock at the door.

"That'll be the Hastingses." She extricated herself, squeezing his hand and releasing it. "I'll just let them in and we'll have you up again in a jiffy."

She ran to the door.

"Why Nora, what's that smell?" Marie Hastings said immediately, pausing with one large hand still on the doorknob.

"Cookies. I've cut bread for cinnamon toast to replace them. But I'm afraid Father's fallen off his bed," she explained grimly.

"I'll see to the toast and the tea," Marie announced with her usual competence, releasing the doorknob and bustling inside. "And Charles, you go with Nora and get Ralph up." Shaking her head, Marie strode briskly down the hall to the kitchen.

Ralph was sitting up, leaning against his bed, when they reached his room.

"Father!" Nora exclaimed angrily. "I'm sorry," she said, turning to Mr. Hastings. "How did you manage that?" she asked her father.

"I didn't want Charles to strain himself lifting me," Ralph said.

"What about your poor daughter straining herself?" Charles said severely. He bent from the waist, grasped Ralph under the arms, pulled him up with surprising strength given his slight build, and seated him on the edge of his bed. "Hmm? Did you expect her, a mere slip of a girl, to get you up without help?"

"No, no. I realized she couldn't. We decided to wait till you came, but I didn't want to trouble you." Ralph seized the minister's hand. "Thank you, Charles," he said. "You're always so kind."

"Ralph, are you hurt or not?" Charles demanded.

"My back aches and my head aches and I think I scraped my arm. But it's not bad," he added bravely, closing his eyes and wincing.

"Do you need the doctor? X-rays?"

Ralph's eyes flew open. "Not X-rays. Not the hospital! If I go there, I won't come back alive. You know what they do there. There was that woman they gave the wrong pills to, and she died. They make mistakes all the time." His voice dropped conspiratorily. "I know. I won't go there, ever. Nora's promised neither of us will, haven't you, Nora?"

"I've promised to try," Nora corrected him. "To try to keep you out. But I can't promise you'll never have to go."

"There are portable X-ray machines." Charles turned to Nora. "I can arrange for one if you like."

"I don't think that's necessary. Is it, Father? I don't think you're really hurt. Right? Tell the truth now."

Ralph closed his eyes. "I can't tell," he said weakly. "My back does ache. Ohhhhh!"

"In most nursing homes," Charles said quietly, pulling Nora into the doorway, "they X-ray patients automatically when they fall. It's hard to tell with some old folks whether they're hurt or not. As you can see."

"What?" called Ralph. "What? I can't hear you!"

"Mr. Hastings is just saying it might be a good idea for you to have some x-rays anyway. He can have a machine come here. I think it would be a good idea, Father, just in case."

"No. Too expensive. I won't hear of it."

The minister went back to the bed. "It'll be paid for, Ralph. I'm sure Medicare will cover it, or most of it. I really do think it would be wise. Put your mind at rest, and Nora's, and mine."

"Tea's ready." Marie appeared in the doorway, filling it with her large frame. "Well, Ralph, there you are back on your bed! Feeling better?"

"Yes," Ralph said gruffly. "Thanks to your good husband."

"And your good daughter, too, I should think," Marie said. "Shall we have our tea in here, make a little bedside party of it?"

"No tea for me." Ralph closed his eyes. "I'm feeling dizzy again. You go on, though. Enjoy yourselves." He swept his arm dramatically across the bed, dismissing them, and leaned back against the pillows. "Nora . . ."

Nora moved to his side, swung his legs up onto the bed, this time without incident, removed his shoes, and covered his feet lightly with a summer blanket that she kept draped over the chair by his window.

Ralph sighed and opened his eyes again as the three of them retreated to the newly cleaned and aired parlor.

"I really think," said Charles, putting down his cup so carefully that it made no sound against the saucer, "that you must have a telephone now, Nora. What if he really *had* been hurt?"

"Or what if your mother has another stroke?" Marie put in, repeating Louise Brice's frequent warning. "It's foolish, Nora, and downright dangerous for you not to have one."

"I know," Nora told them, "but as I've said before, he won't have it."

"Well, he's just going to have to have it, isn't he? I'll talk to him. You let me handle it." Angrily, Marie selected a piece of cinnamon toast.

"He needn't even know." Charles took a piece himself. "Good toast."

"Thanks to your wife." Nora smiled at Marie. "Father

would know. He'd know people were inside the house, installing it, and he'd hear it ringing."

"All right," said Marie, "but what can he do about it, really? I mean, the man is helpless!"

"Ah, but he's not as helpless as he makes out he is," said Charles. "Look at today. I agree with Nora that there wasn't a single thing wrong with him. In fact, Nora, I'm not even sure he fell off his bed. Did you hear a thump?"

"No. As a matter of fact I didn't."

"There you are." Charles drained the remaining tea in his cup. "I think he faked the whole thing to get your attention. Got off the bed and carefully lowered himself to the floor. I'd like to get that X-ray machine in just to prove to him that he's not hurt and to perhaps discourage him from trying such antics again."

"Charles, really!" exclaimed Marie. "We can't be positive he was faking. Anyway, that's neither here nor there. If something really does happen, Nora, you might not be able to leave to get help. And what about thunderstorms, winter, all sorts of things? You can't run out in a blizzard to get the doctor if your mother has a stroke in the middle of one. And suppose there's a fire? With that old stove . . ."

"But even if he'd agree," said Nora, "he'd never stand for the expense. You know how he is about money. Just the other day he complained about the town taxes again."

"Humph," Marie grunted. "I shouldn't think he'd have to pay much, without town water or sewage or anything."

"That's the plan, isn't it?" Charles said. "Doing without those things in order to keep the taxes down? After all, there's all that land. Fifty or so acres, isn't it? But that's beside the point," he went on. "The parish fund can easily manage a telephone."

Nora shook her head. "He'd call it charity."

Marie patted Nora's hand, momentarily enveloping it. "He'll just have to accept it, then."

"No," Nora said firmly. "If there's to be a phone, I'll pay for it out of my proofreading money."

"And," Marie said just as firmly, "the parish fund will reimburse you, pay part of it, something. You need that money for other things, Nora, and you know it."

"No, really," Nora protested, embarrassed. "I insist."

"And so do I. We can work out the details some other time. Meanwhile, I'll call the phone company. So" — Marie got up and fanned her legs once or twice surreptitiously with her skirt — "that's settled then, isn't it? You really do need to be sensible about this, Nora. For your parents' sake as well as your own. Think of them, if not of yourself."

Nora felt too tired to resist any more. "All right," she said dully.

But she knew it would be she, not the Hastingses, who would bear the brunt of her father's wrath.

TEN

The traffic was murderous leaving New York, but Liz had expected that. It thinned out on the Connecticut Turnpike — probably because there's more room for it, she mused. Still, given that it was the first nice Friday that June, she suspected that many of the cars whizzing past her, zipping in and out of lanes, were vacation- or at least free-weekend-bound.

And so am I. She settled back, elbow out of the window of her newly purchased secondhand Toyota, head momentarily against the anti-whiplash headrest. So, if you ignore the botany texts and sketch pads, am I.

* * * * *

Outside Hartford the traffic picked up again, and Liz, day-dreaming about the last day of school when her seniors had actually clapped for her at the end of class, had a near miss when a truck, passing, cut her off as it zoomed in front of her. "Jerk!" she shouted, banging her foot down on the brake and stifling the urge to give him the horn. But then a plaid-shirted arm shot out of the truck's cab, waving, and she grinned good-naturedly as she muttered, "But you're still a jerk, buddy boy."

She stopped for lunch in a town where she knew there was a deli near the road that served good hot pastrami, reasoning this would be her last chance for that till fall, and treated herself to a box of assorted rugelach; they'd last a week if she didn't gorge herself and if she kept them in the fridge.

The fridge, she thought; did I leave it open? Shut it off or leave it running? Oh, Lord! The prospect of cleaning mold out of it if she'd shut it off and closed it made her stomach lurch.

But no, she said to herself. No. I will not spoil this day by worrying.

About anything. I will not think of Megan, or worry about being lonely or being in a town so small it almost doesn't exist.

I will not worry about anything.

When she got to Clarkston's tiny main street, she decided to stop at the post office to ask about renting a box for the summer. She'd told her post office in New York to forward her mail to general delivery but the idea of a post office box filled her with nostalgia. Her family had had one every summer, kept it all year, in fact, till the year Liz's mother had died.

She wondered if Megan would write.

The day before she'd left New York, Megan had called her,

rather stiffly asking about a CD she thought she'd left behind. But she hadn't left anything behind; Liz decided it was probably an excuse.

"Are you okay?" Liz had asked. "How are you and Janey?"

"You want me to be okay, don't you?" Megan said bitterly. "So you won't have to feel guilty."

"I'll feel guilty no matter how you are, Meggie," Liz told her as gently as she could. "And sad. But I'll also know it was the right thing to do. You deserve better than me, better love than I can give."

"You could if you let yourself."

"Maybe, but that's the point, isn't it? If I let myself."

Would I know how, Liz wondered briefly now, pulling the car into the driveway that served as the post office's parking lot.

The Clarkston post office was a tiny brown-shingled cabin, not even a regulation rural post office building. It stood off to one side of the postmistress's matching brown-shingled house. A window box running under the cabin's street-facing window displayed red geraniums; a basket of scarlet and purple fuschia swung brilliantly by the front door.

Inside, old-fashioned brass-and-glass post office boxes covered the wall next to the counter, and Liz was pleased that she recognized the small white-haired woman who was selling stamps to a larger, stouter white-haired woman.

"You'll be wanting the farm's mail, too, I expect, along with this," said the postmistress (Helen Whipple, Liz remembered), handing the stout woman a large flat package. The stout woman looked familiar; so did the blue and white hand-embroidered cotton skirt she was wearing, but Liz couldn't place her. "To Mr. and Mrs. Henry Brice," was scrawled on the package, Liz saw, and then Helen, looking up but not really at Liz, said, "Be right with you, dear," and handed Mrs. Brice — for it must be she, Liz decided — another package and a few envelopes. Liz didn't think her family knew the Brices — not surprising, since summer people didn't mix much with the "natives," as her father had called them privately — but Liz thought she must have seen Mrs. Brice around town or maybe at church, the few times her family had gone.

"Here's another lesson from that poetry school," Mrs. Whipple was saying to Mrs. Brice. "Bless her heart, poor girl. As if she didn't have enough to do already."

"Yes, but, Helen, it keeps her mind occupied. And the proofreading gives her a little independent income. Takes her mind off crochety old Ralph, too, I shouldn't wonder."

"How's Ralph doing, anyway?"

"Grouchier than ever," Mrs. Brice replied. "Especially" — she glanced toward Liz and lowered her voice — "since Corinne's been poorlier. Well, see you tomorrow, Helen." At that point Liz remembered the unwritten rule of the Clarkston post office: any serious conversation had to stop whenever a stranger arrived.

"Neither rain nor snow," quipped Helen cheerfully as Mrs. Brice left. At last looking properly at Liz she said, "Now, dear, what — good heavens, Liz Hardy! My goodness gracious, child, it's been ages. Welcome back! How are you?"

Twenty minutes later, Liz, having been hugged, queried, and warmly welcomed by Helen Whipple, fastened the tarnished brass key to Post Office Box 108 to her key chain, and walked to Clarkston's small convenience store, where she bought milk, eggs, butter, a package of lunch ham, coffee, and bread. She decided to do a proper shopping the next day at the supermarket in the next town; this would do for tonight's supper, with perhaps a salad if she felt like going up to the Davises' farmstand later.

* * * * *

But she didn't. She'd remembered to open the fridge door, thank goodness, so there wasn't any mold. By the time she'd unpacked some of her clothes and put them in the lavender bureau in her parents' upstairs room, and had arranged her botany books and sketch pad and writing supplies on her father's desk in the other upstairs room, she was too tired to do much more than sit on the dock with a glass of wine as the sun set and the air cooled. She sat there till long after the afterglow left the sky, her mind pleasantly blank, or nearly.

Yes, she thought, finally unfolding herself to go inside and cook her solitary supper. Yes, I think I really can do this after all.

The next morning Liz was up soon after the sun and she ran, towel-clad, down to the lake and plunged naked into the still-cool water, startling a small school of fish that scattered as she dove but returned a few minutes later to nibble her toes, making her laugh. She floated lazily on her back till she heard a distant outboard motor; then, cursing it, she swam back to shore, wrapped the towel around herself and ran back to the cabin, suddenly ravenous.

The phone rang.

Cursing again, Liz wrenched the receiver off its hook and barked, "Yes?"

"Liz?"

"Yes?" she said, a little less angrily; it was a slightly familiar elderly female voice.

"Clara Davis, dear. I hope I didn't wake you. Harry thought he saw you in a car yesterday leaving the post office. So you're here now at last! How wonderful!"

Resignedly, Liz edged a chair to the phone and sat. Were the Davises going to be overly attentive?

79

"Yes, I just arrived yesterday, Mrs. Davis. It's grand to be here."

"It's grand to have you here, dear, too. Now, you mustn't be a stranger. I'm sure you'll want company now and then, there in the cabin all by yourself. We'd love you to come for supper tonight; in fact we won't take no for an answer. I wanted to make sure to catch you before you made any plans. Six o'clock?"

Damn! Liz thought. But she knew it would be the height of rudeness to refuse. "Sure, Mrs. Davis," she said, trying to sound enthusiastic. "Sure, that'd be wonderful. Thank you! I'll be settling down to do some work in a day or so," she added, "but it'd be nice to socialize a little before that."

She could almost hear Mrs. Davis's smile.

At six sharp, Liz, wearing a clean, well-pressed light blue shirt and smooth-fitting tan slacks, pulled into the farmstand's parking lot, where she saw to her dismay that a slicklooking black Mazda was parked next to Harry Davis's pick-up truck. Sure enough, as soon as she stepped into the farmhouse's front vestibule, where Harry's barn boots sat muddily next to his wife's herb basket, Clara Davis, after hugging Liz, threw open the inside door and, beaming proudly, stepped aside to reveal a tall, blond, confident-looking man of about forty, dressed as Liz was in a blue shirt and tan chinos. "This is Roy Stark," Clara announced, "a near neighbor, new in town this spring. Roy's renting the old Kincaid place, and he's been teaching part-time at the high school, filling in for someone who left suddenly, so you two have a lot in common. Roy, here's Liz Hardy, who I told you about."

Roy stuck out a very clean, almost hairless hand. "Hi, Liz," he said in a pleasantly deep voice. "I hope you don't mind my being here, but it's all Mrs. D's fault."

"No, no," Liz sputtered politely, minding a great deal. "Not at all."

His grip was firm, his eyes friendly.

"Come in, come in!" Clara led them past a coat rack, bare except for an old-looking maroon cardigan; Liz remembered being fascinated with the rack as a child. On Halloween, the Davises made a ghost out of it, with blinking Christmas-light eyes. It had terrified Jeff once when they'd spent Halloween weekend at the cabin and Dad had taken them trick-or-treating.

Clara ushered them into the living room and sat them down next to each other on the slightly sagging green sofa facing the fireplace. An old border collie struggled to its feet from a rug near the hearth and limped over to Liz, nuzzling her hand.

Liz, giving a little cry of recognition, slid to her knees and held out her hand, which the dog solemnly licked. "This isn't Brinna?" she asked, looking up at Harry, who had just come shuffling in, his cane in one hand and a plate of cheese and crackers shakily in the other.

"Indeed it is," he said, his voice thinner than Liz remembered. "And she still knows you, looks like."

Liz nodded, hugging the dog, who licked her face. "She must be, let's see, how old now?"

"Fifteen," said Clara. "Nearly sixteen. She doesn't hear much any more, or see either, but she still helps pen the sheep when the other dogs bring them in. Mostly she stays by the fire. Do you remember . . ."

". . . the time she woke you up when your barn got struck by lightning? I sure do!"

By then Roy had squatted beside Liz and was making great show of patting the dog, but Brinna leaned against Liz, ignoring him. When they sat on the sofa again, she curled up at Liz's feet.

"That's what you should have, Lizzie," said Harry, passing

the cheese while his wife followed with glasses and sherry on a rather battered tray. "A dog for company, there in that cabin all by yourself."

"I recommend it," Roy said, raising his glass. "Cheers everyone."

"Cheers," the Davises murmured.

"So you have a dog?" Liz asked Roy in the awkward silence that followed.

"Yes, a silly young golden retriever. He's just a pup; you'll have to come and meet him sometime, if you like dogs."

"I do like dogs," Liza said, and quickly added, "but I'm going to be kind of hermit-like this summer, doing some work."

"Oh?" Roy asked. "A teacher working in the summer?" He shook his head. "All work and no play . . . What'll you be doing?"

"Some botanical studies." Liz tried her best to sound serious and boring. "I teach biology and physiology, but I'm kind of weak in botany and need to do some real exploring. I'm looking forward to gathering specimens in the woods around the cabin, to study them."

"Well, if you wouldn't mind company, I'd love to come along. I don't know a thing about botany, but I used to do some surveying so I'm good at carrying equipment." Roy smiled disarmingly and leaned forward. "And a little bird, a realtor I know, actually, tells me you've got a neat summer cabin you're thinking of selling, on a great piece of wooded land."

"I'm not so sure any more that I'm selling it," Liz said, trying not to let her annoyance show, and making a mental note to call Georgia Foley. "At least not for a while."

"And Harry and I are so happy about that!" exclaimed Clara. "As to botany" — she nodded toward Roy — "Roy's not as ignorant as he makes out, at least not in a practical sense. He's been working the Kincaids' big garden. In fact, it's his peas we'll be eating tonight. Now," she added, getting up, "supper ought to be just about ready; I'll go see."

"I'll help," Liz said quickly, jumping to her feet.

But Roy followed.

ELEVEN

"When you were very little," Corinne said lucidly with a wistful smile during her bath on the morning the telephone people were coming, "you called me Mummy, remember? Not Mama."

"Yes." Nora carefully swabbed the remaining soap off Corinne's arms. "I remember. Would you like me to call you Mummy now?"

Corinne's eyes sparkled mischievously. "I think I should call *you* Mummy, don't you?" she said. "I'm the little girl now and you're the mummy."

"Do you mind that very much?" Nora asked. But Corinne stiffened and her eyes stared unseeing into Nora's.

"Mama?" Nora whispered, terror seizing her. "Mama?"

She shook Corinne's arm, then her shoulders, but there was no response.

Ignoring the pain that gripped her heart, Nora put her fingers on Corinne's neck, over her carotid artery. Her pulse was faint, but present; a little uneven, but not erratic. Her skin was cool and clammy, her breathing shallow but regular.

Carefully putting the basin of water aside, Nora reached down to the foot of the bed, pulled up Corinne's terrycloth robe, and wrapped it as closely as she could around Corinne's somewhat rigid body.

"Mama?" she said again. "Mummy? What's wrong?"

Intelligence returned to Corinne's eyes. "Why, nothing, dearie," she said cheerfully. "Are we ready for church now?"

Nora closed her eyes for a moment in relief. "No," she said, "no, it's Saturday, not Sunday. And we've just finished your bath. Now it's time for breakfast. I'll wheel you into the kitchen. Here, lift up now: one, two, three. Good, that's it. There we are." As Nora put the robe properly on Corinne and settled her in her wheelchair, thoughts chased themselves through her mind: another stroke, a quick drop in blood pressure? But why? Good thing the phone's coming today, even though Saturday installations cost more; good thing they didn't have any weekday appointments for a while; first call will be to Dr. Cantor; how many more of these incidents can she survive; God, it would be awful to be old; when I'm old, who'll take care of me; poor Mama, poor Mummy!

"There." Nora settled a thin summer blanket around her mother's knees, adjusted the robe on her shoulders, and pushed her into the kitchen. "Now I'll just go get Father and then I'll start breakfast. Bacon and eggs this morning? Or pancakes?"

Corinne looked confused. "Not that nice turkey? With stuffing and cranberries?"

Nora knelt by the wheelchair. "We'll have that soon, Mama," she said soothingly. "Real soon. But it's June now, see?" She pointed to the big calendar on the wall. Louise Brice

85

had given it to them after Sarah had said that having a calendar in a prominent place would be a good way to keep Ralph and Corinne, especially Corinne, aware of the date. She gave Corinne a hug. "It's strawberry time," she said gaily. "And I" — she stood up, curtseying — "will gather strawberries later for my lady and gentleman. Maybe" — she bent closer, whispering — "I'll even make biscuits and we can have STRAWBERRY SHORTCAKE!"

Corinne giggled delightedly and squeezed Nora's hand with her own good one. "Oh, lovely, lovely! Would you? I'll be so good, really I will."

Nora's throat caught as she kissed her mother's cheek. "You're always good, sweetie. Always."

Her eyes brimming with tears, she wheeled her mother into the kitchen. "I'll be right back," she said, kissing her and going into her father's room.

Ralph, already bathed and dressed in loose-fitting faded black slacks and a blue plaid shirt, was sitting glumly by his window. "You have to take in these pants," he announced when Nora came through the doorway. "All my pants. I've lost weight. I'm getting thin, no matter what I eat. My stomach hurts all the time," he whined. "I think it's cancer."

"If you think it's cancer," Nora said, pushing his new mail-order walker toward him, "then you'd better see Dr. Cantor."

"Ha!" Ralph snorted. "And have him send me to the hospital and stick tubes in me and fill me full of poison? I'd rather die in my own bed in my own house" — he gave her a lopsided smile as she pulled him up from his chair and placed his hands on the walker's front bar — "with my own little girl to take care of me. You'll be sorry when your old father's gone, won't you?"

"Yes, Father," Nora said dutifully, guiding him out of the bedroom. "Of course I will. Do you think your stomach can handle bacon and eggs?"

"What? Bacon and eggs? I don't know. Don't make the

bacon greasy," he said as Nora eased him down into his chair at the kitchen table. "Let me see it."

Nora, with a glance at her mother, whose head was sagging and whose eyes were closed — but her breath was even and regular — fetched the bacon package from the ice box on the back stoop.

"Open it," Ralph commanded. "Let me smell it. Bacon doesn't keep."

"I just bought it yesterday." Nora snipped the package open and held it under her father's nose. "It has a sale date two weeks from now."

"Harumph! Sale date. Didn't have stuff like that in the old days. They could put any date on, Nora, you know that." He looked up at her. "Smells all right," he said begrudgingly. "But it's got too much fat. Don't undercook it. Bacon should be . . ."

". . . crisp and brown," she supplied, for he said this every time she made bacon. "I know, Father."

Corinne woke up long enough for Nora to get some scrambled eggs into her and one piece of bacon, finely minced. Ralph, despite his stomach ache, managed to eat five pieces of bacon and the rest of Corinne's eggs plus his own. He ate slowly, though; Nora's tea was cold by the time he finished, and she kept an anxious eye on the clock, wanting him to be back in his room and out of the way when the phone people came.

"I'll just take Mama back to bed," Nora said when her father had only one limp piece of toast left. "Then I'll come back for you."

"I think I'll stay here today," Ralph said. "Don't want to go to my room yet. Maybe I'll sit in the parlor or — what's that? Sounds like a motor!"

87

Oh, Lord, Nora thought. "I'll go see," she said as calmly as possible, dashing into the hall. "Then I'll settle Mama."

"I don't want that Brice woman here," her father bellowed. "It's bad enough she comes twice a week. This isn't one of her days."

"No, you're right," Nora called. "It isn't. I'll be right back."

A glance out the front door confirmed Nora's suspicions; it was the phone company, half an hour earlier than they'd said. "I'll just be a few minutes," she shouted outside. "Please wait."

But a young man with tools hanging from his belt was already climbing out of the truck.

"Damn," Nora said under her breath. She ran back into the kitchen and tightened the safety belt around Corinne's waist, securing her in the wheelchair, and pushed the chair into Corinne's room, positioning it by the window. "Look, Mama," she said cheerfully, "look what a nice day it is! And there's a truck out in front. I'm going to go talk to the driver and settle Father and then I'll come in to you again, in case you want to go back to bed. Okay?"

Her mother looked confused. "Whyza struck?" she asked, her speech slurred again.

Nora frowned; Corinne was often better, not worse, after eating. The sugar and other nutrients, Dr. Cantor said, increased her energy and awareness.

"I'll explain later," Nora told her. "It's a secret for now."

Corinne giggled. "Goody!" she said. "I never tell."

"That's right. Don't tell." She patted Corinne's hand. "I'll be back in a bit. Don't take any wooden nickels, okay?"

Her mother nodded solemnly. It was an old joke between them, left over from Nora's school days, when they said it to each other every morning as Nora left. "I wooden won't. You either."

"I won't." And Nora, stifling her concern over the intrusive "wooden," hurried out of the room just as there was a pounding on the front door.

"Coming!" she called, runnng to the hall.

Simultaneously, Ralph yelled from the kitchen, "Don't answer it!"

Ignoring both him and the sound of his walker thumping toward the front hall, Nora opened the door.

"Morning, ma'am," the young man standing there said deferentially. He was tall, with a neatly licked-back ponytail, one earring, and the beginnings of a beard. "This is Tillot Farm, right?"

"Right," said Nora, "and yes, I did order a phone."

The man looked puzzled. "New installation, right?"

"Right."

"I couldn't find the box," he said apologetically. "Could you show me . . . ?"

"There isn't one," Nora explained as her father thumped up behind her and stared suspiciously at the young man. "There's never been a phone here."

"And never will be," Ralph thundered. "We don't take kindly to peddlers," he said severely, "and we don't buy anything that comes door-to-door. Didn't know the telephone people were doing that now. But we don't want one."

"But I thought . . ." The man looked from Ralph to Nora. "That is, didn't . . . ?"

"It's all right," Nora said calmly. "You're in the right place. Why don't you start outdoors, and I'll be with you in a few minutes. You do have to do something outdoors, don't you?"

"Yes, ma'am. We've got to bring the line in from the main road. But I need to know where to feed it into the house."

"Feed what into the house?" Ralph roared. "Has everyone gone crazy? There is to be no telephone!"

"Father, please!" Nora pushed the young man gently outside, saying, "I'll be right out; just give me a minute." She closed the door. "Father, I did order a phone. We have to have one."

"We do not have to have one!" he shouted, his face growing very red. "It's too expensive, and too damned annoying. Ringing all the time, people calling up . . ."

"Father, listen," Nora said with forced patience, wondering how she could have been so stupid as to imagine she could have it installed without his knowing. "Mama had another spell just this morning. She came out of it, but what if she hadn't?"

"You'd have gone for the doctor as you did the last time."

"It took me twenty minutes last time to get to the Lorens' house. And it was just luck that they were home. We have to have a phone, Father, for safety. I'll tell people not to call us unless it's an emergency. Suppose something happened to you?" she added, steering him back to his room. "Suppose your stomach pain became unbearable? And you're often dizzy."

"I'm dizzy all the time."

Nora nodded. "Right. And suppose your dizziness made you faint, and you were lying on the floor unconscious and Mama had a spell right then? I'd have to leave both of you all alone to go for help. Suppose it was winter and there was a blizzard?"

"All right! All right! You've made your point," he growled as she eased him down into the armchair in his room. "But the expense! We can't afford it. Unless" — he looked up at her craftily — "unless you were planning to pay for it yourself out of the money you get from that stupid reading job of yours."

"It's not stupid, Father!" Nora shouted. "It's the only . . ." She clenched her fists, bit her lip. "Don't worry," she said quietly. "You won't have to pay for it. It won't come out of your money."

"Put me in the parlor where I can see that boy working. Someone's got to keep an eye on him."

* * * * *

It took all morning and part of the afternoon to bring the line into the house from the road, and most of the rest of the afternoon to install the phone — in the kitchen, Nora had decided, since that was where she spent most of her time and where it would be closest to her parents' rooms in case she had to keep an eye on them when she called for help. By the time the pony-tailed man had left, it was late afternoon, too late to pick strawberries. Tomorrow, Nora thought, starting supper as both her parents napped in their respective rooms, worn out from the disruption. Tomorrow maybe I'll do short-cake.

TWELVE

One more day of sloth, Liz promised herself before she got up Sunday morning. Then I'll fix that window in Dad's study so I can work there. After — she sat up, swinging her legs over the edge of the bed — doing a proper grocery shopping first thing Monday.

She stretched, looking out her window at the lake, sparkling where the early morning sun touched its slightly rippled surface.

Coffee. That's the first thing now.

And another swim.

Fuzzily, still in the t-shirt in which she'd slept, Liz padded down to the kitchen, started the coffee maker she'd brought from New York, and went out to the dock. "Good morning, world!" she shouted, taking a deep breath of the cool but rapidly warming air. A warbler called from the woods behind her, and two darning needles danced, skittering, across the lake's surface; a fish — pickerel, she judged from its size and shape — leapt up, grabbing one. Liz winced; bio teacher or no, she'd never been able to shake off a mild squeamishness when confronted with the food chain in action.

No one seemed up. No boats marred the surface of the lake; no motors disturbed its stillness; no shouts came from the one or two cabins, hidden by trees, that faced hers from one side of a large plot of heavily wooded vacant land on the opposite shore. Liz shucked off her t-shirt and plunged in, diving down to the muddy bottom where soft weeds waved their tendrils in the clear but brown water and rocks made elephant shapes among them. She slid along the bottom for a few frog-like breast strokes, then arced up, breaking the surface with her lungs exploding and her hair in her eyes. Exhilarated, she treaded water till she got her breath back, then swam with sure, clean strokes halfway to the other side, where a barking dog and a shouting child let her know she was no longer alone in the morning. She swam back, this time only mildly annoyed, but thinking she'd better unpack her bathing suit so she could swim without interruption.

She put her hands on the edge of the dock and jumped out of the water, shedding drops and shaking them off like a dog. Then, in deference to the remote possibility that someone on the opposite shore had binoculars, she kept her back turned, pulled her t-shirt on over her head, and ran back up to the cabin for breakfast.

Fixing the study window, a three-over-three casement, was obviously not going to be easy. Much of the frame's wood was warped and rotten and what little putty remained had shrunk with age, then cracked and flaked. Liz scraped and dug at the putty with a screwdriver and a knife, planning to replace it, but soon realized the frame wasn't worth repairing. She put her tools down and studied it. It was probably too old to be a standard size, but they'd know that at the hardware store and could order a new one if it was. If it wasn't, she'd have to get a carpenter. She wasn't sure she was skillful enough to build a rain-and-snow-tight window frame.

Sighing, Liz went back down to the kitchen's tool drawer for a tape measure and measured the window, writing down the dimensions on a scrap of paper which she stuffed into her pocket. At least, she thought, it doesn't look like rain today, and so far the rain didn't seem to have gotten onto the desk. Nevertheless, she pulled the desk out a little further, just to make sure.

She spent the remainder of the morning unpacking the rest of her clothes and giving the cabin another, very minor, cleaning. Then, just as she was making herself a tomato sandwich and contemplating going for a walk in the woods after lunch, there was a rustling outside and a loud, insistent knocking.

Annoyed, Liz put down her mayonnaise-laden knife and answered the door.

Roy Stark stood there holding the screen open, grinning; his Mazda was parked at the end of the stone path. "Hi," he said. "I was passing your driveway, or maybe I should call it a road, it's so long. And I thought I'd stop in and see how you're doing."

"I'm doing fine." Liz blocked the doorway with her body. "Thank you," she added reluctantly.

"I'm thinking of heading into town for the Sunday papers," Roy said, unabashed, "and I wondered if you needed anything, or if you'd like to come with me. There's a good movie in Poscaquill, too; I thought maybe we could go see it later. Or have a walk in your beautiful woods."

"Thank you," Liz said evenly. "But no. I have other plans."

Roy peered beyond her into the kitchen. "Nice looking kitchen," he said. "Ah. You're making lunch."

"Right. And then I'm going for a walk, a working walk. I don't know when I'll be back. Later, I may go to the hardware store, which I think is open Sunday afternoons."

She regretted that as soon as she said it, for Roy seized on it quickly. "Hey, maybe I could help with that! I could pick up whatever it is for you. And you know what? I'm pretty handy. No offense, but this place must need a fair amount of work, especially if it's been shut up for so long. For a part-time English teacher and ex-surveyor, I make a pretty good carpenter."

"And gardener," Liz said dryly, remembering Clara Davis's recommendation. "Is there anything you can't do?"

"Ouch!" He made great show of wincing. "I guess I deserved that. Look, I'll level with you. Mrs. Davis, bless her sweet soul, told me you've recently broken up with someone and she said you might be lonely. I broke up with someone, too, not long ago. So I thought maybe . . ."

Liz sighed. "Roy, I'm sorry. But I — I'm just not ready." No, Liz, she told herself; he won't accept that; she could already see it in his eyes and she imagined him framing the answer: *"Well, when you are . . ."*

Then he said it, with an acquiescent nod. "Okay, I understand that. But when you are . . ."

She sighed again; why was it so impossible to tell the truth? So hard, anyway.

"I don't expect to be ready for a long time, Roy," she told him. "I'm sorry."

He stretched his hand out and patted her shoulder. "No, no," he said. "My sympathies. *I'm* sorry. But maybe" — he withdrew his hand — "we could just have a friendly walk sometime. As I said, I'm good at carrying equipment." He winked.

"Maybe," she said. "But I can manage the equipment."

He shrugged. "Okay. Whatever. As the kids say," he added. "Funny how one picks up their language."

She smiled, trying to be polite without being encouraging, but didn't answer. An insect, possibly a bee, flew past Roy's head, buzzing loudly. He batted at it, letting go of the screen door, which swung closed, not quite slamming.

"Well," he said, "good luck. I'll give you a call sometime, shall I? You know, about that walk."

"Roy, I . . ." Liz began, but he turned away as if to prevent the answer she was about to give him.

"See you later!" he called, walking briskly back to his car. "Bound to, in such a small town."

Liz turned away before he got to the car, and returned to making her sandwich. But she felt oddly violated, her pleasant solitude unpleasantly shattered.

By the time she'd finished her lunch, Liz realized with annoyance that she'd better cut her walk short if she was going to go to the hardware store, so she just strolled for about a mile along the lake shore to the left of the cabin, following a muddy, overgrown path she and Jeff had often explored as children. It took her longer than she expected, for the path was tangled with weeds, and the cedar boards she and Jeff and their father had placed there long ago to bridge the muddy places were rotting and slick with bog slime where they weren't carpeted with moss. Another project, Liz decided, somewhat cheered by the thought. She turned back, planning to bring clippers and a saw with her the next day to start restoring the path.

Before she left for the store, she checked in the tumble-down toolshed for what she'd need and found her father's old bow saw, a small pruning saw, and two pairs of loppers. They were a little stiff and rusty so she added WD 40 to her list and headed off to town.

As she passed the road into the Tillot place, she saw something light-colored in the clearing at the edge of the woods. Slowing down, she realized it was a person, bent over and searching for something, it looked like, in the grass and weeds. She was about to speed up again when the figure straightened and turned, and Liz recognized Nora Tillot.

She slowed more, and pulled over. "Hi," she called. "Liz Hardy. I borrowed your jack last month."

Nora shaded her eyes, then walked to the car, smiling. "Yes, of course," she answered. "Hi."

"Hi." Nora's smile was warmer than Liz remembered and again she was struck by the green flecks in her eyes. The sun was catching them, bringing out their slight gold tinge. "Did you lose something?"

"What? Oh." Nora laughed and picked up a basket that had been hidden in the weeds. "No, I was picking wild strawberries. I'm going to make shortcake, but" — she laughed again, a gentle, musical laugh — "but I've picked enough for an army. Hey," she said, cocking her head, "come by later and do me a favor by taking some. Or I could make extra biscuits and give you some shortcake; there'll be plenty of cream, too."

"My mouth is watering already." Liz wondered if the smile she knew was forming on her face looked as silly as she felt it must, for it had grown without her knowing it or planning it. "But your parents . . ."

"I know." Nora laughed again. "I'm probably crazy to suggest that you come over. I don't know what got into me. Something, though. Come anyway? After supper, maybe around seven? We have a telephone now," she added shyly. "I haven't used it much yet. But you could call if you change your mind. Here." She fumbled in the pocket of her ever-present apron, withdrawing a pencil stub and a scrap of paper, and scribbled something. "Here's the number."

"Let me give you mine, too, then." Liz tore a strip off Nora's scrap and reached for the pencil. "In case something comes up with you or *you* change *your* mind or your cat eats all the cream or something."

Nora laughed, taking the paper. "He won't," she said, "eat all the cream."

When she drove away, Liz's smile had broadened and she was humming, though unconsciously.

THIRTEEN

Liz took a shower in Mom's Hippo after a hasty meal of broiled chicken and salad, and laughed at herself for dressing with such care. "It's not as if it's a date, stupid," she said into the mirror as she brushed her newly washed hair and straightened the collar of the red and white striped shirt that she knew set off her dark skin.

She reached the Tillots' dirt road at a few minutes before seven, so she stopped as soon as she'd pulled into it, not wanting to be early — or to appear eager, she thought, again amused.

Am I eager, she wondered, turning off the engine and switching on the radio.

For the next several minutes she chased that thought around in her mind, and then, still without an answer, switched the engine back on and rolled slowly down the road.

The house looked even bleaker than she'd remembered it, its siding cracked and weathered, its roof sagging, its trim peeling. Needs more work than my place, she thought, getting out of the car and then kicking herself for not having brought something. But what? Wine? Not for strawberry shortcake, probably. Flowers? But Nora had plenty of those; Liz could even see them, though she didn't know all their names. Irises and lilies she recognized, interspersed with something blue and white and something else that looked like fading yellow daisies, nodding in the light breeze.

Nora answered the door so quickly that Liz was sure she'd been waiting at a window. She'd washed her hair, too, since that afternoon, Liz could see, and she'd put on an old-fashioned-looking pale yellow dress trimmed with blue piping. The warm smell of something baking made Liz's mouth water.

"You look nice," Liz said before she could wonder if she should. "I hope I'm not too early. And I'm sorry I didn't bring anything, but . . ."

"Bring anything?" Nora's smile was wide and welcoming. "But what would you bring except yourself?"

"I don't know. Wine. Flowers."

"No, don't be silly. Come on, come in. The old folks are asleep." She led Liz into the kitchen, which was warm, almost hot, from the stove. "At least I hope they are." She closed two doors at opposite ends of the room. "They go to sleep pretty early."

"That must mean you've got hours at night with nothing to do."

Nora motioned Liz to a chair. "Not quite nothing. Night's when I catch up on things like mending and ironing, things I usually can't do during the day."

"Ironing? But you don't have electricity."

Nora looked amused. "Neither did your great grandmother, I bet." She gestured to a shelf above the stove, along which marched several old-fashioned sadirons. "You heat them on the stove," she explained. "When one gets cool, there's another ready and waiting."

"They look heavy." Liz reached for one, momentarily startled by the envelope of warm air that surrounded the stove. "May I?"

"Sure. Be careful, though. They *are* heavy!"

"Whoa!" Liz laughed, hefting one. "They sure are." She put the iron back and for a moment they faced each other, not speaking.

"Let me get the cream," Nora said finally, turning away. "Biscuits are in the oven. I think they're about ready."

"Surely you didn't make fresh ones!" Liz exclaimed, calling after her.

"Why not? They're better fresh." Nora went outside briefly and returned with a bowl of whipped cream, which she set on the table next to a breadboard. Then, holding a dish towel bunched up in her hand, she pulled a sheet of golden-brown biscuits out of the oven and placed it on the breadboard. "There." She handed Liz a knife. "Maybe you could slice the biscuits while I get the berries?"

"Sure. Of course." Awkwardly, wondering why she felt so clumsy, Liz sliced two of the biscuits horizontally and put them on the gold-trimmed white plates that Nora handed her before she reached onto the counter and produced two bowls, one of crushed juicy berries and the other of small whole ones. "They're wild," Nora said. "But some are wilder than others. The big squashed ones are ones we planted eons ago; I don't take much care of them any more, but the plants still produce berries. And the little ones are Alpines, very sweet but not always very juicy. These" — she ladled crushed berries onto the biscuit halves — "have been sitting in sugar, rendering their juice, and these" — she topped the biscuits with cream and then added a few whole berries to each — "are the garnish. Dig in!"

"I would," Liz said, feeling around on the table for a fork, "but . . ."

"Oh, good grief!" Nora clapped her hand to her head. "Forks!" She leapt up, brushing past Liz on her way to a drawer under the far counter. Liz, charmed, fought off an absurd desire to seize her around the waist and hug her, for Nora's consternation at having forgotten the forks had turned her efficiency into a most appealing fluster.

"What a goose I am!" Nora came back, handing Liz a fork. "Here you are. Now you can dig in." She watched anxiously as Liz took a bite, chewed, swallowed. "Okay?"

"Okay!" Liz exclaimed. "Perfect. I have never," she said solemnly — sincerely, too — "tasted any strawberry shortcake this good."

"It's all right that it's on biscuits?" Nora asked, still anxiously, taking a bite herself.

"Absolutely," Liz said with her mouth full. She waved her empty fork before cutting the next piece. "In New York, if you ask for strawberry shortcake, they usually put it on cake, but my mother used to make it like this, and as far as I'm concerned, anything else is a cheap imitation."

"You must be a New Englander, then. Or your mother must be."

"I am," Liz said. "Born in Boston, transplanted to Connecticut at a young age, and moved to New York City right after college. Mom was from Maine, Dad was from New Hampshire. And since the cabin's here in Rhode Island, we've hit almost all the New England states."

"Was?" Nora said, looking solicitous.

"Hmm?" Liz was busy with another mouthful.

"You said 'was,' about your parents."

"Oh — yes. Mom died of breast cancer five years ago." Liz tried to sound matter-of-fact. "And Dad of a heart attack this past spring."

"I'm sorry."

"Thank you. It's okay. I miss them, but . . . Well, maybe

102

it's better than living on into old age and going through all the stuff old people go through, you know? Well, of course," she added, flustered herself then. "Of course you know!"

"Yes." Nora spooned up berries. "I do. I certainly do."

A noise behind one of the closed doors made them both turn, and Liz was conscious of a clumping sound right before the door opened. Nora's father appeared in the opening.

"Who's that?" he said crossly. "I thought I heard voices!"

Nora got up and went to him, steadying him with her arms; Liz stood as well. "This is Liz Hardy," she said. "You remember. She stopped in last month . . ."

"I'm the one who borrowed the jack." Liz held out her hand, but Ralph ignored it. "How are you, Mr. Tillot?"

"Not well," he growled. "So you brought the jack back finally, did you?"

"She brought it back weeks ago," Nora said. "I told you that, Father."

"And I sure was grateful to have it," Liz said quickly, struggling to be polite and cheerful, but appalled all over again at this brusque, grizzled man whose eyes flashed equal amounts of anger and suspicion. He seemed more stooped than when she'd first seen him, and much more hostile. "It just about saved my life that day."

"Harumph. Shouldn't need a jack if you're a careful driver."

"Father!" Nora said in a loud whisper. "You know that's not true. Accidents happen."

"I think I ran over a nail," Liz said. "Or maybe there was a nail already in the tire when I left New York. It was a rental car."

"Don't hold with rented things." Ralph lurched toward the table. "Nora, I'm dizzy."

"Maybe you should go back to bed, then, Father." Nora moved swiftly behind him and put her hands on his waist.

But he pulled out a chair and toppled into it. "More short-cake?" He peered at the half-full plates. "No wonder you didn't eat much at supper. Planning a secret party, weren't you?"

"Would you like some?" Nora asked.

He shook his head. "My stomach's no good." He turned to Liz. "Cancer," he whispered behind his hand.

"I'm sorry." Liz glanced at Nora, who shook her head. "That must be very difficult."

"It is. Maybe," he said to Nora, "a small piece."

She cut him half a biscuit and passed him the bowls. He ladled berries and cream generously over the half, and then topped it with the other half, adding more cream and a single berry to the top. "There," he said triumphantly.

"It's nice that you've got such a good appetite," Liz couldn't resist saying.

"Some days it's not too bad," he said. "But I didn't eat much all day, did I, Nora?"

"Well . . ." Nora began.

But he interrupted, saying to Liz, "You'll be going back where you came from soon, I expect."

"I'll be going back to my cabin on Yellowfin Lake. I'll be staying there all summer. And," she added impulsively, "I was hoping Nora could give me some gardening pointers."

"Nora's too busy to give 'pointers,' " Ralph growled. "She's got work to do in the house and when she's outside, she has to tend her own garden, not teach. Isn't that right, Nora?"

"I think I could spare a little time now and then." Nora smiled at Liz. "I'd like to, in fact."

"Now and then." Ralph pushed his plate away. "Make sure it's more then than now. Help me back into bed, Nora." He struggled to stand, and then slipped. But it's as if, Liz thought, grabbing for one of his arms as Nora grabbed for the other, he's purposely teetering.

"Don't push me!" Ralph barked angrily at Liz.

"I'll be right back," Nora said, steering him and his walker hastily out of the room.

While Nora was gone, Liz took the empty dishes to the sink and worked the pump handle up and down till a thin stream of cold water emerged. She looked around for a pot, then saw there was a black iron kettle already on the stove over one of the warm, lid-covered burners. Remembering a toy old-fashioned cook stove she and Jeff had played with at their grandmother's, she looked around for a handle for the burner lid, found one, and moved the kettle. Then she dipped the handle into the hole on the lid, lifting it and exposing the glowing coals inside the stove. She replaced the kettle and sat down to wait for the water to get hot enough for doing dishes.

She was just getting up again to look for some kind of soap when Nora came back carrying a plastic urinal. "Sorry," she said, "He's like a little boy. Has to — to go to the bathroom, wants a drink of water, etcetera, etcetera. I'll be right . . . You've got the kettle on! And you've cleared the table, and rinsed the plates, too!"

Liz grinned. "Even us twenty-first century types can — I don't know . . ."

"Cope with time travel?" Nora smiled. "Thank you. Back in a jiffy."

When she came back, she disappeared into her father's bedroom again and Liz could hear her voice and Ralph's through the walls. They seemed to be arguing about something, so she rummaged under the sink, where she found a dishpan and a long-handled wire pouch full of soap ends. Liz filled the dishpan and managed to make soap film on the warm water by swishing the pouch back and forth. She washed the plates and was just rinsing them by pouring hot water over them in their rack when Nora came back in and leaned against the door frame watching her.

"You are a marvel," she said. "This is the first time anyone but me has washed a dish in this house in years. Nothing like making your guests work. The least I can do is offer you some coffee. Or tea."

"Coffee," Liz said. "Thank you. That'd be wonderful."

While the coffee brewed, Nora and Liz sat companionably at the kitchen table, talking in low voices, mostly about gardening, and Nora agreed to answer Liz's questions whenever she had time. "Maybe I could even come over and have a look at your garden," she said, "some Friday. That's usually the day Mrs. Brice takes me shopping."

"I could do that," Liz offered, "take you shopping. And give your Mrs. Brice a break."

"I think Mrs. Brice likes doing it," Nora said. "But maybe you could take me on the day I come to look at your garden."

"How about this coming Friday?" Liz asked quickly, afraid that if she didn't pin her down, Nora would never come.

Nora got up to get the coffee. "Maybe," she said. "I'll check with Mrs. Brice. She did say something about her daughter and son-in-law coming to visit. She'd probably welcome the time off then."

"Great!" Liz accepted a large stoneware cup of coffee. "That's settled, then."

"Well," said Nora, "almost, anyway."

FOURTEEN

At midnight, Nora sat sleeplessly at the kitchen table trying to proofread. Pink-gold light from the kerosene lamp made a flickering pattern on the galley page in front of her; moonlight cascaded disturbingly through the window. "Moon's nearly full," she mused, seeing Thomas sitting in the path it made across the floor. "No wonder I'm restless."

The book she was proofing was absorbing. It had been hard, so far, to concentrate on finding typos, for the story had sucked her in and she liked the characters; she'd had to read many a page more than once.

But now it was even hard to concentrate on the story. She felt oddly excited, as if a new chapter of her life had begun that evening while she'd been having strawberry shortcake

107

with Liz. How silly, she told herself; it was only strawberry shortcake!

Yes, but a friend! Another person "my own age," as in: "Play with someone your own age. Pick on someone your own age. Isn't there anyone your own age around for you to have fun with?"

There hadn't been since high school. Then there had been Marsha. Nora leaned back, her pencil making absent-minded circles on a blank sheet in front of her. Marsha was married now, with, how many was it? Two? No, perhaps three children; Marsha with her long pony-tailed hair, her red lipstick (but only on weekends), and the dates she told Nora about each Monday lunchtime. Nora remembered Marsha's first kiss. (Did Marsha?) The boy was named Tim, and he had the beginnings of a mustache; Marsha said it tickled. They'd giggled over that; Nora smiled, remembering.

Three years ago, soon after Corinne's stroke and the birth of Marsha's most recent baby, Nora and Marsha were still writing each other regularly, and they'd joked about how now they both had diapers to change, Marsha, the baby's and Nora, her mother's. But the joke had worn thin, and the letters gradually slowed until now they arrived only at Christmas. Since her marriage (to a man named Victor, not Tim), Marsha had sent annual computer-printed accounts of skiing and camping and Victor's and her own work, plus, later, enthusiastic descriptions of how well the children were doing in school/music lessons/sports. Nora had read those letters with envy at first, but for the last few years, their contents had seemed so remote, so outside her own life, that they bored her. And she'd stopped writing Marsha, for what was there to say?

Her other friend (Nora got up and pumped herself a glass of water, then settled again with Thomas on her lap, curled and purring) — her other friend had been Peter, gentle handsome, kind Peter. He'd walked her home from school and after a while had asked her to the movies, but she wasn't allowed to go. "Never mind," he'd said and had gone on

108

walking her home, but he'd asked other girls to the movies. Sometimes, when Ralph was away on one of his infrequent sales trips, Corinne had let her have Marsha or Peter to supper; they were fascinated by the way the Tillots lived. Marsha had wanted to learn how to use the big cook stove, and Peter had sometimes chopped wood for them if they were running low. For the last ten years or so now, Ralph had claimed to be unable to do that job, and since he wouldn't let Nora do it, he'd arranged to buy stove-length wood by the cord, although he'd grumbled at the cost.

Peter, Nora thought, stroking Thomas, made me laugh. She remembered the day he'd done cartwheels in the front yard and pretended to walk on a tightrope; Mama had laughed, too. And he'd told them the plots of movies, elaborately, with gestures and different voices for the different characters.

She'd tried to imagine herself going on a date with him, necking in a car, the way Marsha told her "everyone" did, letting him touch her, put his hands on her breasts, stick his tongue in her mouth and dart it back and forth the way Marsha had described.

But it was hard to imagine, somehow. It had made her shiver, feel vaguely — what? Half sick, half excited.

There hadn't been any other friends.

But Ralph had been a friend to her sometimes, back when she'd been little, telling her stories and taking her fishing, taking her and Corinne out for Sunday drives in the old Ford. He'd even taken them out to lunch a few times, calling them "my two best girls," and opening doors and pulling out chairs for them. He'd never taken them to dinner, for that was too expensive, but lunch had been fun.

He hadn't let Nora have lunch out with Marsha, though, when she was in high school. He'd changed by then, guarding her more closely, growing more suspicious of outsiders, angry, it seemed to Nora, at the world.

What would it be like to have lunch with a friend?

To *have* a friend?

Restlessly, thinking again of Liz, Nora got up, easing Thomas into his basket by the stove. The moon had moved a little now; the path on the floor was a half-path, and shadows lurked in the back yard. The woodshed looked like a large prehistoric animal hunched near the back stoop, the barn loomed beyond the garden, and the outhouse looked more tilted than it really was. What will I do, she wondered absently, when it falls down?

She could recall Liz's laughing eyes — that is how she thought of them: "laughing eyes," like the Longfellow poem, only that was Edith, wasn't it? But Allegra was the one who laughed: "Grave Alice and laughing Allegra — yes, but wasn't it "Edith with laughing eyes"? Or was it some other kind of eyes? She'd have to look it up.

Liz's eyes had laughed, but had seemed pain-filled once, when she'd glanced away. And they'd held sympathy when she'd looked at Ralph. How nice she'd been to him, how kind! And yet exasperated, too.

A kindred spirit.

Would it be charity, letting Liz take me shopping?

Perhaps not if I helped her with her garden.

And perhaps we could become friends, just for the summer, till she has to go back. For she will go back, of course, to her teaching; Liz had mentioned that she taught high school.

What would that be like, Nora wondered, teaching great huge children, high school boys and girls in New York City? One would have to be brave and firm to do that. Brave and firm . . .

"What in thunder are you doing up?" Ralph, shoving the door open, clumped his walker into the kitchen. His pajama top was flopping around his waist and his bathrobe was open. As usual, when he was ready for the night, he wore no bottoms and the moonlight fell on his thinning pubic hair, his incongruously heavy, sagging testicles and limp penis.

A wave of disgust swept over Nora. "Father, cover yourself!" she said sharply. "I might ask you the same thing, about being up."

He looked down at his body in surprise, then clumsily pulled his bathrobe closed, swaying as soon as he let go of the walker.

"Too much noise," he said, though Nora had heard nothing but Thomas's quiet purr. "I'm dizzy." He reached for the back of a chair.

Nora had an overpoweringly evil desire to push him over, to wrestle him to the ground; it blinded her with its intensity. She forced a smile, she hoped a sweet one, to counter the feeling, pushing it back, denying it. For of course it wasn't a true desire, really; it was the fault of the hour, the moonlight, her wandering thoughts resenting interruption.

"I'm sorry you're dizzy," she said, but not as kindly as she'd planned. "Would you like some cocoa?"

"My stomach . . ." he began, but then gave her a little-boy smile, one she still found charming, one that still moved her. "Yes," he said, sinking into the chair.

So they sat having cocoa while Thomas purred, and Nora read Ralph the page she was working on, first telling him the plot so far. He probably missed some of it, she realized, not that it mattered, for his eyes soon closed. When cocoa-spittle dribbled out of his mouth, Nora shook him awake and led him, she hoped gently, back to bed.

An hour later, when the moon had moved to the front of the house and Nora had reached the end of the galleys, she went outside and sat in the dark near the garden, quietly stroking Thomas, enjoying the quiet. Later still, when she checked on her parents as she always did before sleeping, she found Ralph sitting by Corinne's bedside, holding her hand. There was a faint sweet smile on Corinne's sleeping face, but there were dried tears on Ralph's. Nora thought again of stories and fishing and long-ago excursions, and found tears welling up in her own eyes as she helped her now-docile father once again to bed.

When Liz got back to the cabin that night, she found a note stuck in the screen door. "Came by to say hello and invite you to come see my garden tomorrow. Took the liberty of walking around a bit. Nice piece of land! Still would like to see more of it. Will call later. Roy."

Angrily, she squeezed the note into a crumpled ball and tossed it into the fireplace.

And when the phone rang half an hour later, and half an hour after that, she ignored it.

The third time, she took it off the hook.

FIFTEEN

At eight o'clock the next morning, the phone rang again, and this time Liz did answer it, barking "Hello?" angrily into the receiver.

But it was Nora.

"I was thinking," Nora said shyly when Liz had apologized for answering rudely, explaining that someone she didn't like had been trying to get her, "about what you said about your garden, and my shopping and all, and — well, I was right about Mrs. Brice having company. So if it's still all right with you, I could give Mrs. Brice Friday off, and see you. I mean if . . ."

"That's wonderful!" Liz said, filled with unexpected (but was it really unexpected?) pleasure at hearing Nora's voice.

"Friday's fine. What time shall I get you? We could make a day of it if you'd like."

"I *would* like," Nora said, "but I can't be away very long. Just a couple of hours. Maybe one, one o'clock, I mean, not one hour? Or two o'clock?"

"Could you come here for lunch?" Liz asked quickly. "We could eat while we're looking at the garden if you're really in a hurry."

Nora laughed. "That's too much of a hurry." She paused a moment. "Lunch?" Her voice was softer when she spoke again, almost shy, Liz thought. "Yes, I think so. I could leave my parents' lunch with the girl who takes care of them when I'm out. Yes, wonderful! Thank you. And then . . ."

"And then I could take you to do your shopping. No problem. I'll probably have to do some of my own by then. What do you like for lunch? Sandwiches? Salad? Soup? What do you usually have?"

"Oh, anything. Any of those is fine."

"What about fish?" Liz asked recklessly. "I make a mean grilled salmon."

"Oh, but that's far too much trouble! And too expensive." But Liz could hear longing in her voice.

"Grilled outdoors," Liz said. "That gives it a wonderful smoky flavor. If you like that."

Nora laughed again, even more shyly this time. "Yes," she admitted. "Yes, I do. It's been ages since I've had salmon. Father doesn't trust fish."

"Then that's settled," Liz told her happily. "Settled." She paused for a moment, but Nora didn't seem to be going to say anything more. "I'll see you Friday, then. What time should I pick you up? How about twelve-thirty? Or is that too early? You said . . ."

"No, that's fine. I'll have to check with Patty, though; that's the girl. But I'm sure it'll be fine."

"Great! Hey, you're using the new phone! Good for you. Does it feel weird?"

"Yes. Yes, it does. Very weird. A little bit like magic."

"If you think that's magic," Liz said, "wait'll you see my TV set."

"Gee, I don't know if I'll be able to stand it! Too much technology all at once. I bet you've got a modern stove, too, and a refrigerator, and a dishwasher. "

"No dishwasher," Liz said, "but the others. And lots and lots of electricity. Sitting around in — in bushel baskets, just waiting to be used. I'll lend you some if you like."

"I'd love it." Here Nora's voice faded and Liz could hear Ralph's in the background, gruff and angry. Damn him, she thought; damn that old man!

"Liz, I've got to go now. But I'll see you Friday, half-past twelve unless Patty can't come then." Ralph's voice grew louder. "I'll call you if there's any need to change it," Nora said hastily. " 'Bye."

Before Liz could say goodbye, a click told her Nora had already hung up.

"I told you you are not to use that infernal machine!" Ralph thundered, his eyes bulging with anger. "You promised it was just for emergencies. Do you see an emergency? I do not see one. There is not an emergency, damn it. Jesus Christ almighty, Nora, the minute my back is turned . . ."

"No!" Nora shouted, letting go; it felt wonderful. "It was not an emergency. But it's high time we were able to be in touch with the outside world."

"Ha! What outside world? We don't need an outside world. Who were you talking to? You talked to someone else before you talked to whoever that was. Who was it?"

You don't have to tell him, Nora's mind said to her. You really don't.

But she did.

"I called Mrs. Brice earlier," she explained, reluctantly

trying to calm her temper. "I called her because she's having company and it'll be difficult for her to take me shopping this week."

"Don't go shopping then. We spend far too much on food as it is. We can have soup. Some of that meat you bought so extravagantly. There's lots of things in the garden now; we can have them. We don't need to have such big meals. My stomach can't take them anyway."

"Then don't eat so much!" Nora shouted. But when her father flinched, she regretted it and put her arms around him. "I'm sorry," she said. "I'm sorry I yelled. But it's all arranged now. That nice Liz Hardy is going to take me shopping, and Patty Monahan will come as usual and sit with you and Mama. See how helpful the phone is? If it hadn't been for the phone, I couldn't have arranged any of that."

But he was staring at her, rigid, reproachful. "Liz Hardy," he said, his voice taut with what Nora could only diagnose as loathing. "That woman. I don't want you seeing her, letting her come here. It's her doing we got that phone in the first place."

"No, it's not, Father," Nora said in what she hoped was a soothing tone of voice. "It's not. It was the Hastingses' idea. Remember? I told you."

"Interfering busybodies! You can't trust anyone," he said dramatically, turning away, "but your mother and your wife."

"Not even your daughter who takes care of you?"

"No. Not even my daughter who takes care of me."

"That makes me very sad," Nora said. "Father, listen." She put a hand on his walker, then on his hand, but he remained rigid. "Father, I'm forty years old. I'm a grown-up. I have very little life of my own. I don't ask for much, really I don't. But once in a while I'd like to be with" — she smiled slightly — "with someone my own age."

"There's church," he said gruffly. "There must be young people at church."

"Yes, there are," she answered. "But Mrs. Brice whisks me

116

off to buy the paper right after the service, and then brings me home, and I can't go to any other church events because I can't get to them. If I could drive . . ."

"Oh, no," he bellowed, furious again. "There you go! You are not going to drive. That's not for women; women can't drive anyway. It's too dangerous, honey," he whined. "What if you had an accident? What would I do then? I can't take care of your mother. I'm too sick. I need you, Nora. I need my little girl."

Sighing, Nora patted his hand and led him back to his room.

SIXTEEN

After talking with Nora, Liz set off whistling down the lake path, carrying a saw and clippers and wearing her oldest jeans and a faded t-shirt with "HOLDEN ACADEMY" emblazoned across the front. For two hours, she worked steadily, chopping and sawing, disregarding both the scratches on her arms and hands and the nervous thoughts about Friday's lunch that crowded into her mind whenever she let down her guard.

By 10:30 the sun was already hot, her shirt was clinging to her sweaty back, and she was cursing herself for not having brought water. Then, just as she lifted the shirt's hem to wipe the sweat out of her eyes, the board she was standing on vibrated and Roy appeared at its other end, wearing a wide-brimmed cloth hat and khaki shorts, and carrying a red-and-white cooler with "PLAYMATE" printed on its side. "Hey, there," he called. "Thought I might find you here."

Liz, speechless, could only stare.

"Beer?" he offered, lifting the cooler, holding it out to her. "Water? Lemonade? I came equipped. Whew, it's hot, isn't it?"

Rejoinders chased themselves rapidly through Liz's mind. But she knew she couldn't say any of them out loud.

"I'm for beer myself," Roy said, taking a brown bottle from the cooler and twisting off its cap. Holding it out to her, he said, "You, too?"

"No. No thanks," she sputtered.

"Water? Lemonade?" he asked again. "You've got to be thirsty. You even look thirsty. And," he added, stretching his hand toward her face, "you've got a very charming smudge right" — he rubbed his thumb along her cheek — "there."

Instinctively, Liz twisted her head away. "Roy, I don't want to be rude," she said carefully, "but I came here to be alone. I really don't want company. I don't know how to make that any clearer." She cringed inwardly at the stiffness of her words. But why shouldn't I say them, she thought. He really is being impossible.

He gave her a long look, then downed more beer and resumed staring. For a moment her stomach lurched in fear, but that's ridiculous, she told herself; surely he's perfectly safe!

"I guess you really do mean it," he said finally. "Okay. Sorry. Again. My last girlfriend always said I come on too strong." He put the half-empty bottle back in the cooler and snapped the lid down. "I'll be going, leave you to your — your project."

"Thank you. It's not you, really."

"What a relief," he said sarcastically. Then he shook his head. "No, sorry once more. That wasn't fair. I do come on

119

too strong, I know, especially when faced with an attractive woman. You *are* an attractive woman, you know, even with a smudge on your face and a dirty shirt. But I think I misjudged you. Truce?"

Reluctantly, Liz shook the hand he offered her.

"Nice job clearing the path," he called over his shoulder as he left.

Later that afternoon when Liz had finished the path, had a swim, arranged for a carpenter to fix the upstairs window, and was looking out toward the lake from inside and planning what to clear and what to leave standing, the phone rang.

"Oh, good, Liz, you're in," came a cheerful female voice when Liz finally answered. "Georgia Foley here. First, how are you?"

"Fine." Liz groaned inwardly, angry at herself for not yet having asked Georgia to take the cabin off the market. "How are you?"

"Good, thanks. Listen, Liz, I'm calling as an emissary, you might say, a messenger of peace. Have you got a moment?"

Liz pulled a chair over to the phone and sat. "Just about," she said cautiously.

"I'll be as quick as I can. Now, I know you've met Roy Stark." Georgia paused significantly.

"Yes."

"He's such a nice man, don't you think?"

"I don't really know him, Georgia."

"No, no, of course you don't. Not yet, anyway." Georgia laughed. "Well, I do know him, and poor lamb, he can be so inept socially. You know how men, especially good-looking ones, think all they have to do is turn on the charm and all women flutter . . ."

Liz leaned her head against the wall.

". . . and Roy's no different. But it just so happens Roy's a client of mine as well as a friend. In fact, he's the client I mentioned a couple of months ago who's interested in buying your place. He's got some really wonderful ideas for it, Liz, and . . ."

"Georgia, it's not for sale."

"What? But . . ."

"I'm sorry. I should have told you earlier. I was planning to, but I hadn't gotten around to it yet. My fault. My brother and I have decided not to sell."

There was a pause during which Liz found herself actually smiling. So that was Roy's interest in her! Maybe now he'd leave her alone.

"Is that a firm decision?"

"Yes, for now." Immediately she regretted the "for now," which Georgia repeated quickly: "For now? How long is now?"

"I don't know. Maybe it's permanent. Please tell Roy, would you? I wouldn't want to give him false hopes."

"I'll tell him if you insist, Liz, but I should tell you that he's prepared to make a very handsome offer. So do let me know if you change your mind or if you want to discuss it further. I'd really hate to have you miss out. Of course he can't wait forever."

"No," said Liz. "I wouldn't want him to. I don't think I'll be changing my mind for a long time, Georgia, if at all. So Roy should probably go ahead and buy something else. There are other cabins on the lake."

"Actually," said Georgia, "there aren't any available, especially not any with land. The only thing on the market is a bit of acreage across . . ."

"Georgia," Liz interrupted, "I don't want to be rude, but I really have to go. Thanks for calling."

"Oh, no trouble, no trouble at all." But Georgia's voice still sounded strained and disappointed. "I'm glad you told me. And I do hope you're enjoying your charming little camp.

I can understand your wanting to hold onto it. But if that changes . . ."

"I'll let you know," Liz said. "Goodbye, Georgia. Thanks again. And my apologies to both you and Roy for not letting you know sooner."

SEVENTEEN

Dingy, Nora thought at noon on Friday, brushing her hair and eyeing the faded flower-sprigged paper covering the walls of the maid's room, now her room, off the kitchen. They hadn't used the old house's second floor since Ralph had begun to complain about dizziness, long before Corinne's stroke.

But it doesn't matter, she thought; Liz Hardy will never see this room.

Will she?

Of course not, Nora admonished herself sharply, rummaging in her narrow closet for a clean dress.

Or a blouse and skirt; yes, she thought, pulling out a calico skirt, green with tiny blue and white flowers. "Like the wallpaper," she muttered, amused, as she pulled it on and topped it with a white scoop-necked blouse she hadn't worn in years.

But it, she was glad to see, unlike the wallpaper, wasn't dingy.

The time was twelve-fifteen.

Thomas, perched on the sill under the open window that looked out over the back yard, barn, outhouse, and the neglected fields beyond, jumped down and wound around her legs, mewing plaintively.

"You've got plenty of food, you old faker." Nora picked him up and cuddled him, her cheek against his purring side.

There is no reason to be nervous, she said silently to herself, putting the cat down. Reaching to the bureau for her old gray pocketbook, she checked inside for money, the house keys she seldom had to use but always carried, and the shopping list that she'd already looked over many times. No reason to be nervous. None. What could happen? What could happen today, with Patty here the way she's been every Friday for ages, that hasn't happened before? Why should today be different?

But she felt it was; the fluttering in her stomach told her it was, the dampness on her palms, the catch in her throat.

"See you, Tom," she said to the cat, decisively closing her pocketbook and darting into the kitchen, stopping to look around the corner into her mother's room. Corinne, freshly bathed, breakfasted, and nightgowned, was snoring lightly. Nora tweaked the sheet to one side; it had slipped. Quickly, she crossed the kitchen to her father's room.

"I'm just going," she announced. "As soon as Patty comes." *And Liz*, she added silently, swallowing guilt for not saying it out loud.

But why should I feel guilty?

"Ermmm." Ralph, in his chair by the window, grunted and held out his hand. "Let's see that list."

"You already looked at it."

"Don't remember. List."

Nora snapped open her pocketbook and handed it to him. A car drove up outside; a car door slammed.

"Father, it's time. Here's Patty."

He looked up from the list and peered out the window. "That's not Patty," he said. "That's your precious Miss Hardy. We don't need those paper towels." He held the list out to her. "What's wrong with cloth ones?"

"Cloth ones need washing. And I don't like to use them for wiping up spills and accidents."

"What's wrong with rags, then? No paper towels. That's an extravagance."

There was a firm knock at the door.

Nora took the list, resisting the impulse to snatch it roughly. "I may be back a little later than usual," she said. "Come in," she shouted, though she doubted that Liz would be able to hear her.

"Oh, you may, may you? And if I fall or have a bad dizzy spell, what then?"

"Patty will be here."

"I don't want you off gallivanting."

"I promised Liz I'd have a look at her mother's old garden."

"And a generous promise that was," Liz said, appearing in Ralph's doorway. "Hi, Nora. Good afternoon, Mr. Tillot. I brought in my newspaper just in case you'd like to have a look at it. I've finished with it."

"Harumph! Infernal lies in papers. I would not like to have a look at it."

"Father!" Nora admonished him sharply. "You could at least say thank you."

"Why? I didn't ask for the paper."

"Sorry," Nora said to Liz in an undertone.

Liz shrugged, and whispered, "It's okay. I didn't mean to offend you, Mr. Tillot," she said to him. "You're right that there's a lot of ridiculous stuff in the papers these days. But I didn't know but what you might be interested in the sports or the business section or something like that."

"Sports are a waste of time," he said gruffly. "Have been ever since big money took them over. And business is full of crooks. Politics, too."

Liz grinned. "I guess that about covers it, then, unless you like recipes and movie reviews."

Nora suppressed a laugh; Ralph eyed Liz suspiciously, grunted, and turned back to the window.

With immense relief, Nora heard Patty drive up, and tugged Liz out of the room.

"I probably shouldn't say this," Liz said a few minutes later as she drove Nora out toward the main road, "but, again, I don't know how you stand it."

"Sometimes I don't. Mostly I don't think about it. And they sleep so much, Mama does, anyway. In the summer I can stay outside a lot, and that helps; Father does make more demands when I'm in the house. In the summer I try not to think about the winter." Nora glanced at Liz. "That must sound pretty Pollyanna-ish."

"No. But I still can't help thinking you must be some kind of saint."

"You wouldn't think that if you could read my mind sometimes." Nora looked out the window, watching the trees. Liz drove smoothly, confidently, unlike Mrs. Brice, who tended to weave and look from side to side as much as straight ahead. "My mother's a sweetheart. And Father wasn't always so gruff. And I do like it here. Besides, I don't know what I'd do if I didn't have them," she added. "My parents, I mean. I know I won't always. But it's hard to imagine life without them."

"Yes," said Liz. "I suppose it is." She turned onto the main road. "Think of all the free time, though. Unless you got a job or something."

"I have a job now," Nora said — proudly, defensively, Liz thought. "Not much of one, but I've been thinking of expanding it. Proofreading," she added before Liz could ask. "For a small publisher. They send me galleys and I correct them. The author corrects them, too, of course, and so does someone at the typesetter's, but the publisher doesn't have a very big staff so they use freelancers. I've been thinking of asking for more work from them, or asking another publisher."

"What kinds of books?" Liz asked.

"Oh, everything. Novels, poetry. Poetry's hard, because of course some things that look like errors, aren't, so you have to read against the manuscript. Nonfiction, too. I did a Civil War history last winter, a big thick book, but it was fascinating."

Nora's cheeks had flushed and her eyes sparkled; she's come alive, Liz thought, suddenly no longer sorry for her; she's not a dowdy careworn drudge at all now.

"Sounds great," Liz said. "Any science? I'm biased," she explained hastily, "being a bio teacher and all."

"No, no science." Nora chuckled. "I don't think I could manage that. Not smart enough, I guess."

There she goes again; Liz turned down the long drive to the cabin. "I don't think it's a question of smart," she said carefully. "I'm smart, but I could never manage poetry."

"Poetry's just words," Nora said absently.

"And thoughts and ideas and feelings. Plus beauty, no?" Liz stopped in front of the cabin and turned toward Nora. "No?"

"Well, yes, that's right." Nora seemed surprised. "But when I write it, I don't think of it that way. It just sort of comes out, you know?"

"Wow! So you write poetry?"

Nora nodded. "I'm taking a correspondence course. I don't

think I'm very good at it. The instructors are told to encourage the students; it's pretty transparent. But it's fun. And sometimes a kind of — relief, I guess."

"Are your poems very private?" Liz switched off the ignition. "Or do you show them to people?"

"Who would I show them to?" Nora looked out the car window at the cabin. "I love it," she said. "What a sweet little house!"

"It wasn't so sweet when I arrived," Liz said, getting out of the car. "At least not inside. But, yeah, I guess it does look pretty nice." She went around to the passenger side.

Nora had jumped out by then and was looking toward the lake, shading her eyes. "How wonderful," she said, "it must be to wake up here in the morning. It must be so peaceful, so calm!"

"It is. I usually take my coffee out to the dock. Or I have a swim and then take my coffee out to the dock. If it's really early, there's no sound but the birds and there are lots of them. Come." She held out her hand impulsively, without really noticing. "Come see the garden."

Nora took her hand, whereupon Liz did notice and felt instantly wary, self-conscious. But she managed to lead Nora around the side of the house to her mother's perennial plot, with the rock garden beyond.

"Oh," Nora exclaimed, dropping Liz's hand and falling to her knees. "Oh, but this is marvelous!"

Liz knelt beside her. "Is it? I wouldn't know. I mean, it looks pretty and even exciting, with stuff coming up and all, but I only know maybe two or three of these flowers and I have no idea" — she pointed to a cluster of stubby gray-green leaves — "if something like that is a weed or a rare exotic plant."

"Neither. It's a sedum. It'll spend the summer growing and then in the fall it'll have flowers. They'll probably be a sort of maroon-reddish, but they might be yellow. There are lots of different kinds of sedum," Nora explained, carefully moving twigs and leaf mold off some small multi-lobed leaves. "Look," she said, "here's a little chrysanthemum plant. It's been neglected, but if you keep an eye on it and pinch it off several times during the summer, it should form a nice mound and then flower in the fall."

"Chrysanthemum! You mean those huge fall flowers?"

"Some of them are huge, but this one will probably have lots of smallish ones. That's the goal of pinching off, usually, to help plants form mounds covered with flowers. Now here" — Nora stood up, brushing dirt from her knees; her legs were bare, Liz noticed, and her feet, with neatly trimmed nails, were in sandals — "here's phlox coming, lots of it." She pointed to several tall leafy plants with buds at the ends of their many branches. "These will flower fairly soon. You might put some fertilizer in, though; everything's kind of spindly, probably undernourished."

"What kind of fertilizer?" Liz asked, enjoying watching Nora move around the garden, examining, bending over the plants, touching them delicately, confidently.

"You could get some all-purpose commercial stuff at a hardware store. Or you could get a soil test kit and find out exactly what the soil lacks." Nora cocked her head. "That should interest you," she said. "Mixing chemicals."

"I'm not a chemist, but, well, yes, I guess it would. Really? Mixing chemicals?"

"It depends on the kind of kit. Some involve more work than others. They sell all kinds at Greely's. You know, the hardware store in town."

Liz nodded. "Maybe we could go there when we're through grocery shopping. And you could show me which one to buy."

"Sure," said Nora, "if there's time."

"When do you have to be back?"

"An hour ago, if Father has his way," Nora answered with a rueful smile. "I'm usually out for about two hours with Mrs. Brice, but this time I tried to tell him it'd be a bit longer. It can't be too much longer, though; he gets very anxious."

Liz looked at her watch, swallowing a less-than-charitable reply. "Then I guess we'd better get going. Tell you what. You stay out here and grub around in the garden so you can tell me more about it, and I'll see to lunch."

"But can't I help you?"

"Nope." Liz scrambled to her feet. "Seems to me you deserve an occasional meal you don't have to prepare."

"Thank you. That's very kind."

For a moment they looked at each other, and then Liz, struck by the intensity of the look, said, gruffly, "I'll give you a shout."

Recklessly, Liz served chardonnay with the French bread, the grilled salmon, and the Caesar salad, and they lingered over it, looking out over the lake from the living room. She wondered how often Nora drank wine; not often, she suspected. But she seemed to appreciate it, sipping it delicately, sometimes holding it in her mouth before she swallowed as if savoring its flavor as appreciatively as she'd seemed to savor turning the knobs on the stove and the TV, and examining the refrigerator.

"No motorboats," Nora commented after a comfortable pause. "I was afraid there'd be many, roaring by."

"Not yet. But come July, there'll be more. At least there always were. By August I'll probably want to scream at them to shut up. I like to watch the water skiers, though. Once one of them let me try her skis. It was terrifying and wonderful, all at once."

"You seem like a daring sort of person." Nora held up her glass, squinting through it at Liz. "The kind of person who'd do anything if she had a chance. Climb mountains, traverse the Arctic, cut your way through the jungle."

Liz laughed and poured them both more wine. "I'm afraid I'm the type who likes to read about adventures more than

130

have them. When I was a kid I used to think I'd do that kind of thing, or maybe become an Olympic athlete. But somehow I never found time to train for anything, and it's my firm belief that if you put a dream off by saying you don't have time for it, you really don't want it enough."

"You're probably right." Nora sipped, then put down her glass. "It must be wonderful to want something that much, enough to work hard for it. I never did. I never knew what I wanted. So it's just as well I'm doing what I'm doing. No thwarted dreams."

"No dreams of marrying, even?" Liz asked casually. "Of a husband and kids?"

"Not really." Nora's eyes went to the window again. "There was a boy, Peter, in my class in high school. We were friends. But I didn't date like other girls. Too shy, I guess, or just not interested. And not allowed to anyway." She turned back to Liz. "What about you?"

Briskly, Liz stacked the plates. "Boys — men — never interested me much either. How about a little carrot cake?"

"Do we have time?" Nora, seeming nervous, glanced at her watch. It was an old-fashioned ladies' watch, Liz noticed, with a black string-like strap. "Oh, my! Could we have the cake some other time? I think I'd really better get at the shopping."

"Sure," said Liz, standing there holding plates. "If you promise that we'll do this again. Lunch, I mean. The garden."

Nora stood up. "Oh, we will, don't you think? And I'll fix lunch here for you, if you'll let me. I'd love to learn how to use your stove, and I'd love to run water in your sink, and — oh, and turn lights on and off." Laughing, she flipped a nearby switch, then said, soberly, "If it's not too boring for you. If I'm not."

"You are not," Liz said before heading for the kitchen, "in the least boring."

EIGHTEEN

"He's in rare form," Patty said, meeting Nora at the door when Liz dropped her off at around 3:30. She was a cheerful girl with a fresh, open face who had graduated from the local high school a year earlier and since then had been earning a meager living by expanding her former baby- and elder-sitting jobs. "He's on a rampage. I kept telling him you'd said you'd be later than usual, but it didn't seem to make much difference. Here, let me have one of those." She took a grocery bag from Nora and followed her into the kitchen. "He even tried to use the phone," she said, setting the bag down on the table.

"He didn't!" Nora put her own bag down, her pocketbook next to it.

"Yeah." Patty grinned. "He did. I thought he was going to, like, rip it off the wall. He grabbed the receiver and then he yelled, 'Where the hell's the dial? How do you work this infernal thing?' I figured he must've used old-fashioned phones long ago at work or something, so I tried to, you know, explain about the buttons and stuff, and I gave him the number you left me, but he like freaked and banged at the buttons so hard I was afraid he was going to bust the phone through the wall. So I called the number for him, about eleven times; he kept making me do it again. No answer."

Nora groaned. "Oh, lord, I'm sorry, Patty! We were out shopping by then, probably. My friend and I." She said 'my friend' carefully, then realized she was savoring it as she had the wine, tasting it, almost.

"Yeah, that's what I figured. But he — uh-oh." Patty stepped back as Ralph thumped through the door, his shirt buttoned wrong.

"It's about time!" he thundered, banging his walker against the floor. "Where the hell were you?"

"Shopping," Nora said mildly, indicating the bags. "As you can see. I told you I'd be later than usual."

"Gallivanting!" Ralph roared. "Neglecting your duties." He reached into a bag, pulled out a package of Oreos, his favorite; Nora had gotten them as a peace offering.

Or, she thought, opening the package for him, as a bribe?

"Want some tea?" she asked him. "Patty?"

"No, thanks. I'll be going." Patty glanced at Ralph, who was stuffing cookies, and lowered her voice. "Um, you probably should have a look at your mother; she seems — I don't know. Kind of, you know, dopey. Not dumb, I mean," she added hastily. "Like sleepy-dopey. She didn't say much the whole time I was here, didn't want much either."

"I will," Nora said. "Anything else?"

"Nope. Good luck," Patty whispered, giving Nora's arm a little squeeze as she left.

"Thanks," Nora called.

"For what?" said Ralph, dark brown crumbs cascading down his chin.

Nora reached up and brushed them away. "For looking after you. Sit down, Father. I'll put the kettle on, then go check on Mama. Come on." She took his arm and settled him in a chair. She felt calmer, more amused than angry, as if the glow of her afternoon out with Liz was protecting her, insulating her from her father.

"You got those towels," Ralph said reproachfully, peering into a bag after he was seated.

Nora handed him another cookie. "Yes, I did." She planted herself in front of him. "Father," she said boldly, "since I'm the one who does the cooking and cleaning and everything else, don't you think I ought to be the one who decides what to buy? If I need something in order to make my job more efficient, I think I should get it. Don't you?"

"Well, Miss Fancy Pants, I'm the one who pays for everything around here."

"Not quite everything." But Nora felt the protective wall begin to crumble. She stopped, built it up again, and said, "In any case, what's done is done. Paper towels are cleaner than rags and cloth towels." She bent close to him and playfully tweaked his nose. "Fewer germs," she whispered sepulchrally, then turned and filled the kettle.

"My back aches," Ralph whined. "I have a lot of gas, Nora. I can't move my bowels. You better find the magnesia or something."

Nora reached the blue bottle down from the cupboard and handed it to him with a spoon, took the tea out of the canister, and headed for the door leading to Corinne's room. "I'll be right back."

"Help me," Ralph said softly. "Help me."

She turned, alarmed; he'd unscrewed the top of the bottle and was holding it out in one hand, the spoon in the other. Both hands were shaking.

In an instant she was at his side and had taken both bottle and spoon, pouring out the dose and feeding it to him.

"Thank you," he whispered, closing his eyes. "You're a good girl."

"Father," she said. "Hold up your hands."

He did, and it was just as she thought; there was no tremor. As an experiment, she handed him a glass. "Here, hold this, please, while I put some water in it for you."

"What for?" he asked suspiciously, his eyes snapping open. But he took the glass and held it while she transferred water from a pitcher by the sink into it.

Again, it was as she expected. No tremor.

Well, maybe the shadow of one, but nothing like before.

"Oh, I just thought you'd like a water chaser," she told him. "Be right back.

"You're a good girl," he called after her.

Corinne's eyes were closed, her breathing heavy. She looked a little pale, Nora thought, bending over her. "Mama," she said, touching her shoulder. "Mama?"

Corinne didn't stir.

"Mama?" Nora said more loudly, shaking her gently. "Mama, it's me, Nora."

Corinne's eyes fluttered, twitched, finally opened. She stared at Nora blankly, then said "Ahhh!" weakly and recoiled.

"Mama, it's me, Nora, your daughter." Nora kissed her and brushed back her hair. But fear caught at her throat.

Corinne smiled crookedly. "Oh," she said. "Dearie. I was dreaming. A bear, I think, a big bear."

"Chasing you?" Nora asked. "How horrible!"

"No, staring." Corinne's gaze shifted and she clutched Nora's arm, her eyes wide with fright. "Oh, there — there, see?" Shakily, she pointed to the corner where her rocking chair was heaped with clothes. "What's he doing there, Nora? Is that Peter? I don't want him in my room, Nora. Make him go."

"No, Mama, no, it's not Peter. It's just your clothes on the chair. Look." She picked up the clothes and took them to the bed. Corinne fingered them doubtfully. "See, Mama? Not Peter."

Corinne shook her head. "He was there," she insisted. "He must have left quickly. You wouldn't let him do anything, would you, dearie?"

What would he do, Nora wondered. "No, of course not. I never would."

"That's all right then," Corinne said comfortably. "How was school?"

"Fine, Mama, fine. Would you like a cup of tea?"

"Oh, my, that would be lovely." She struggled to sit. "But mustn't neglect horse — horsework. No, that's not it." She put her hand to her head, rubbing it, frowning.

"Homework, I think you mean. I don't have any today."

"How nice for you, dear."

In the kitchen, the kettle shrieked and Ralph yelled, "NORA! The tea!"

Corinne moved her good leg off the bed.

"Coming, Father!" Nora called. "Mama, wait just a minute, okay? Let me set the tea to steeping and then I'll come in and help you get up."

"Help me?" Corinne asked, obviously puzzled. "But why on earth? I don't need help." She wiggled her hips and arched her back, inchworming herself forward, then tugged at her paralyzed leg. "Something's wrong with my leg!" she cried. "You knew that. Did you know that?"

"Yes, Mama," Nora said. Ralph's walker thumped toward the bedroom. "You had a stroke a while back. You have trouble walking. That's why I said I'd help you."

"Nora, what the hell are you doing?"

"Helping Mama."

"Hello, sweetheart." Ralph pushed Nora aside as he moved to the bed. Bending clumsily, he put his arms around his wife.

"Ralph," Corinne said tearfully, "Nora says I had a stroke! Is that true?"

"Yes, sweetheart. Yes, it's true. But it's all right. You'll be fine."

"But I can't move my leg! Or" — she looked at her useless arm in surprise — "or my arm."

"I know, dearest," Nora heard Ralph say soothingly as she left to start the tea. "I know."

Thank God, she thought, he's still gentle and sweet to her.

NINETEEN

"Dear Mrs. Brice . . ." Nora began after church that Sunday — it was almost July now, hot and humid; Nora felt the backs of her thighs sticking to Louise's car seat through the thin fabric of her summer Sunday dress. "Dear Mrs. Brice, you've been so wonderful to me for so long. I've been thinking, that nice Liz Hardy, you know, the woman who's fixing up the old cabin at the lake?"

Louise wove the car around an object in the road; a plastic bag, it looked like. She glanced at Nora, her raised gray eyebrows making horizontal ridges in her forehead. "Yes?" she said tentatively, more a question than an answer.

"Well, you know she took me shopping that time when you

had company. And she's offered to do it regularly, for the summer. She's a teacher, so she'll be going back to New York in the fall. But in the meantime . . ."

"But Nora, dear!" Louise veered toward the right as she fixed her eyes more firmly on Nora. Nora winced, trying not to be obvious about bracing her body; there was a tree at the edge of the road, and a ditch. "It's no trouble at all for me," Louise said, "since I do my shopping then, too. It's nice of Miss Hardy, but wouldn't it be silly to bother someone else when I'm willing, ready, and able?"

"Oh, I know you are! And you've been so wonderful. I don't know what I'd have done without you all this time! Or what I'd do without you come fall, but . . . ."

"That's settled then." Louise patted Nora's knee; the car lurched a little to the left.

"Well, but you see," Nora said, avoiding Louise's eyes, "Liz — Ms. Hardy — has asked me to help her restore her mother's garden. In exchange for taking me shopping," she added hastily, though that was not true; there'd never been any question of "exchange."

"Oh." Louise's voice was flat, abrupt. "I suppose that's different, then."

"The trouble is," Nora said apologetically, "I don't think I can get away on another day. Father pretty much accepts Friday shopping and Sunday church, but I don't think he'd take kindly to my going out another day as well. You know, to help with the garden."

Louise turned down the road to Tillot Farm. "No," she said stiffly. "I suppose not." She swung — literally, Nora said to Liz later, on the telephone, "Literally *swung*" — the car around the bend at the front of the house. "I'll see you next Sunday then."

"Yes, of course." Impulsively, Nora leaned over and gave Louise a quick kiss on her cheek; it tasted of powder. "Thank you for understanding. We'll probably meet in the grocery store anyway," she said, "since Friday's your day, too."

139

But they didn't. "I do not," Louise said stiffly to Henry, her husband, "like that Hardy woman. I think she's interfering."

"Nonsense." Henry peered through thick glasses over the top of his newspaper. "You're just jealous. You'd think Nora was your own daughter the way you fuss over her like a regular mother hen. You're too protective, Louise."

Louise sniffed. "Well, perhaps if we'd *had* a daughter . . ." Henry glared at her, and she let that go. "Mark my words," she went on, "the Hardy woman will do more harm than good, befriending Nora like that. She's going to make that poor child long for things she can't have."

"What, a garden?" Henry said. "Nora Tillot's got the best one in the county already!"

"No, not a garden."

"What then, Louise?"

"Young friends. The modern world."

Henry put down his paper, revealing a spot on his yellow sport shirt. "Wouldn't you like that for her?" he asked curiously.

"Yes, of course I would," his wife snapped, noticing the spot with annoyance. Grease, perhaps butter from the breakfast muffin he'd taken out to the shed in which he frittered away countless hours each day and evening, fiddling with that ridiculous short wave radio of his. "But it's just not possible, don't you see? Ralph will never let her out of his clutches till he dies, and he shows no sign of doing that. And she's too meek to break free."

"Maybe this Hardy woman will give her the strength to break free. Wouldn't that be good?"

"For Nora, of course, although I suspect she couldn't function without someone to take care of. But what of Corinne and Ralph? How would they cope?"

Henry shrugged. "I thought long ago they should both be in a home of some sort."

"I doubt very much there's any money for that." Louise shook her head mournfully. "It would be far, far better to let everything stay as it is. You'd better let me have that shirt, Henry; there's a spot on it."

By the following Friday, everyone in Clarkston agreed they were in the middle of the worst heat wave in many years. Nora used the cook stove as little as possible, and that night even wheeled her mother into the back yard and fanned her till she slept. Luckily, there were few mosquitoes, it had been so dry. Ralph sat nearby in a chair she had lugged out for him, drinking glass after glass of ice-chip filled tea till there was no ice left. "And there'll be no more coming till Monday," Nora said, handing him the last glass.

"You could use that infernal telephone to call what's-his-name and get another block in the morning," said Ralph. "No reason why he has to stick to his regular day."

Nora shook her head. "I tried, but he said there won't *be* any more till Monday anyway. He's having trouble making it in this heat." She leaned forward. "Father," she said, "he also told me that he's probably going to go out of business soon. There's not enough market for his ice any more, except for campers and fish stores, and he wants to retire anyway. So I think we'd better get the electric company to hook us up, and buy a real refrigerator."

Ralph banged his glass down on the table she'd put beside him; the amber tea sloshed out, puddling. "Someone must still

make block ice," he bellowed. "Find out who does, and we'll
get it from there."

"What? Where?" Corinne whispered, opening her eyes.
"Oh, dear. Oh, dear."

"What is it, Mama?"

"That man, that man!" Feebly, Corinne lifted her good
arm and pointed across the yard.

"There's no man there, Mama. Just the trees at the far
edge of the garden. It's getting dark, so it's hard to see."

"Nora's right, sweetheart," Ralph said, leaning forward.
But Nora noticed he, too, had peered into the growing darkness.

"Where is the house?" Corinne cried in alarm, her eyes
darting around and her good shoulder twitching as she tried
to move. "Did it" — she clutched Nora's arm, panic in her
eyes — "did it burn down?"

"No, no, sweetie," Nora soothed her, "no. See?" She
turned Corinne's chair around. "You just had your back to it.
We're all out here, you, Father, and me, even Thomas, out in
the yard to catch the breeze, it's so hot inside. Would you like
some cool water? There's no more tea or ice, I'm afraid."

"Thomas?" Corinne twisted around to face the garden
again. "That man? Thomas?"

"No, Mama," Nora said patiently, "There's no man.
Thomas is the cat. You remember." She scooped up Thomas,
who'd been lying at her feet, panting, and held him out for
Corinne to see.

"Oooooh, no, not a dead thing!" Corinne moaned, recoil-
ing. "Not that dead thing from the road!"

"He's not dead, Mama, he's very much alive. Here, touch
him, see how warm he is!"

But Corinne shook her head and pulled away.

"It's the time that dog was hit on the road," Ralph said to
Nora, "and the people came here thinking it was our dog. It
frightened her." He edged his chair closer to Corinne's and
took her hands. "Sweetheart," he said. "My sweetheart. It's

all right. The dead thing's not here. 'In my sweet little Alice blue gown . . .' " he began singing.

Nora put Thomas down again and looked up at the sky, trying to let his crooning comfort her, too. A star fell as she watched.

TWENTY

A slightly revised pattern emerged. Sarah Cassidy, the nurse, continued her regular visits, and on Sundays, Patty still came to stay with the old folks while Louise drove Nora to church and to get the Sunday paper. But Patty's Friday sessions lengthened, matching Nora's lengthening visits with Liz for lunch, gardening, and grocery shopping.

In late July, at Nora's urging, Sarah brought Dr. Cantor, who examined Corinne and told Nora gravely that her increasingly frequent hallucinations seemed to be "a result of an irreversibly deteriorating neurological condition brought about by the stroke and by the numerous small strokes that apparently have followed it."

"But I can't confirm this," he said, "unless I put her in the hospital and do some tests."

"And that," Nora had said, sighing, "as you know, Father won't allow."

Dr. Cantor opened his mouth as if to object, but Nora quickly added, "Besides, it would terrify her. And anyway, there's not much you could do for her, is there, even if you knew what was happening?"

"No," Dr. Cantor admitted, slightly bending his tall body in a courtly, acquiescent half-bow. "I'm afraid there probably isn't. But" — he handed Sarah a hastily scrawled prescription — "try these. They may help."

So Sarah picked up the new drug, which did seem to make Corinne calmer and more docile; at least she was less frightened of the hallucinations and more easily soothed when they were explained away. "But she still has them," Nora told Liz one Friday.

They were sitting on the dock; Liz had lent Nora a pair of shorts, and Nora was dangling her legs, dabbling her feet in the water, which was almost as tepid as the air.

"Poor lady," Liz said. She splashed Nora's leg gently. "It must be so hard for you to see her like this."

"It is," Nora said. "She was such a sweet, strong woman. Even though she always gave in to Father, she was strong. And she and I used to have little conspiracies whenever he wasn't around, especially once I was in high school and he got more like he is now. He'd been fun sometimes when I was little, but something must have happened, maybe to do with his work, to make him change. Anyway, Mama and I would take long walks in the woods, looking for wildflowers; we'd cook extravagant desserts — we even invented some; we'd read aloud to each other. She'd make up stories . . ." Nora felt her eyes fill, and to her horror tears spilled over. "Sorry," she gasped, batting at them with her fingers. "Sorry, I . . ."

"Shh," Liz said. "Shh." She put her arm around Nora, and

for a moment Nora leaned against her, weeping silently. "It'll do you good to cry," Liz said softly, stroking her hair.

"I can't seem to stop." Nora pulled away and laughed through her tears in a surprised sort of way. "I'm sorry. Let's do something."

"Okay. But no apologies. I know." Liz stood up. "How about a swim? I could lend you a suit. I've got an extra one."

Nora sniffed; her eyes, Liz saw, were still bright with tears, her cheeks slightly flushed. And her hands still had dirt caked under the nails from weeding. "All right," Nora said, scrambling to her feet. "But guess what?" She looked embarrassed. Sheepishly, she said, "I don't know how to swim."

"Then I'll teach you." Liz hesitated, then rushed to say what she'd been thinking for a few days: "I could teach you to drive, too. And if you want, I could get my dad's mechanic — I found out he's still in business — to look at your father's old Ford. If he can make it run, you wouldn't be dependent on anyone for errands. Or emergencies."

Nora looked so startled that Liz said quickly, "Just think about it, okay? Come on. Race you to the house!"

When they got there, laughing, at almost the same time, Liz steered Nora into Jeff's old room to change, and went upstairs. Am I crazy, she thought, stripping off her clothes and pulling on her suit. Am I crazy? What do I think I'm doing? What do I think I'm feeling? For she knew that the emotion growing inside her was no longer compassion or pity — well, compassion, sure, was part of it — but it was also admiration for Nora's pluck, her industry, the way she doggedly carried on despite the obstacles her dreary life cast in her way. It was her enthusiasm, too, that drew Liz to her, when Nora exclaimed with pure joy upon discovering a new plant in the garden, or a new bird, or a sunset; by now Liz had gone to the farm several times in the evenings after the old folks were

146

asleep, and sat with Nora and Thomas in the garden as the setting sun touched the sky with color and made dark silhouettes of the trees. Once, too, at the cabin, when a sudden rainstorm had beaten the lake into a frenzy and sent lightning whips to lash the opposite shore, Nora had watched from Liz's table, an expression of rapture on her face, without a trace of the fear that Liz had expected and that Liz had even felt herself when a sudden loud crack and flash told her a tree (she hoped it was only a tree!) had been struck nearby.

Just the other night, when they'd been sitting near Nora's garden, Liz had found herself talking about her own parents, remembering and facing, as she had not before, memories of her mother's pain, of her mastectomy scars, of the infection that had followed her surgery and of how she, and later, Liz, had had to change the dressing and clean the drain that oozed pus. She'd told Nora about the radiation burns, the chemo nausea, the destroyed hair and appetite, the thinness, and, toward the end, the morphine-induced confusion. And at last she'd broken down for the first time, crying five years' worth of tears in Nora's arms.

What's happening to me, Liz thought now, passing a brush through her hair before going out to meet Nora again, surveying her own swimsuit-clad body in her mirror.

You know damn well, kiddo!

She had never cried in front of Megan, never talked with Megan about anything deeper than the latest fracas at school or the latest political scandal she'd read about in the paper. And it was not only, she knew, that Megan hadn't really cared, hadn't really been interested, hadn't been able to contribute much beyond a kind of generalized sympathy. That was part of it, certainly, but only part . . .

"Liz?"

"Yes. I'm ready!" Liz opened her door and Nora stood there, clad in Liz's old red, white, and blue suit. It was a little small, revealing the tops of Nora's breasts, but it clung smoothly to the rest of her compact figure, softly curving in at the waist and out again where her hips merged into rounded thighs which in turn led to incongruously boney knees and then tapered to gently muscled calves.

"Hi." Nora turned, an awkward pirouette. "How do I look?"

Liz choked back *beautiful.* "Fine! Come and see." She turned Nora toward the mirror.

"It's a little skimpy at the top." Frowning, Nora tugged at the straps.

"I guess. But, hey," she said breezily, "as my high school phys ed teacher used to say when she walked into the locker room and a couple of kids shrieked and threw towels around themselves, you don't have anything I don't have."

Nora laughed. "Did they really do that? The kids?"

"Yeah, we had a couple of weirdos." Liz decided not to say that this had happened only after it was rumored, incorrectly, that the phys ed teacher was a lesbian. "So, ready for your lesson?"

"Yes, ma'am."

"Careful," Liz warned as they waded in. "The bottom's sandy at first but then it gets rocky. Right about here . . ."

"Ow!" Nora exclaimed, clutching Liz as she hopped on one foot and grabbed her stubbed toe with the other hand. "Yes, I see what you mean!"

"Sorry." Liz steadied her.

"It's not your fault."

"No. But I'm apologizing for my lake, which I told to behave itself for you."

Nora looked amused. "Did you?" she asked, still holding onto Liz.

"Yup. Now" — Liz dropped Nora's hand — "out here a little way it gets deeper."

"It's so warm!" Nora said, following Liz.

"Wait. You'll hit a cold spot soon. What's the matter?" Nora had squeaked and stopped.

"I hit the cold spot." Nora was breast deep now, and Liz saw her shiver.

"Duck down," Liz commanded, "so you'll be wet all over before we start."

"Yes, teacher," Nora answered demurely, bending her knees. Then, with a mischievous look, she held her nose and put her head under, walked bent-kneed along the bottom to Liz, and playfully tickled Liz's leg before she popped up beside her, hair and face streaming.

"Whoa! It's that way, is it?" For a moment they chased each other, running clumsily in the water away from the rocks, splashing each other.

"Are you sure?" Liz asked, panting after a few minutes, "that you don't know how to swim?"

"That's right. And I do want to learn. Okay, lesson one. I bet it involves putting one's head in the water and tipping it out again to breathe, like this." She demonstrated.

"You do know how to swim," Liz said, disappointed.

Nora shook her head. "Wrong. I know how to breathe for swimming. One summer the town offered lessons. Mama let me go, but when Father found out, he made me stop. So I never got beyond the first lesson, which was about breathing — on dry land."

"Why did he make you stop?"

"The lessons were at a public pool and he was afraid of germs. Or so he said."

"God! You poor kid."

"I was pretty upset. But resigned. I mean, it was what he always did anyway whenever I tried anything new. Girl Scouts, too. After I went once, he said he didn't want me going any more. It was a Commie organization, he said. Come on, let's swim!" Nora waved her arms enthusiastically, making swimming motions.

"Okay. The first thing you have to do is sort of lie down

in the water. At the same time, kick with your feet and make the same motions with your arms that you were making."

Nora complied, stretching out and saying, "And I'll sink like a — oh!"

"No, you won't." Liz had lunged forward and put her hand under Nora's stomach. "Now go on with those motions and I'll hold you up till you're afloat. Don't panic, just swim."

"What about breathing?" Nora gasped.

"Never mind breathing."

Nora twisted around, looking up at Liz. "What, not breathe?"

"Hey, take it easy!" Liz laughed, struggling to hold her. "Just breathe normally," she said, when Nora was again lying properly in the water. "You can do the fancy stuff later. There, good. Keep that up. That's it, keep going." Liz dropped her hand an inch or two away; Nora turned again, looking at her nervously and beginning once more to sink, but Liz shot her hand up and caught her.

"See?" Liz said. "Whenever you stop the motion and thrash around, you'll sink. But as long as you keep moving you'll be okay." She walked carefully along the bottom, avoiding rocks as Nora moved forward.

"Like riding a bike," said Nora. "But I thought one could float without moving."

"One can. That's the key: not moving. And staying flat on your back or on your stomach. But let's go on swimming first for a bit." Liz held her and walked again as Nora swam tentatively forward.

"Hey!" Nora cried after a few minutes. "Where's your hand?"

Liz held it up. "You're swimming. Well," she added when Nora floundered and stood up, "you were swimming. Congratulations!"

"Holy smoke!" Nora grinned, and squeezed Liz's hand. "I was, wasn't I?"

"Yup. Come on. Try again."

150

Dutifully but still a little uncertainly, Nora stretched out in the water and Liz hovered next to her, her hand barely supporting her this time. "You're fine," she said. "Now concentrate." She removed her hand once Nora was moving steadily forward and stood watching as Nora swam a few yards away before realizing she was on her own again. But then Nora panicked, dunking herself once more.

"You did it!" Liz called when Nora surfaced, sputtering. "You did it! Next thing you know you'll be swimming across the lake."

Proudly, Nora swam back to her. "But it was friendlier," she said, standing up and smiling into Liz's eyes, "when your hand was under me."

TWENTY-ONE

Nora woke in the night and lay in the dim light of her room, her eyes fixed now on a chair, now on a table, the window, her dresser. That is my chair, she thought, with my clothes on it; that is my dresser. Those lumps are my brushes, my jewelry box; that brighter oblong opposite the window is my mirror.

When she was very small and all the Tillots slept upstairs, she'd had a larger room. Objects were harder to identify; she had woken up many nights seeing bears and robbers and had lain frozen in terror, waiting for them to move toward her, attacking, until she could summon enough voice to call her parents.

Like Mama now, she thought.

It was usually her mother who came, bringing a kerosene lamp, soothing Nora and rubbing her back, turning up the lamp and handing her clothes to her to prove there was no bear and that the robber was a bulge in the curtain at the left side of her window. (It was always the left side, though Nora never figured out why.)

Her father had come a few times without a lamp, told her she was silly to be imagining things, and left without demonstrating that nothing was threatening her. But then one night he sat on the edge of her bed and told her a funny story about the bear and the robber. It was so funny it made her laugh, and it quelled her fears from then on.

Nora missed that Ralph. She had loved that Ralph, long ago.

Nora passed her hands over her body, remembering the feeling of the water as she had lain in it at Liz's cabin; she rested her hands on her stomach, remembering Liz's hand there, supporting her till she could support herself.

"No one has ever touched me there," she whispered to the unhearing darkness. "I am not a person who is touched."

"Damn!" Liz dropped the potholder with which she'd been about to move the chicken she was roasting so she could baste it (the Davises were coming for dinner), and ran to the phone. She wanted to let it ring. But it might be Nora, she reasoned; Nora had taken to calling sometimes in the evenings just to chat, though she hadn't called last night, the night after the swimming lesson, when Liz had expected it. No, Liz corrected herself. Wanted it. Not expected.

It was Jeff.

"So how's it going?" he asked, his voice hearty. "You haven't called in a while, so I thought I'd check in. About ready to go back to the teeming city?"

153

She chuckled, though she was mildly annoyed at the interruption and disappointed that it wasn't Nora. "Nope, happy as a clam. And making dinner for the old Davises, remember them?"

"Lord, yes! Harry and — what was her name?"

"Clara. Still is. And they still have the stand. They look older, and Harry's feeble and deaf as a post, but they're still sweet. Even if they did try to fix me up with some guy."

"That must have been awkward as hell."

"It was." Liz found she could just reach the oven by stretching the phone cord. She opened the oven door, then had to close it again to get the baster. "I wanted to tell him I'm gay, but I didn't."

"Find a chick and make out in front of him," Jeff said.

"You're disgusting," she answered affectionately. "Anyway, it turns out he was probably more interested in buying the cabin than in me, and he's left me alone now that he knows it's not for sale." She opened the oven again.

"Good. But hey, at least that shows it's salable, you know? In case we change our minds. Say, listen, why I called? I can't talk long, I'm at work, but we've been scheduling vacations and I need to know if you still want to invite us to the cabin."

Liz paused, the baster dripping in her hand. Did she?

She'd have to. It was his house, too.

"Sure." She squirted the chicken, slid it back in, and closed the oven door.

"Great, when?"

"I don't know." Her mind leapt ahead. What was going to happen with Nora? Anything?

No. Probably nothing.

Still . . .

"I've got a sort of standing thing on Fridays with this woman who lives at the old Tillot place."

"The Tillot place! Whoa! I figured they'd all died off and the house had fallen down long ago."

"No, the old couple's still there and their daughter takes care of them."

"And you've got a — a 'standing thing' with her? Lizzie? What're you up to?"

"No, no," she said hastily. "I'm just, well, sort of helping out. She's helping me restore Mom's perennial garden and teaching me to identify cultivated plants, and I'm giving her swimming lessons in return."

She could almost hear his raised eyebrows. "*Swimming* lessons?"

"Don't, Jeff," she said, more defensively than she intended. "She's really sweet and she's very lonely. Think of taking care of two sick old folks, one of whom's crochety as hell."

"Okay, okay. So you'd rather we weren't there on a Friday, right?"

"Yeah, maybe, except . . . Look, there's nothing really going on between us, and there probably won't be anything. She's probably straight, if she's anything. I mean, she must be. And I'm not ready, even though . . ."

"Even though you sound like you're getting ready, and even though she's sweet and needy, and . . . Sorry. None of my business."

"But it wouldn't make sense for you guys to come just for a couple of days."

"Why not?"

"All the way from California?"

"You may not have noticed, babe, but there are lots of neat places in New England for vacationers. How about we come some Saturday in August, stay a couple of days, and then go on to someplace else? The Cape, the Berkshires, Maine, the White Mountains? I want Gus to see where his daddy's roots are."

Liz chuckled. "Like he's sure to remember what he sees at two."

"Going on three." Jeff's voice was indignant. "You'd be surprised. Look, sis, I've got to go. How about the — oh, say, the third weekend in August? Or the fourth? Yeah, the fourth. That's right before Labor Day, so we can add Labor Day on."

"No," Liz said quickly; she'd have to go back to New York soon after Labor Day. "The third weekend would be better for me."

"Oh, that's right. You'll be going back to the city. And you'll want some time with . . ."

"Jeff!"

"Sorry. But what's her name, anyway? Just so I'll know."

"Nora."

"Nora. God. Sounds like something out of Ibsen. Doesn't he have a Nora in a play?"

"Yes. She's nothing like that Nora."

"Thank God! Ibsen's women are awful."

"They weren't when he wrote them. They were strong for their time."

"And suicidal."

"That's Hedda Gabler. But even she was strong. You'd go for Solveig, I bet."

"Which one was she?"

"The one in *Peer Gynt*. The one who waited forever while her man went off and had adventures."

"Yeah, that was pretty cool. Whoops! Now I've really got to go. I've got a meeting." He said something to someone else, muffled. "So, see you in August, babe. Don't do anything I wouldn't do, you hear?"

"Don't worry. I wouldn't even dream of doing half of what you'd do! 'Bye."

" 'Bye. Love you."

"You, too."

Liz replaced the receiver and started peeling potatoes. Heavy-handed though Jeff's kidding could be, she always felt warm and loved when she talked to him. Thank God for him, she thought, now that Mom and Dad are gone.

What would it be like, having Jeff and Susan and Gus all there? It might be fun; they'd be a family again. She'd give Jeff and Susan the master bedroom upstairs and she'd put a cot in the study for herself; Gus could have one of the downstairs rooms. Or — yes, better — he could sleep in the study and she could move back into her old downstairs room.

She remembered lying in bed downstairs as a child, falling asleep to the murmur of her parents' voices in the living room. Mom and Dad had often read up in their bedroom, though, or sat outside when the mosquitoes weren't too bad, till long after she and Jeff were asleep. Funny arrangement, having the kids' rooms downstairs off the living room.

Still, we managed.

She popped the potatoes into a pot and looked at her watch. Yes, she should start them boiling and then trim the beans she'd bought from the Davises earlier that day.

What, she wondered, is Nora doing?

TWENTY-TWO

"That's right," Liz said the following Friday, giving Nora a driving lesson. "That's right. Now ease up on the clutch. Hey, gently!"

"Sorry. I'm still nervous."

"It's okay. When I was learning I confused the brake and the gas. At least you haven't done that."

"No." Nora laughed nervously, and, as if driving over eggs, made a cautious right turn.

"Good! Go back into third now, once you've gotten a little more speed. That's it. Fine. Nothing much happened because luckily when I mixed up the pedals, I was on a back road. But I did leap ahead when Dad wanted me to stop."

"You were really close to him, weren't you?"

"Eyes on the road, Nora. Yes, I was. He was a great friend to both of us. Both me and Jeff."

"What was he like?"

"Gentle. Intelligent. Unflappable. Nothing shocked him. When I told him . . ." She broke off; she'd been about to say *When I told him I was gay.*

"When you told him what?"

"Oh, anything. He never reacted with anger or condemnation, no matter what it was. He'd just think about it, and then respond very carefully, very fairly. If he felt anything negative he'd keep it to himself till he'd thought it through, and then he'd discuss it with me, still carefully, not so much as a father but as a wise teacher. Watch out!" A squirrel ran across the road but by the time Liz spoke, Nora had already applied the brake. Not the clutch, though; the car jerked and stalled.

"Sorry. I forgot. What do I do now?"

"Start it again with the key. It's okay. It's hard to remember everything at first. With practice, things like that will be automatic."

"That wasn't what you were going to say," Nora said when the car was moving forward again. "Was it?"

"What? When?"

"When you were talking about how your father reacted to things. You started 'When I told him . . .' as if you were going to say something specific." She glanced at Liz. "Or am I prying?"

"Yes," Liz said quietly. "I'm sorry, but I guess you are a little. It's my fault, though. I shouldn't have started to say what I was going to say."

Nora smiled ruefully. "Secrets. That's too bad."

"Why?"

"Oh, because secrets — I guess secrets stand between people. Between friends. Not that I ever had many friends. Just two, really, in high school. And I was only close to one of them, Marsha."

"What about the other one?"

"That was Peter. I told you about him."

"Umm." Liz nodded. "The boy you didn't go out with. And weren't much interested in."

"Right." Nora glanced at her again, then looked back at the road ahead. "Your turn. You said you weren't much interested in men either. But for all I know, you might even have been married and divorced four or five times!"

Liz laughed nervously. Then, even more nervously, she said, "Nope. I did live with someone for a few years, but we broke up." She was about to add "a woman" when the car lurched forward. Nora took one hand off the wheel and quickly squeezed Liz's. "Whoops! Sorry. Sorry for the leap ahead and for your break-up. Did he leave or did you?"

"I left," Liz said, deciding not to correct her. The moment had passed. Or was it, she wondered, my courage that passed?

"Good," Nora said. "I mean, not really good, but I guess it's not as bad for the person who leaves. Of course I wouldn't know. I guess it'd be because of the reason. I mean if he beat you or started seeing someone else, then it would be bad and good, bad that he'd hurt you but good that you left."

"It wasn't like that," Liz said stiffly.

"Oh. I'm sorry again. I'm asking too many questions. It's just that I like you so much and I want to be your friend. And I'm curious about you. You have a whole huge life in the city that I don't know anything about. It's been so long since I knew, really knew, anyone from — from the Outside is how I think of it. As if I were a nun or a prisoner."

"You are, kind of. Aren't you?"

"Yes. I guess I am. In a way."

"Turn left here. Slow down — good. Now downshift. Good. Turn. Easy does it with the wheel, Nora. That's it. Okay. Now — beautiful! You remembered to go back into third. Well done." Liz relaxed again. "Do you think you'll ever get out? You know, leave the farm, leave your parents?"

"Not while they're living. They do need me. I'd feel guilty and I'd miss my mother. Well, I already do miss her. Like I told you, she's not who she was. Neither's my father, but with him, it's that all the bad things about him are worse and the few good things are mostly gone. But Mama was always gentle and we were always friends. She taught me everything I know about running the house. And now she doesn't remember how to do much of anything." Nora paused; her voice had wavered a little. Liz wanted to touch her, to comfort her, but was afraid of distracting her, both from her driving and from what she was saying.

Finally Nora looked toward her, smiling. "I do like a lot of what I do, Liz, living in that old house, reading and proof-reading and writing poetry, and going to church and tending the garden and putting up the things I grow and making jam from the berries I pick. Sometimes it's lonely and hard, yes, but I'm not sure I'd know how to cope if I left. Now my life has a predictable rhythm along with the seasons and the chores that go with each one." Her smile broadened. "I don't understand how people can live in places where there's only one season, do you?"

"Like Florida? No. My brother lives in California, near San Francisco. He has half-baked seasons. In the summer the grass turns brown, and in the winter it rains instead of snows."

"But there's snow nearby, isn't there? In the mountains?" Nora laughed. "I read a lot."

"Yes, you're right. And he does go skiing. Or he did, before the baby came."

"Baby!" Nora said wistfully. "It must be nice to have a baby. I wish . . ." She broke off, shaking her head.

"What?"

"Oh, it's crazy, but sometimes I do wish I could have a baby. No husband; just a baby."

"Maybe you could adopt a baby. Single people can, these days."

Nora gave Liza a look. "Sure," she said. "As if anyone would let someone in my situation adopt a baby. No electricity, no running water, two old folks who need as much attention as the baby would."

"Yeah, you're right. But maybe when . . ." She stopped.

"Maybe when they die? Maybe. I've thought about it. But I'll probably be too old then."

Liz studied her face. "Tell me if this is rude," she said, "but have you thought about what you'll do when they're gone?"

"A little. You're not rude. I don't know what I'll do." Nora sped up — thirty, thirty-five; Liz watched the speedometer, but it steadied just short of forty. "Probably nothing. I'll probably go right on doing what I'm doing. As I said, I'm not sure I'd know how to cope anywhere else. I suppose I might get the house fixed up, though, someday. Gradually modernized."

"But not move?"

"I love the house," Nora said. "I might get some sheep, make a farm out of it again." She paused as if considering that. "But Father's healthy as a horse, for all his complaints. He'll go on forever, I think. What about you? Would you like a baby? A husband?"

"No," Liz said, startled, then uncomfortable again. Her mind shouted TELL HER!

But she found she couldn't. "Not a husband," she said. "But I'd consider a baby." *If I had a partner*, she added silently. A real relationship, an honest one.

"You could adopt a baby easily, I bet."

Liz pulled her thoughts back. "Not with my schedule. The kid would have to be in day care a lot, and that's no good."

"You could take time off. Couldn't you? At first?"

"Maybe. But I'm not going to do that. I don't think I'd want to be a single parent. I'm not as good as you at taking care of people by myself, I'm afraid."

"But you are good," Nora said, "at teaching, teaching swimming and driving, anyway. Who's that? Should I stop?" She slowed down.

162

A figure was waving at them from the side of the road, a golden retriever by his side. Liz, annoyed, recognized Roy.

"Oh," she said, "he's a guy the Davises, you know, at the vegetable stand, introduced me to. Roy Stark. Let's just wave; you don't need to stop."

But Nora had already braked and now Roy was striding toward the car, the dog bounding ahead of him.

"Down, Zeke," he ordered as the dog jumped enthusiastically on the passenger door, making Liz laugh in spite of herself. "The mail carrier on my route has biscuits in the car so Zeke thinks all cars are full of Milk Bones. Sorry." Roy pulled the dog down and made him sit. "I don't think he scratched it," he said to Nora over Liz's head, then looked at Liz. "Hi, Liz! Isn't this your car?"

"Yes," Liz said.

"She's teaching me to drive," Nora explained.

"This is Roy Stark," Liz said. "Roy, Nora Tillot."

"Oh, so you're the woman from the Tillot place." Roy, with what Liz was sure was meant to be a dazzling smile, held out a hand, stretching it through the window across Liz. "Nice to meet you." He winked at Liz. "Told you we'd run into each other," he said. "By the way, I got your message from Georgia."

But Nora was already saying "Nice to meet you" to him. "We've got this old car at the farm," she went on, "and Liz thought if I learned how to drive, then maybe we could get it running again and I wouldn't have to depend on other people for transportation."

"Good idea," Roy said. "Hey, listen, if you need help with the car, I'm a pretty good mechanic. And I'd love to see your farm."

"Are you really?" asked Nora. "A good mechanic?"

"I've already asked my dad's mechanic," Liz said quickly, then felt ashamed. Can I actually be jealous, she wondered. "Thanks anyway."

"You're welcome. So, I'll leave you to your lesson. Good to

163

see you again, Liz." Roy winked again and stood there watching as they drove off.

"He seems interested in you," Nora observed after a few minutes of silence.

"More in you, I think. Actually, Nora, I . . ."

But another squirrel ran across in front of the car, making Nora swerve, brake, and stall again.

Once more, the moment passed.

TWENTY-THREE

"There she is, ma'am."

Ned McNeil, junior, who looked more like his father's younger brother than his son, straightened up with a wrench in his hand, beaming first at Nora and then at Liz. Ned, senior, Liz's father's mechanic, gave something on the underneath of the Tillots' old Ford sedan a quick wipe, and then stood, his grizzled face also beaming. The Neds had worked tirelessly all weekend and for two days before, almost camping out in the Tillots' barn and at one point towing the car, which hadn't run when the Neds had first tried it, to their garage on the other side of town so they could put it on the lift. Ralph had grumbled and fought at the idea, first of Nora's driving lessons and then of having the Neds fix the car. "Emergencies, my foot," he'd growled, when Nora told him that was the purpose of both projects. "Like the telephone. That woman's a bad influence, Nora. Next thing I know, you'll be bringing in the electric." Ralph had refused to take an open interest in the car repairs, but Nora had caught him more than once at the kitchen window. He was there again today, she saw, perhaps because she'd told him this was the day the car would be ready. "And we'll celebrate tonight," she'd told him at breakfast, "if it *is* ready."

Ralph hadn't reacted, so she thought it wise not to tell him Liz would be staying for supper.

"You'd best take her for a spin, Miss Tillot, see how she runs," said Ned, senior.

"Call me Nora, please," Nora said for the third or fourth time. She glanced nervously at Liz. "I don't know if I . . ."

"Sure, let's!" Liz opened the driver's side door and gestured to Nora to climb in.

"You'll come, too?"

"Try and stop me." Liz went around to the passenger side, stopping on the way to say to the Neds, "Can you guys stick around for a bit? Just to make sure she runs okay? And" — she nodded toward Nora — "to reassure Nora; she's a little nervous."

Ned, senior, grinned. "Sure we'll stick around, Lizzie. But she looked like she did pretty damn well again yesterday, practising in your car. You're a good teacher, I'll bet."

"That's my job, Ned, that's what I do." With a wave, Liz slid into the Ford. She took the key from the dashboard and handed it to Nora.

Nora hesitated. "Where's Father?"

"Still at the kitchen window. Don't worry. The Neds'll handle him, if need be. Come on, Nora, you'll do fine. And so will old Esmerelda, here."

Nora inserted the key and turned it. The car coughed, bucked a little, then turned over and whirred smoothly; the

Neds both cheered. "Esmerelda?" Carefully, Nora shifted into reverse.

Liz shrugged. "Maybe Ermentrude. I always name my cars."

"Oh really?" Looking over her shoulder, Nora backed away from the barn. Her voice shook a little, but Liz could tell she was excited as well as nervous, and silently thanked the Neds again for making this bid for freedom possible.

"So what's your car's name?" Nora asked. "The one you're driving now?"

"Sally. Mind the outhouse."

Nora braked, a little too hard. "Whoops," she said, reddening as the Neds, who had sprung aside, both grinned. Ned, junior, wagged a finger at her; his father grabbed his hand and pulled it down.

"It's okay," Nora shouted. "I deserved that! All right," she said to Liz, taking a deep breath and squaring her shoulders. "We're off."

And she drove slowly but smoothly down the driveway. Esmerelda-Ermentrude coughed again once or twice, but otherwise did fine.

At the main road, Nora stopped. "Now what?"

"Go on, why don't you? Let's go down to, oh, Greely's Hardware. That's only about five miles, Nora."

Nora bit her lower lip and smoothed her hands on her skirt. "Okay. If you don't mind taking your life in your hands."

"I don't mind, but I'm not worried. You'll do fine. Just keep your eyes open and . . ."

". . . your wits about you," Nora finished in unison with Liz, who had claimed earlier that that was all one needed to remember once one got the hang of driving; Liz laughed and said, "Right."

"Well. Here goes." Nora headed slowly out onto the main road, braking as a car full of teenagers passed her, yelling, "Get a horse."

167

"Costs too much to feed!" Nora yelled back.

I love you, Liz said silently. *Lord, help me, but I love you!*

When they got back to the farm and Nora, flushed with victory, fairly flew out of the car, Ralph broke clumsily away from the Neds with whom he'd obviously been standing for a while, leaning white-knuckled on his walker. "What in tarnation do you think you were doing?" he roared.

"Driving the Ford," Nora said calmly. "Someone had to test it. It runs fine," she said to the Neds, shaking their hands, ignoring Ralph, who was still sputtering. "I can't thank you enough. Let me just get my wallet."

"No need," said Ned, senior. "Like we said, Liz, here, is an old friend, and I owed her father a favor. He died before I could pay up, so I figure this is it, since it was Liz who asked us to do the job."

"It was fun," Ned, junior, said. "Lots of fun. I love old vehicles. And," he added, smiling broadly at Nora, "if you ever have any trouble with her, just give me, I mean us, a call. I'll be happy to come give her a once-over now and again, too. Or go on with those driving lessons. There's some differences between old cars and new ones. Not that you're used to either, much, I guess," he added sheepishly, "but you did learn on Liz's, and . . ."

"You're right," Nora said, looking amused. "But thanks to you and your dad, and Liz, I think I've just about grasped most of them by now."

"Oh, there are a few obscure differences," Ned, junior, said.

"Come along, you young scoundrel." Ned, senior, cuffed his son affectionately. "Miss Tillot has better things to do than ride all over the countryside with the likes of you."

"She certainly does," Ralph said belligerently, glaring at Ned, junior. "Don't you get any ideas, young man!"

"Crusty old bastard," Liz heard Ned, junior, exclaim under his breath as his father pulled him away.

"Come along, Father." Nora patted Ralph's arm. "We've just got cold meat loaf and salad for supper. But Liz is staying, to help us celebrate. She's brought a yummy-looking carrot cake and some ice cream."

Liz ignored the poisonous look Ralph gave Nora. "And as it happens," she said, "I've also got a nice bottle of red wine in the car. We can really celebrate!"

"We'll need to save leftovers from the meat loaf," Ralph grumbled. "And I can't drink wine. Too much medication. It harms my stomach."

"The meatloaf's already leftovers," Nora said, winking at Liz. "And if you can't drink any wine, Father, there'll be all the more for the rest of us."

"Your mother can't drink it either," Ralph retorted. "And a whole bottle's too much for you girls. Now listen, Nora," he said as Nora and Liz helped him maneuver up the two steps to the back door. "Just because that old car's working again is no reason for you to go gallivanting all over the county. Remember you said that it's just for emergencies."

"But, Mr. Tillot" — Liz held the door for him — "the car's got to be used regularly or it'll seize up again the way it did before. I don't think you can count on the Neds to fix it again for free."

"No, and I wouldn't ever ask 'em to. Are you sure," he said, facing Liz, his eyes bright with suspicion, "that they did owe your father a favor?"

"Positive. There's no debt to you or Nora. You're not beholden to them in any way."

Ralph grunted. "Sure better not be. It's not as if I asked 'em to fix the damn car." He grunted again as Nora and Liz eased him down into his chair at the table and Nora went to get Corinne. "And listen." He leaned forward and pointed at Liz, who was standing there awkwardly, uncertain whether to sit down or start setting the table. She still wasn't sure where some things were, or what china Nora would want to use.

"Listen," Ralph said to her again. "I don't want Nora going off all the time. She belongs here. Her mother and I need her at home, you understand? I know she's been seeing you a lot, helping with the garden and all."

"And she's done a wonderful job. I'm very grateful."

"Yes, but now it's over. No more. She needs to go back to her regular schedule."

"Mr. Tillot," Liz said hesitantly, "with all respect, I think it's good for Nora to get out once in a while. When I go back to New York in the fall, I guess she'll go back to her regular schedule anyway. But shouldn't she have a little fun in the meantime? It's summer, after all, and . . ."

"Nora is a grown woman, Miss Hardy, not a child. She doesn't need 'fun.' That's all right for you New York folks, probably, but here in the country we believe in hard work and the satisfaction we get out of it. Where *is* Nora? Nora," he bellowed. "Bring my pills! My head's killing me." Dramatically, he ran his hand over his forehead.

"Let me get you some water." Quickly, Liz pumped a glass full of water and handed it to him.

"Water's no good without the pills, you damn fool!" Ralph waved the glass away just as Nora tossed the pill bottle to Liz from the doorway. "Here you go," she called. "Mama and I will be right in."

"Shall I open the bottle for you?" Liz asked.

He snatched it from her. "I'm not a cripple," he shouted. "At least not yet."

Liz, giving up, pulled out a chair, but before she could sit, Thomas mewed at the back door, so she let him in. He wove himself in and out of her legs, purring.

"You remember Liz Hardy, Mama," Nora said cheerfully, rolling Corinne's wheelchair into the kitchen.

Liz was startled to see that Corinne's head lolled and that one side of her mouth drooped, leaking a thin thread of saliva.

"Hello, Mrs. Tillot." Liz bent closer. "How are you?"

Corinne lifted her head a little. "Hello, dear. Have you come for the eggs? Get a dozen, Nora, for the lady."

"No, Mrs . . ." Liz began, but Nora held up her hand.

"Yes, Mama," Nora said. "I will." She pushed her mother's wheelchair to the table and began opening cupboards, handing dishes, cutlery, and napkins to Liz.

"Now, Mama," she said after a minute or two. "What do you think? This is Liz Hardy, my friend. She's going to stay to supper. Isn't that nice?"

Corinne smiled sweetly at Liz. "Nice," she said. "Hello, dear. What's your name?"

"Liz, Mrs. Tillot." Liz shook Corinne's limp hand.

"Are you in school with Nora?"

Nora nodded, so Liz said "Yes," and the conversation, such as it was, went on from there while Nora served the meat loaf and they began to eat.

"Today she's stuck in my junior year in high school," Nora whispered to Liz as they cleared the first course; Corinne had called Liz "Marsha" several times and asked about someone named Peter; Liz remembered they'd been Nora's friends. Ralph had eaten silently and messily, staring down into his plate, not speaking except, once, to bark, "Where the hell's the salt?" and, later, to say, "Those damn pills don't do any good."

"Does your head still hurt?" Nora asked, pouring Liz more wine. "I'm sorry, Father."

"My head hurts, too," Corinne said softly. "A little. Maybe it's bedtime?" she said to Nora. "And Marsha needs to go home or her mother will worry."

"Wouldn't you like some dessert first, Mama? Liz — um,

171

Marsha — brought a lovely carrot cake and some ice cream. We have to eat the ice cream," she said merrily, "before it melts. I'll get it, shall I?"

"And I'll get the cake." Liz followed Nora out to the back stoop. "You didn't tell me she'd gotten worse again," she whispered.

"Didn't I?" Nora opened the ice box and took out the carton she'd placed against the rapidly melting ice block. "She does seem kind of fuzzy tonight, but no worse than at other fuzzy times, except for the headache. That's unusual, but not unheard of; she's had them before, now and then. Nothing's consistent with her. The doctor's not sure why. Something about the blood supply to her brain, he thinks."

"I wish you could take her for tests."

"So do I, but she'd be terrified and Father would never stand for it."

"You managed the car."

"With your help." Nora leaned over, standing on her toes, and to Liz's astonishment, gave Liz a quick kiss on the cheek. "Thank you for that. For the car. For the driving lessons. For — for a taste of freedom. And for you yourself."

Before Liz could say anything or react, Nora fled back into the house.

Later, when the old folks were in bed, Nora and Liz sat out near the vegetable garden, facing each other with their lawn chairs almost touching as they finished the wine.

"I'd forgotten," Liz said, "how bright the stars really are till I came back here to Clarkston."

"They must be even brighter at the lake, reflecting off the water."

"They are. You'll have to come some night and see them." She leaned forward. "Come now? Come tonight. We could have a midnight swim."

172

Nora leaned forward also and gave Liz's hand a squeeze, then held it. "I'd love to. But I can't leave them alone,"

"No." Liz squeezed Nora's hand back. "I know. Of course you can't."

"Maybe sometime I can get Patty to stay with them for a couple of hours at night. Sometime before you go back. I'd like that."

"I'd like it, too." Liz said, stroking Nora's hand.

And then they both leaned forward a little more, till their faces were close together, and they kissed.

TWENTY-FOUR

For a long time neither of them said anything, but Nora rubbed her cheek against Liz's and then slipped off her chair to the ground, kneeling, her head in Liz's lap, while Liz stroked her hair.

Awkwardly, Liz, too, slipped off her chair. She took Nora in her arms, hoping Ralph wouldn't get out of bed and look outside, then was annoyed with herself for thinking that. She felt heady, a little dizzy, and she realized, as her mind leapt ahead, that she was beginning to do what she had done with Megan: editing her feelings, verbalizing them as she felt them, putting words between them and herself so that she, or some part of herself, remained distant — even as she stroked Nora's back, tipped her face up to her own, looked into her eyes, and,

174

seeing trust in them and no fear, kissed her mouth, first gently, then more insistently.

Her internal commentry receded.

"All right?" she whispered, smiling at Nora. "Are you all right? Is this?"

"Oh, yes. Oh, yes!"

Nora snuggled closer. But then she turned her face away from Liz's, and Liz quickly pulled back.

Nora caught her. "No," she said. "No. Don't move. I don't understand this, but I . . . Well, maybe I do understand it. Do you?"

"I understand," Liz said, "that I care for you deeply and that . . ."

"I care for you, too," Nora whispered. "I never felt this way before. Did you?" She sat back on her heels. "You must have," she said, "for the man you lived with. Did you?"

Clumsily, Liz shifted back onto her chair. "Nora, I didn't live with a man. The person I told you about was a woman. I'm gay, Nora. A lesbian."

Nora stared. "Oh," she said in a very small voice. "Oh." For a long moment she looked at Liz, her head cocked in the way that had charmed Liz in what now seemed centuries earlier. Did I fall in love with her then, Liz asked herself, when she first did that? But she felt as if she'd loved Nora for a very long time.

"I think I sensed that," Nora was saying. "All along."

"Does it matter to you?" Liz asked quietly.

"Not in the way you think. It matters only in a good way, in that it means you can — can care about me in a special way and I can care about you. I — I don't know what I am. I don't know if I'm anything. I've read about lesbians, but it's feelings that matter, isn't it, more than labels. Maybe since I never thought much about men, or cared much for them, I'm a lesbian, too. I don't mind that. I just care about how I feel about you."

"Maybe it just means you haven't met the right man."

"Maybe. But now it feels as if I've met the right woman. And it also feels as if I want to kiss you again, want you to kiss me . . ."

A cry from inside the house made them both spring apart, made the blood drain from Liz's head and fear clutch at her stomach.

"NORA! NORA! GOD! OH, GOD! NORA!"

For a moment Nora and Liz clumsily held each other back, tangling together as they tried to run. Then Nora broke free and ran ahead of Liz, stumbling over roots and nearly falling up the steps to the back door.

Ralph stood there, ashen, trembling. "Corinne," he cried brokenly. "Mama! Oh, God, oh, Jesus!"

Nora clutched his shoulder briefly, then ran past him. Liz tried to steady him, her hands on his waist, steering him back inside, to the kitchen table, to a chair. "Here, Mr. Tillot, sit down. It's all right; Nora's with her, it's all right . . ."

"You!" Ralph choked out the word, making it an accusation, his hands thrusting at her as if to push her away. "You — you interfering — you! Get away from me! It's your doing, your fault; you did it with your lessons and your mechanics and your, your damn carrot cake! Yes! The carrot cake! You — I . . ."

"Liz," Nora called in an oddly conversational tone from Corinne's room. "Liz, please. Please come."

Awkwardly, Liz reached over to pat Ralph's shoulder, then thought better of it and of saying anything to him; she withdrew her hand and, dreading what she'd find, she went into Corinne's room.

Corinne lay on the bed, her face distorted, her eyes open, but obviously unseeing. No breath stirred her chest, and she looked absent from herself, as if she no longer inhabited her body.

"Oh, God." Liz put her arm around Nora. "Oh, Nora, dearest . . ."

"I can't tell," Nora said, looking up after a few moments

during which she'd clung to Liz, her head buried in Liz's neck. "I'm not sure. Would you . . . ?"

Liz bent closer, put her hand on Corinne's chest, then felt for the pulse in her neck, but there was nothing. "Do you have a mirror?" she asked, not at all sure if that was the right thing to do. "A small one?"

Nora fumbled among objects on Corinne's dresser and at last gave Liz a small hand mirror. Liz held it up to Corinne's mouth.

It remained clear, fogless.

Liz felt for a pulse again, fruitlessly.

"I'm afraid . . ." she began, and then stopped, for Ralph had lurched into the doorway.

"I'm sorry," Liz began again, this time to him.

"Murderer!" Ralph howled, flinging himself on Corinne's body as if to protect it. Or to merge with it, Liz thought; that's what he wants, poor man.

"Murderer!" he shouted again, twisting around to look at Liz over his shoulder.

"Father!" Nora, terror and horror mingling on her face, tentatively touched his shoulder. "Father, it was another stroke! It has to have been."

"Brought on by her." His eyes snapped with brittle fire. "Lessons, taking you away, the car. And then that carrot cake. Poisoned, she poisoned my Corinne!"

"You had some cake yourself," Nora said, swaying a little.

"Steady." Liz put an arm around her again. I should be terrified, she thought. Terrified. But she felt oddly removed, and fascinated. Yes, that's it, she thought, as she watched Ralph pull Corinne's body closer. His mouth was slack and he was drooling a little; saliva was dribbling onto Corinne's nightgown, onto her neck. His eyes still burned, but tears showed in them along the bottom lids, little contained rivulets of tears.

"No, I didn't have any cake," Ralph said, his voice muffled, for he was lying across Corinne now, awkwardly, holding her, cradling her head. The rivulets overflowed, sending tears down his grizzled cheeks. "I didn't."

"Well, I did," Nora said, "and so did Liz."

"She served it," Ralph said. "She cut it. She could have put anything in it. But it's all right," he crooned to Corinne. "It's all right, my sweetheart, my best girl. It's all right. I've called them; they'll come, they'll take her away and punish her. Don't you worry. She won't get away with it."

"Father!" Nora said as Liz felt cold sweep over her, and terror at last, and disbelief. "What? Who did you call?"

"I called the police." He twisted around, facing Liz, and his eyes gleamed coldly, triumphantly. "I called that 911 number for emergencies. I told them there'd been a murder."

III

III

TWENTY-FIVE

For a moment none of them moved.

I must remember to breathe, Liz thought, realizing she had stopped and seemed to be standing outside herself, watching strangers: a dead woman, a crazy man practically lying on her, two horrified women staring . . .

Then Nora cried out, "Father, no!" and seized Liz's hand. Liz, herself again, felt a sharp stab of fear and her stomach knotted, for he had said, hadn't he, that she had killed Corinne?

"The phone," Nora gasped, dropping Liz's hand and rushing from the room. "Maybe . . ."

Liz followed her.

The phone was dangling from its cord; Nora picked it up

delicately, as if handling something hot, and held it to her ear. "I'll call them back," she whispered to Liz. "Tell them that . . ." Then her face changed, and she said into the mouthpiece, "Yes? Hello? . . . No, I — Nora. Nora Tillot . . . Yes, he's here. He's in with my mother . . . Yes, I think so . . . Yes" — she glanced at Liz — "my friend, Liz, Elizabeth Hardy . . . What? . . . No, of course not! . . . We were outside in the yard. My father yelled and we went in . . . Yes, into my mother's room and — and found her . . . No, she wasn't . . . Yes, my father's here." Nora put her hand to her forehead.

Liz moved swiftly to her. Why couldn't the police — for it must be them, she reasoned, still on the phone after Ralph's call — why couldn't they leave her alone instead of badgering her with questions?

". . . in with my mother," Nora was saying; she was leaning against Liz now, heavily; Liz felt the slightest change in her own position would topple her. "Well, all right. Just a minute and I'll . . . What?"

A moment later, Nora put her hand over the mouthpiece and said to Liz, "He doesn't want me to leave the phone, but he wants to talk to Father. Would you get him, please?"

"Are you going to be okay?"

Nora nodded, but Liz dragged a kitchen chair over to her and pushed her gently into it before she left the room.

Ralph was lying full-length next to Corinne now, tears on his cheeks, caressing her face and murmuring. In spite of herself, Liz felt a pang of sympathy for him. It seemed cruel to disturb him, to intrude on his grief, but she leaned over, touching his shoulder. "Mr. Tillot?" she said quietly. "Excuse me, but the police want to talk with you. They're on the phone."

Ralph twisted around and looked up at her, his eyes glazed with grief and then, as he recognized her, grief gave way to fury and hatred. "You!" he said, pushing her away, then gripping her arm painfully. "You! Get out of my house, get away from here. Poisoner! Murderer! Get out! Get out!" His face reddened and sweat beads stood out on his forehead as he shook her arm violently.

"I can't leave," Liz said, wincing in pain, "as long as you're holding onto me. The police really do want to talk with you, sir. Won't you go to the phone?" She realized she was shivering inside, as if she'd caught a sudden chill.

He shook her again. "You'll come with me, then." He pulled himself up via Liz's arm; she nearly fell over onto him as he tugged. "You won't stay with my sweetheart." He turned, still gripping Liz, awkwardly forcing her partway down on the bed as he twisted down again, kissing Corinne. He'd closed her eyes, Liz saw, or someone had. Had she? Had Nora? But they weren't all the way closed; she could see white in the slit between the upper and lower lids.

"I'll be back, my sweetheart," Ralph said, caressing Corinne's face. "I'll be back."

Roughly, he sat, then stood and, shoving Liz in front of him, went to the kitchen and snatched the phone from Nora. "I've got her," he said into the receiver, his eyes snapping.

Crazy, he's crazy, Liz thought, shaking her head at Nora, who, standing again, was trying unsuccessfully to pry Ralph's fingers away from Liz's arm, which was turning red and white where he was gripping it.

"I'm holding onto her. But she's strong. You'd better come and get her . . . Well, good, but where the hell are they, then? It's been hours since I called, God damn it! . . . What? . . . No, it has not been just fifteen minutes, young man. Who the hell are you anyway?"

As Ralph barked into the phone, Nora edged the chair over to Liz and tried to steer her into it. But Ralph's grip was too strong and too high for her to be able to sit, and Liz, again feeling oddly disconnected from what was happening, found herself on the verge of laughing. But if I laugh, she thought, shrugging helplessly at Nora, I'll never stop, I'll have hys-

183

terics — I'm almost having hysterics already. That thought in itself made the urge to laugh stronger, so she forced herself to listen to Ralph's meanderings:

"Supper, yes, like a viper. She's been taking my daughter from me, disrupting us, making trouble, nothing but trouble . . . Oh, something with her car — wanted to borrow a jack, she said, but it was a lie, just to get in here, just to destroy us, to kill my sweet Corinne and then me next, I suppose, and maybe Nora, too, and then take the house and all our land, our money."

"Father," Nora whispered, her face stiff with renewed horror, pulling at his hand where he was holding Liz, "Father, don't. That's not true, none of it is true."

But Ralph shot his elbow out, catching Nora under her ribs and she gasped, clutching her side, and reeled away emitting loud, rasping, painful sobs that seemed to rise from deep inside her, as if they'd been buried for years — for all her lonely life, perhaps, Liz thought, reaching for her as best she could.

But Nora slowly collapsed to the floor, gradually curling into a ball, as if first her knees, then her hips, then her waist and shoulders melted. Liz struggled toward her, but Ralph, still barking, now into the phone, now at her, wouldn't release her.

And so they stayed till the police — for it must be them, thank God, Liz thought — pounded on the front door and at last burst into the kitchen.

TWENTY-SIX

Ralph cried, "My sweetheart — in there!" and one of the officers ran into Corinne's room. It was only then that Ralph finally released Liz, shoving her toward another officer. Purplish-red welts appeared on her arm where Ralph had gripped it, and now the officer was holding her, more gently at least than Ralph, and saying, "Are you all right, ma'am?" Liz heard herself answering, "Yes," and the officer said, "Are you Miss Hardy?" and Liz told him she was and the officer said, "Let's go where we can talk, shall we?" He led her into the parlor.

As they left, Liz saw another officer bending over Nora, asking her who Corinne's doctor was, and a fourth prying

Ralph loose from the phone and sitting him down in a kitchen chair. Then the officer holding her closed the door, steered her to the sofa, sat her down, and flipped open a notebook.

"Now, Ms. Hardy, your full name?"

"Elizabeth Mary Hardy," Liz said.

"And you reside at?"

"I live at 448 West 98th Street in New York City, but I'm staying this summer at my family's cabin on Yellowfin Lake. I think you folks keep an eye on it in the winter. It's called Piney Haven and it's been in my family for years."

The officer nodded noncommitally and scribbled in his notebook. Liz rubbed her arm furtively, but when the officer looked up, he smiled and said, "I'm Detective Morris. That's a nasty bruise, where the old man was holding you. Maybe you need some ice on it."

"No," said Liz, "it's okay. But thanks for noticing, um, Detective Morris."

"Your folks haven't used that cabin for a long time, have they?"

"No." Liz explained about her parents' deaths and her own summer plans, and then, as he questioned her, told how she'd met the Tillots and what had happened that evening.

"You all had that carrot cake, is that right?"

"Yes. Except Mr. Tillot. He might not have had any; he said he didn't, anyway. I didn't notice."

"Is there any left?"

"Yes. It's in the kitchen. Should be right on the table. I brought ice cream, too, vanilla. I think Nora put what was left back in the ice box on the back stoop."

"Why do you think the old man accused you?"

Liz hesitated. "Well, he doesn't seem to like me and he seems to resent my friendship with Nora. I think he's afraid I'll take her away from him. He resents that I've taught her to drive, for example, and I can understand that. I mean, as

186

long as she can't drive, she can't leave. I think — it's my impression that he's a little unbalanced. And he also seems to love his wife very much, so naturally he's upset at her death."

"Hmm." Morris wrote for a few minutes, then looked up. "What's his financial situation?"

"What?"

"What's his financial situation?" he repeated blandly.

"I have no idea!" Liz felt shocked, resentful, at the question, and guilty, as if there were some truth in Ralph's accusation, because it seemed as if Morris thought there could be. Motive, she thought, that must be it; he's trying to see if there's a motive.

"What's your relationship with Miss Tillot?"

Oh, God, Liz thought, what in hell do I say to that?

"We're friends," she answered, trying to make her face unreadable, trying to ignore the sudden rapid beating of her heart. "We — we seem to be becoming quite close friends, in fact."

"Hmm," said Morris again, writing in his notebook. "Was Mrs. Tillot ill at all, do you know?"

Liz told him about the stroke and the TIAs and he asked if she'd been in pain recently or had had a recent "episode." Liz told him about the headache Corinne had had at dinner and said that she'd seemed vaguer than usual.

Morris nodded, writing rapidly. After a moment or two, he closed his notebook and stood up, smiling, holding out his hand. "Nice to meet you, Ms.— er" — he glanced at his notebook — "Ms. Hardy. We're going to have to ask you to stay here for a bit while we search the house, assuming Mr. Tillot gives his permission. That's routine when we have a case of this kind. There'll be someone from the district attorney's office here soon, and state police, probably, and after that, probably, the medical examiner. Assuming, of course, that Mrs. Tillot is actually, er, deceased."

Liz suddenly felt dizzy. This is not happening, she thought, it can't be. I'm a murder suspect. I've just fallen in love and now I'm a murder suspect.

"Will I . . ." she began, planning to ask if she'd be going to jail, if she'd be held, but instead she asked, "May I go back to Nora now?"

"Yes, of course." Morris opened the door for her. "At least I think so. Let me just check. Ken?" he called to an officer Liz could see talking on the phone. Nora was sitting at the table, her back very straight and tense. "All clear?"

The officer named Ken put his hand over the phone's mouthpiece and said, "All clear." Then, into the phone (he must be talking to Dr. Cantor, Liz realized), he said, "So you've been expecting something of this nature?"

"There you go." Morris stepped aside to let Liz precede him through the door.

Liz's legs didn't feel like her own when she walked to the kitchen, and she felt Morris's eyes, then his colleagues', on her as she entered — as if they're watching my every move, she thought, to see if I walk like a murderer.

Nora jumped up from the table when Liz came in, and hugged her. "Are you okay?" she whispered. "How's your arm?"

"Oh, my arm," Liz said. "I'd forgotten it. Are you okay?"

"I think so." Nora led Liz to the table, and they both sat down.

"Where's your father?"

"One of them's got him in the other room," Nora said softly. "He looked at Mama first, and then he took Father to the parlor. There's a policeman in with Mama. We can't go in, he said, till the medical examiner's been here and says we can." Nora stood up unsteadily and gripped the back of the chair she'd been sitting in. "But she's my own mother!"

Liz reached for Nora's hand as Nora looked at her, her eyes liquid and bewildered. "I know; that seems awful," Liz said lamely. "But I guess it's because of your father's — you

188

know, what he said about me. I'm so sorry, Nora." She could see the officer named Ken with Detective Morris at the other end of the kitchen; they were both rummaging in cupboards.

"After he looked at Mama," Nora said, "he told me they'd probably want to fingerprint us. 'Elimination prints,' he called them. He actually asked for permission." Nora's face softened. "I don't think they suspect you, really," she whispered. "I told them I certainly don't. I told them about Mama's stroke, and they called Dr. Cantor; they had to page him at the hospital. And I told them Father's, well, pretty near crazy. They know that anyway; they must. Everyone in town does. It'll be okay, Liz; I'm sure it will. Except Mama . . ."

Nora's voice broke.

She turned away, crying quietly. Liz got up and put her arms around her; Nora leaned her head against Liz's breast and sobbed.

A few minutes later, the state police arrived.

TWENTY-SEVEN

It was a long time before everyone left. While the state police searched the house, Nora and Liz sat in the kitchen — the police still wouldn't let them into Corinne's room — and Ralph sat in the parlor with a police officer, who was again questioning him. Nora felt wooden, devoid of emotion, devoid almost of thought. She saw Liz — Liz whom I love, she thought with mild surprise left over from earlier, although it seemed like years since she'd realized it; Liz who loves me — she saw Liz watching her anxiously, but she could manage no more response than a vague pat on Liz's arm. It had become, after the first flurry and the first reaction, as if it were all happening to other people, as if she herself were someone else.

An ambulance came at one point and the police sent it away. So it's really true, Nora thought, as Liz went to someone who beckoned from the kitchen door; Mama's really gone, really dead. She knew she'd known that before, of course, but having someone official acknowledge it — although no one had actually said the words, which, Nora thought vaguely, seems odd — having an outsider really acknowledge it somehow made it more true.

"Nora," Liz said quietly, coming back in and putting a hand, then two hands, on Nora's shoulders. "The state police want to talk to you for a few minutes. Just a few. It's all right," she added with a thin smile when Nora looked up at her. "They're nice. They already talked to me, and one of them's with your father." She put a hand under Nora's elbow and lifted her up — carefully, Nora thought; she's handling me carefully, as if I might break. I wish I *would* break!

She barely noticed what the state trooper looked like, except the word "grave" popped into her mind when she looked at his face, like "grave Alice" in the poem, and she barely noticed his questions; they seemed the same, anyway, as those the local police had asked. Tiredly, she went through the facts again, sitting outside with Liz, hearing Ralph's cry, finding Corinne's body, hearing Ralph's accusation, seeing the phone swinging on its cord, picking it up, finding the dispatcher still on the line . . .

"They're trained to do that, ma'am," the state trooper explained. So I must have asked about it, Nora thought fuzzily. "Trained to stay on the line when they get a call about — a call like this — till the officers come. Just in case, you know, of danger."

Then he asked her about Liz, about how long she'd known her, what she thought of her, whether Liz seemed to have an interest in . . .

"In money?" Nora asked, horrified, her mind now fully engaged. "Why no, of course not, not at all. She . . ." Then, having realized the implications of what the trooper was saying, she broke down again and wept, and the questions stopped.

Much later, or so it seemed, the two sets of police finally finished combing the house, even going upstairs to Nora's old bedroom, to her parents', to the other unused rooms, dusty and mouse-ridden, she was sure; this was after she and Liz and Ralph — whom she realized she hadn't seen for what seemed like hours — had been fingerprinted. "To eliminate you," a very young-seeming officer said, rolling Nora's fingers on a little pad; the "elimination prints," Nora thought; yes. "You see, you'll have touched lots of things around the house, and we don't want to find your prints on something and say you're a suspect."

"But I am, aren't I?" Nora asked. "A suspect?"

"Oh, no, ma'am, I very much doubt it," the officer said. "I can't say anything for sure, but I very much doubt it."

"How about my friend? How about Liz?"

"Well, again I can't say, ma'am, but, well, we have to take into consideration your father's — your father's state of mind. Time will tell." He snapped his little pad shut and gave Nora a tissue with which to wipe her fingers. "But I wouldn't fret."

That was what he'd said: "fret," as if he were a much older person: *fret!*

Then the medical examiner arrived and spent what seemed like a long time in the room with Corinne. He came into the kitchen afterward, a square man, Nora thought, square face, square body, even a square mouth when he smiled as he did now, sympathetically, at her. "You might want to go in to your mother now, ma'am," he said. "To say goodbye."

Nora looked up at Liz, who was standing beside her; she couldn't think what to do. But Liz nodded and squeezed her shoulder, so, obediently, feeling more as if she should than as if she wanted to — but she also did want to — Nora went, alone, into her mother's room and stood for a long time looking down at her, thinking, This is my mother, and she is dead. Her eyes were dry now, though they stung.

She knelt by the bed and took Corinne's hand. It was cold and a little stiff. There were her clean nails, neatly trimmed by Nora only yesterday; there was her engagement ring, her wedding ring. (Later the medical examiner would say to her, "You'd best take her jewelry, miss," and Nora did, slipping her mother's rings onto her own finger, then giving the wedding ring to Ralph, who asked for the engagement ring as well. So Nora gave that to him, too. She hadn't wanted it, really, except for the fact that it had been on her mother's finger and she thought it would be nice to have something that had touched Corinne's body. But then so must Father, she reasoned, and she felt his was the stronger claim.)

Holding her mother's hand, looking at her face, vacant and uncannily still in death, touching her hair, Nora tried to summon memories, thoughts that might make her weep again, for she could feel grief knotted painfully inside her. But the memories skittered through her mind, like waterbugs, she thought, the memory of waterbugs on Liz's lake interrupting the one of her mother showing her how to grease cookie tins when Nora had been, what? Five, maybe, or six. She remembered the games they'd played with bedmaking, with Tisane, one of Thomas's predecessors, for they'd always had cats — where was Thomas? Nora looked vaguely around the room and noticed there was the barest beginning of light around the edges of the windowshade; the false dawn, she thought; where *is* Thomas?

Abruptly men — more ambulance attendants? But why, since Mama was dead? Maybe they were just police? — men brought in a long stretcher on wheels. Liz came in, too, and Nora clung to her, and the police held onto Ralph while the men wheeled Corinne's body, now an elongated package encased in black plastic, outside. Ralph struggled to get to it, Nora saw without being able to react, and when the ambulance . . . But it looked like a van. It wasn't a hearse, surely? Not yet!

When it drove away, Ralph lunged at Liz and another policemen had to help the first one hold him.

"I think," the first policeman said to Nora, ducking out of range of Ralph's flailing arms, "that it might be a good idea to give your family doctor another call. Maybe a sedative . . ."

"Yes," Nora agreed, obediently again, and dialed Dr Cantor. But his wife answered; Dr. Cantor was still at the hospital, Mrs. Cantor said sleepily; she was so sorry about Corinne; could she help? And Nora, speaking as clearly as she could, oh, very clearly, said, "My father accused my friend Liz Hardy of poisoning my mother. Would you please tell Dr. Cantor about that when he comes home and tell him the police think Father needs a sedative?" She glared at Ralph. "It's not true, of course, what Father said about Liz."

Ralph lunged toward her, nearly breaking free of the police, shouting, "She's bewitched you, you're under her spell, she'll destroy us, she's evil, evil, a murderer!"

"See," Nora said calmly into the phone. "Did you hear that? He's snapped. He's crazy. Please tell Dr. Cantor."

"Of course," Mrs. Cantor said, sounding wide awake now. "Oh, Nora, I'm so sorry, dear, so sorry. He shouldn't be long. I'll have him paged again and ask him to go straight to your house from the hospital. Are the police still there? You're not alone, are you? If you are, why don't I come over?"

"No, no," Nora said. She realized she'd been rubbing her forehead, hard, with her free hand, and forced herself to stop. "It's all right. Thank you. I'm not alone. Thank you, Mrs. Cantor. I should go now. I — goodbye." She replaced the phone, smiled at Liz and the police officers without looking at Ralph, who was now slumped in a kitchen chair, sobbing, and said, "Shall I make some coffee?"

She saw the police officers glance at Liz and then nod. Liz handed her the coffee pot and the coffee can and pumped water for her while Nora, wooden again, stirred up the stove.

* * * * *

Across town, in the shed where he went nearly every night, especially when he couldn't sleep, Henry Brice sat staring at his shortwave radio. It was a little hard to piece together from the faint police calls which he'd run into accidentally (I really should buy a scanner, he thought), but it sure sounded to him as if the local police and an ambulance and then the state police and then the medical examiner had been dispatched one by one to the Tillot place because Corinne Tillot was dead and Ralph had accused that new friend of Nora's, that New York woman who'd been taking her to the grocery store instead of Louise taking her — Ralph had accused the New York woman of killing her.

TWENTY-EIGHT

By the time the sun came up, the doctor had arrived and had given both Ralph and Nora sedatives. Two police officers were still sitting outside in their cruiser. "Just in case," one of them had murmured, nodding toward Ralph when the others had left.

"Call me," Dr. Cantor now said brusquely to Liz, scribbling on a piece of paper. "Here's my beeper number. Call me if anything happens. Mr. Tillot should sleep a good long time, but I gave Nora a lesser dose; she should wake in a few hours. Here are a few more pills." He shook some from a bottle into an envelope. "If she needs more, give her one, but no more than one till I come back. I'll need to look at Mr. Tillot again later. Don't give him any more. He might bluster a bit, but he's too weak to do any real harm. And I'll come back later, as soon as I can."

Liz nodded.

"Are you all right?" Dr. Cantor added almost as an after-thought.

"Yes." *Sure,* she wanted to say, *I've just been accused of murder by a crazy old man who wants to kill me, too, probably, and who's succeeded in terrifying the woman I love. Sure, I'm fine.*

"Sure," she said out loud, leading Dr. Cantor to the front hall. "Thanks for coming."

"They're old friends of mine, the Tillots," he said, shaking his head. Liz wondered if he always looked so mournful or if it was just that he was sad about Corinne. His eyes, Liz could see, looked pained; no, defeated. "I'm so sorry this has hap-pened." He hesitated a moment, then reached for Liz's hand. His own, Liz noticed absently, was long-fingered and pale, with exquisitely cared-for nails. "Ms. Hardy," he said gravely, "I doubt anyone will put much stock in that accusation. Everyone who knows Ralph Tillot knows he's a, well, a difficult person. Difficult and troubled." He paused again, as if weighing his words carefully. "His wife's death has clearly aggravated his, ah, his problems. I will try to reason with him later today and see if he'll be willing to see a colleague of mine who may be better equipped to prescribe for him than I."

Shrink, Liz thought; good. It's about time.

With his free hand, Dr. Cantor patted the hand he held. "I wouldn't worry too much, Ms. Hardy, about what Ralph, Mr. Tillot, I mean, said."

Liz smiled thinly. "I'll try not to. And thank you."

"You're welcome. Now I must check in at the hospital. There are a few patients I have to see, but I'll come back as soon as I can. Please remember to beep me if you need me. Thank God they finally got a phone here!"

197

"Yes, thank God," she said politely as Dr. Cantor bowed stiffly and left. But she thought: If they hadn't gotten one, Ralph could never have called the cops and accused me.

She stood at the door for a few minutes watching the doctor walk to his car.

I could leave, too, she told herself. I could get in my car and escape from this madhouse. I could go home to the cabin or even home to New York; I could stay with someone till my apartment's free again, till the sublet's up. I could leave this crazy town, this crazy place. I could even go out to Jeff and Susan's in California for a while.

But you can't leave Nora, her internal voice said. *You know that. You can't leave her now.*

"I do know that," Liz said aloud almost crossly. God, do I know that!

Would I have stayed with Megan if this had happened to her, she wondered as she turned and walked back toward the kitchen.

Oh, hell, who knows! And does it really matter?

It doesn't matter, not any more, she thought, opening the door to the kitchen, seeing Nora at the table with Thomas on her lap; she was patting him absently while he purred. But she doesn't even know Thomas is there, Liz realized; she's trying to shut herself off from what's happened, as I, she thought, startled, shut myself off from feeling with Megan, because . . .

But nothing followed "because," so she went to Nora and sat next to her, carefully touching her arm. "Nora, forgive me," she said, "but how about bed? You should probably try to get a little sleep. You must be exhausted, and that pill Dr. Cantor gave you should help you sleep."

Nora turned to her, pools of unshed tears in her eyes. "I never said goodbye." Her voice was small, like a child's, and full of self-reproach. "I never said goodbye to Mama. All I said to her tonight when I put her to bed was 'Goodnight.' I don't think I even said, 'I love you.' I often said that, and she'd take my hand and smile and say, 'I love you, too.' But we didn't do that tonight."

"You didn't know," Liz said, "what was going to happen. Neither did she. But she knew you loved her, Nora. Look at how you took care of her, how gentle you always were with her, how . . ."

"She took care of me, too. Even after the stroke, she took care of me." The tears spilled over, without sobs, and Nora shook her head as if in wonder. "She protected me from him, in a way. She knew, she knew how, how awful he was some-times and she'd make me laugh at it. Never directly, she couldn't go against him, but she'd distract me from him. And now . . ." Nora buried her face in her hands and her shoulders shook, but still silently.

Liz tried to gather her in her arms, but Nora was tense, unreachable, so she drew back. "How about bed?" she asked again after a few minutes. "You need to sleep, and the pill will help you. There'll be things to do soon, people to call, probably. Won't there?"

Nora lifted her head, moving her hands away. "Yes, I sup-pose so. Although there aren't many relatives. A few cousins. I'll have to ask Father about some of them, I guess. Or go into his desk. No one cared, though. I almost don't need to tell anyone."

"No one cared?" Liz asked incredulously. "But your mother was so sweet!"

"Yes, but no one liked Father. No one liked Clarkston either. Everyone moved away after a while and drifted away from us, too. When I was little we did have some family parties." Her eyes brightened. "Even here. People came back to Clarkston a few times for them, and I had cousins to play with then. But after a while Father got angry at everyone, I think because they wanted him to change, you know, elec-tricity and a telephone and plumbing. Finally he got so angry he wouldn't see anyone in the family any more, so of course they stopped coming and after a while they stopped writing, too. They've never come back."

"What about the cousins you played with, though?" Liz managed to pull Nora to her feet and steer her into her room. "Didn't they want to go on seeing you?"

"Maybe, but when they were kids I guess they couldn't have done anything about it if they did. I guess they couldn't go against their parents, but I bet they didn't really want to. Father was okay for a while when we were all little, but when he started to change, they seemed afraid of him. One cousin did write to me for a while. Andrew, his name was. We were good friends, I guess, for a while when we were pretty young."

Liz sat Nora down on the edge of the bed, drew the windowshade, shutting out most of the strengthening sun, and bent to remove Nora's shoes.

"Andrew wrote to me for a while after the family parties stopped being here, and of course we never went to them anyway when someone else had them. But then he stopped. He went away to boarding school, I think, and I don't know what after that."

"Maybe you could get in touch with him." Liz swung Nora's legs around onto the bed and eased her shoulders down till her head touched the pillow. "I'm sure he'd like to know about your mother. He'd probably like hearing from you again, too, if you were friends. Maybe if you could find him, he could help you find the others."

"Yes, maybe."

Nora's eyelids, Liz could see, were getting heavy and her voice was getting softer, her speech slower.

"Tell me about Andrew," Liz said, sitting on the edge of the bed and taking Nora's hand. "Is he older or younger than you?"

"Older," Nora said sleepily. "Two or three years older. Once when he was here he killed a snake and cut it open and showed me its eggs and we went running into the house to

200

show the grownups. Father got mad that we were dripping on the floor, but Mama said we were real scientists. I remember that: 'Real scientists,' she said and looked at the eggs and marveled at them. You could see the baby snakes curled up in the eggs and the eggs were all strung together. Like beads, Andrew said. I remember that, too. 'They look like beads,' he said. I thought that was clever."

"He sounds nice. What else do you remember about him?"

"Oh, he had — had brown hair — curly." She yawned. "I'm so sleepy." She squeezed Liz's hand. "And you're being so dear. Thank you."

"Shh. Shh. Sleep now." Liz stroked Nora's hair, her forehead.

Nora moved Liz's hand to her lips, kissing, then holding it. "Thank you," she said again. Then, looking shy and embarrassed, she said, "Would it be, I don't know, rude, presumptuous, of me to ask you to sleep here? I mean right here, next to me? It's not a very big bed so if you'd rather not, it's okay. It's childish, I know, but I don't want to be alone, suddenly. I feel — I feel — I don't know. Little, I guess, like I want to crawl into a hole. I didn't feel anything before," she said, sounding surprised, "but now I feel — that way. It's a foolish request, though, I know and I . . ."

"Shh," Liz said again, pulling her shoes off quickly and sliding onto the bed, taking Nora in her arms and cradling Nora's head against her breast. "Not foolish at all," she whispered. "Sleep now, love. Sleep."

Nora closed her eyes and was soon breathing evenly and deeply.

But Liz stared into the rapidly brightening room. I called her "love," she thought first. As if I was already used to it. Then she thought: Murder. I've been accused of murder.

Even though she knew by then that the police put more stock in Ralph's mental state than in his accusation — indeed, had even seemed to suspect him when he'd balked at the autopsy the medical examiner told him he would have to per-

201

form — and even though the police had been apologetic when confiscating the leftover carrot cake and ice cream, and even though she knew their search of the house and the barn had turned up nothing — no telltale vial of poison, not even any mouse or rat poison, although they had taken samples of some medication — even though the medical examiner had agreed that Corinne had probably died of a stroke — Liz felt herself shivering violently, and she moved away from Nora and sat in a chair so she wouldn't disturb her. She tried relaxing her muscles, then tried holding herself rigid, then relaxing again till the shaking finally stopped enough for her to go back to Nora's bed and fall into a restless sleep.

TWENTY-NINE

By nine-thirty that same morning, Louise Brice had the story down pat.

"Good morning, Marie," she said as soon as Marie Hastings answered the phone with a cheerful, "Good morning, the Parsonage."

"Marie, I have some sad news and some disturbing news that I think you and Charles need to know before anyone else does and before you hear it from someone else or see it in the papers, which, inevitably, you will."

"Goodness, Louise," Marie answered; Louise was annoyed to hear water running and dishes clattering in the background. "Whatever can you mean? Charles is already working on next Sunday's sermon."

"No need to disturb him right away. Not till you know, anyway. Last night," she said, speaking very clearly, "poor dear Corinne Tillot died."

"Oh, no!" (Louise was glad to hear silence after one last ring of crockery against crockery; the running-water sound stopped abruptly.) "What a shame! Oh, that poor, poor girl! And Ralph! Whatever else one can say about him, he did dote on Corinne. Charles and I . . ."

"I know, I know. But the terrible thing" — Louise lowered her voice dramatically — "is that the police were involved. Henry picked up several police calls on his shortwave; you know, he spends simply hours out in the shed listening in to other people's business, and . . ."

"Police?" Marie sounded bewildered. "Why on earth . . ."

"Because," Louise explained with considerable relish, "of that girl, that erstwhile friend of Nora's."

"That nice summer person, Miss Hardy? But I don't see . . ."

"Apparently, she was involved. Hurrying Corinne's death along, or so the police seem to think."

"What? But I don't . . ."

"My dear, it's not hard to understand, is it? First she befriends Nora, takes that poor girl out for drives and to her cabin and for all I know, to restaurants and movies and Lord knows what. Sucks up to her, I believe is the vulgar expression. It's very likely, after all, that Ralph has money put by. But in any case, that woman has been luring Nora away."

"But I still don't see . . ." Marie Hastings's voice hardened. "Louise, just exactly what did Henry hear?"

"First," Louise said, probably unaware that she was settling into a comfortably gossipy tone — but Marie was aware — "first he heard the dispatcher call for the patrol car on duty to go to the Tillot place, and for any other available

204

cars to go, too. Then he heard the dispatcher say there'd been what appeared to be a murder. "

"A *what?*"

"You heard me. That's exactly what Henry said to me he heard: that there 'appeared to have been a murder.' And that whoever went there should 'use caution,' that Ralph had called and said the accused perp, that's perpetrator, of course, was still in the house and so was the daughter. Well, now who else can that have been but Miss Hardy? And anyway, later when I drove over there, I saw her car."

"Louise, I just can't . . ."

"I know, Marie, I can't either. But one never knows, does one? Anyway, later the state police were called in — at least Henry heard something from one of them over his radio — something saying that they were on their way and that someone should call the medical examiner. Can you imagine?" she said with what sounded, to Marie's horror, like satisfaction. "I always knew that Hardy woman was up to no good. Stepping in where she wasn't wanted and filling poor Nora's head full of goodness knows what. Anyway, I did think you and Charles should be the first to know."

"Yes, certainly," Marie said — stiffly, Louise thought. "I'll tell Charles. We will of course go over there. Thank you for letting us know."

"You're welcome. I'll call again if I hear any more."

By around eleven, Helen Whipple had an eager crowd clustered around her counter in the Clarkston Post Office. There was so much chatter she couldn't get a word in edgewise, as she put it to her husband later.

"I just can't imagine her . . ."

"She used to play with my Betsy every summer!"

". . . became a teacher in New York, I think. Some fancy school."

"I wonder if she was after money, somehow. I hear those private schools don't pay much."

"Funny way to get it, I'd say. Besides, the Hardys had money, I always thought. Most summer people do, anyway."

"You never can tell about people!"

"Poison, they think."

"Yes, in the dinner. Roast beef, I think it was."

"No, no, dessert. Some kind of cake."

"Must've been rat poison."

"No, that makes you dry up. Probably arsenic. Or strychnine."

"They say she's in jail now. You know, being held for questioning anyway."

"Must be."

"Who," asked Roy Stark, coming into the post office for his mail, with Zeke trotting amiably behind him, "is in jail?"

The women, for the crowd was all female, fell silent and looked as one toward Helen.

"So far it's just talk, Mr. Stark," Helen said, scanning the crowd severely.

"Oh, it's more than talk," one of the women burst in. "It's Liz Hardy. Surely you've met her, Mr. Stark, that New York woman who's been staying in her family's cabin on Yellowfin Lake."

Roy, Helen thought, looked both amused and interested.

"Good grief, yes, I've met her. Nice woman. What's she done?" he asked.

Maryann Loren, who lived down the main road from the Tillot farm, stepped closer to Roy, her eyes bright but her voice lowered, as if sharing a confidence. "Of course a person's innocent till proven guilty." She glanced at Helen as if for approval. "But they say she poisoned Corinne Tillot last night."

Roy looked startled and his interest seemed to escalate; it made Helen uncomfortable. "Poisoned who?" he asked, his key poised in front of his post office box.

"Corinne Tillot," several of the women chorused.

Roy turned. "Not that young woman from the farm?" he asked.

"No, no," said Maryann. "Not Nora. Corinne. Nora's mother. We live near Tillot Farm," she explained to Roy. "You know, the old place tucked away down that really bumpy dirt road off the main road?"

"Yes, yes," Roy said. "The crazy farm, the kids call it. A big house, no electricity, lots of land."

"Around fifty acres," Maryann said, nodding; Roy, Helen noticed, raised his eyebrows.

"Well, we've known the Tillots for ages, of course," Maryann continued, "quiet people who've always kept to themselves. The parents are ill, and the daughter, Nora, poor thing, has cared for them for years, devotedly, I might add." She glanced around again; the others nodded. "And last night my husband and I heard sirens and we saw flashing lights passing by."

"Maybe she'll sell the old place," one of the other women said, "now that Corinne's gone."

"She certainly should," Maryann agreed, nodding emphatically. "It wouldn't be healthy, staying on with such memories. And Ralph's bound to get worse. But mark my words, he'll never hear of it. Nora will have to hold onto the place till he dies. Then I bet she'll get out in a hurry, poor child."

Roy's eyes, Helen noticed, darted from woman to woman as the conversation about the possible fate of the farm continued excitedly near the counter.

But Maryann tugged at Roy's sleeve. "Ralph's Corinne's husband, Nora's father," she explained. "And apparently he told the police that Liz Hardy poisoned Corinne. Liz Hardy's been seeing a lot of poor Nora all summer."

Roy unlocked his post office box and pulled out a few envelopes. Helen couldn't see his face when he spoke. "I've gotten to know Liz a little, and I can't believe she'd do murder," he told them all slowly. "You say she's in custody?"

The Greek chorus of women nodded. "That's what we heard," one woman said.

"That's just a rumor," Helen said sternly. "We don't know that for sure."

"Well, maybe I'll just go over to the police station and see." Roy stuffed his mail into his jacket pocket, whistled to his dog, and strode out of the post office, leaving Helen and the other women staring after him.

"I heard he went out with that Hardy woman," someone whispered. "Poor boy."

"I think it must have been only once, though," said someone else. "Clara Davis — you know, the Davises took him under their wing — Clara told me he couldn't get anywhere with her. That she's getting over a broken heart."

"A broken heart will do a lot of things," remarked Maryann, "but I don't think it usually leads to murder. I daresay there's more to the story than just that! I must say, I do wonder about the money angle."

Helen Whipple had had about all the gossip she could take. "Nonsense," she said crisply. "I've known Liz Hardy for years, summers, anyway, and so have some of you. This whole thing is utter nonsense." Angrily she began stamping postmarks — the Clarkston Post Office wasn't automated — on the outgoing mail.

At the police station, Roy found out nothing except the fact that Liz was not being held.

"Is she a suspect?" he asked.

The dispatcher shrugged. "I can't say."

"Why the hell not, man?"

"Because no one's told me," the dispatcher snapped. "And if they had, I wouldn't be able to tell you. Call the chief if you like. All I can tell you is that she's not here and wasn't ever brought in."

Thoughtfully, Roy left the post office and made a quick call from the phone booth on the corner. Georgia Foley wasn't in, but he was able to leave a message with her secretary. Then, whistling to Zeke, he climbed into his car, driving straight to Liz's cabin and then to the Tillots', where he lingered about halfway down their dirt road, out of sight of the house. After a while he got out of the car and walked slowly through the woods and across the back fields.

Quite a while later, Liz, pale and with dark circles under her eyes, opened the Tillots' front door in answer to Roy's knock.

"Well," he said cheerfully, "you don't look much like a murderess."

Liz stared at him, blankly, he thought.

"May I come in?"

"Uh — no, Roy, sorry. I don't think so. Mrs. Tillot . . ."

"Yes, I know." He put a hand on her shoulder. "I'm glad to see you're not in jail. I've heard lots of rumors. Of course they're ridiculous."

"Yes," Liz said expressionlessly. "They are. Would you please let go of me?"

"I just thought you might need a little support."

"No. Thank you. I'm all right. Roy, please!"

He moved his hand away, letting her go. "I just wanted to offer my condolences," he said blandly. "To you, especially. And to ask if there's anything I can do. Or that Georgia can; I'm sure she'd want to help. You know, if things get too unpleasant."

"Georgia?" Liz asked. "Georgia Foley? But what . . . ?"

Roy shrugged. "Just an idea," he said. "If things get nasty." He paused. "For instance, if you decide to leave after all, to sell, or if Nora does. I mean, it seems to me a lot has changed, for both of you."

For a moment she stood motionless, staring at him. Then very quietly she said, "Go away, Roy. Please just go away."

Roy nodded and without saying anything more, he turned abruptly and left.

THIRTY

"Who was that?" Nora asked when Liz went into the kitchen; Nora was standing in the doorway, still wearing the clothes in which she'd slept, as was Liz. It was 3 P.M.; they'd just gotten up.

"Roy Stark." Liz reached for the coffee pot and pumped water for it.

"What on earth did he want?"

"I'm not sure. Partly to find out if I was in jail, I guess."

"In jail!" Nora sank down into a kitchen chair. "But how . . . ?"

"He said he's heard rumors. So I guess people are talking. Do you want some coffee? Or tea?""

"Please." Nora stood up stiffly. "Coffee, I think. I've got to

211

see to Father. I've got to get their baths ready and . . ." She stopped, her head on one side, her eyes swimming with tears again. "No, his bath. Only one. Only one now."

Liz put down the coffee pot and held Nora till she broke away and went to the sink, filling the bathwater kettle and putting it on the stove, which, Liz saw, was nearly cold. Trying not to think about what Roy had said, she moved Nora gently aside and blew on the coals, putting on kindling and then, when it caught, a fresh log. "Right?" she asked. "Am I doing this right?"

Nora nodded, then groaned as Ralph yelled, "NORA!" from his room.

"Coming, Father," Nora answered. "I was just getting your bath water started. Would you like some coffee?" she asked when she got to the door of his room. How had he gotten to bed, she wondered, last night? He was still in his clothes, but she had no memory of putting him to bed. Maybe Liz had, or the doctor.

"I'm dizzy," he complained, rubbing his head. "My stomach hurts. I'm dizzy. You'd better call the doctor."

"He'll be coming anyway, soon, I think."

Ralph struggled to sit up. "How's your mother?" he asked.

Nora felt her eyes fill again; she wiped them with the back of her hand. "Father," she said, kneeling by his bed and taking his hands. "Don't you remember? Mama — Mama passed away."

"I know that!" he shouted angrily. "But she didn't 'pass away'! She was murdered, poisoned by that woman. I want to see her. To see my wife." He swung his legs over the edge of the bed, talking very fast, his eyes wild. "We'll keep her here," he said. "We'll keep my sweetheart here where we can care for her. We'll go on just as always. You'll bathe her and dress her and we'll take her into the kitchen for her meals and outside to sit near the garden. And we won't tell anyone until that woman is tried and convicted and punished, and we'll show them my sweetheart in court and they'll all see how well we take care of her, so they won't make us put her in the ground, and . . ."

"Father, stop!" Nora shouted, shaking him. "Stop!"

Liz appeared in the doorway. "Nora? Are you all right?"

"You!" Ralph shouted, rising to his feet, swaying tipsily. "You!" He grabbed his walker and, shoving it angrily ahead of him, staggered into the kitchen, groping for the phone. "911!" he yelled into the receiver; Nora could hear the dial tone, but Ralph paid it no heed. "The police, damn you! Operator! Get me the police! There's a murderer here, a murderer! The police, damn it, the . . ."

At that moment, Dr. Cantor walked into the kitchen and took the receiver from Ralph's hand. "The door was un-locked," he said over his shoulder to Nora. "I heard shouting so I came right in. Ralph," he said sternly, as Nora sank down into a chair, with Liz standing beside her, "Ralph, calm down. You've already called the police. You don't need to call them again."

"Are they coming?" Ralph asked in a thin voice, like a little boy's, Liz thought, watching again in fascinated horror. "Are they coming? They killed my sweetheart," he moaned, still in the childish voice. "Those two." He pointed to Nora and Liz. "Those two, they killed her, and the police have to come and take them away."

"Shh, Ralph," said Dr. Cantor, leading him back to his room. "That will do. Let the police decide. Water, please," he said over his shoulder to Nora as they shuffled past. "I'm going to give him another sedative."

Liz put her hand out, stopping Nora. "I'll get it."

Nora sat still when Liz had left with the water. She watched the pattern the early afternoon sun made on the floor. Thomas, who had fled into Nora's room when the shout-ing started, emerged and jumped into Nora's lap; Nora, trying to absorb the silence, sat stroking him. I will not go mad, she said to herself. I will not. There will be an end to this, a solution. But nothing will be the same as it was, ever. Everything will be new. And eventually, life will continue in a new way, and I have to be ready to meet it, somehow. "I will be," she said aloud, reaching for a pad and pencil she kept on the shelf above the table for when a poem struck her, *"a new person, whole but forged from fragments,"* she wrote, *"pieces of bone and skin and sinew, painfully ripped away and mixed anew, pasted carefully onto my old frame . . ."*

"He's quieting down," Liz said, coming back in.

Hastily, Nora tore off the page on which she'd been writing and stuffed it into her pocket.

"Dr. Cantor said it's the shock," Liz went on. "He doesn't think he's cracked completely. But he's arranged for a psychiatrist to come and see him this afternoon. Dr. Cantor actually came right out and said that. I don't think he dared say the word to me before. It's as if it's hard for him to admit your father's mentally ill. Funny, elegant, sad-looking man. Nora? Are you all right?"

"Yes."

"Do you want that coffee now? I think the water's ready."

"No. Yes. All right. I don't care. I don't know what I want."

"For it all to be over, I imagine." Liz bustled around, filling the coffee pot, finding the cups. "I'll make some for Dr. Cantor, too, shall I?'

"Yes. That would be nice." Nora tipped Thomas off her lap and got stiffly to her feet. "I'll just feed him," she said, opening a cupboard. "I don't think I fed him last night."

"No," said Liz, tending the pot. "I don't think you did. He hid under the back stoop, I think, during all the — commotion." She bent, running her hand along the cat's sleek body. "Poor kitty."

The telephone rang.

Nora stared at it while it went on ringing.

214

"Shall I answer it?" Liz asked.

"No. Well. Yes, I guess so. It might be for Dr. Cantor."

But it wasn't. It was, Liz explained to Nora reluctantly after she'd hung up, a newspaper reporter.

THIRTY-ONE

The psychiatrist, a Dr. Herschwell, who was unexpectedly, to Liz anyway, round and florid, spent more than an hour closeted with Ralph in his room, while Nora and Liz cleaned all of the house that they could clean quietly, both for something to do and in expectation of funeral guests. When Dr. Herschwell emerged, he took Nora's hand gravely, saying, "I think your father is seriously ill, Miss Tillot. I leave you with these tablets" — he handed her a sample packet — "which will calm him somewhat until we can do a more careful evaluation. Give him one twice a day, morning and evening, starting this evening. I shall make a full report to Dr. Cantor and, after your poor mother's service, I'll arrange for a thorough evaluation. We'll see then what is to be done. I'm

216

deeply sorry for your loss." Then he added, twisting his spherical body awkwardly toward Liz, "And for the accusation made against you. I think you have nothing to fear on that score."

Early that evening, while Nora and Ralph were both napping, Liz drove back to the cabin to shower and get a change of clothes. She managed to keep her mind blank while she drove, but standing under the shower in Mom's Hippo, letting the warm water sluice over her sticky body (for the weather was still hot), a sense of unreality again suffused her. It's as if I'm acting in a play, she thought, tipping her face up to the showerhead, letting water pound onto her skin, or in a soap opera. That's more like it, a soap opera; it's melodrama, not drama; it can't be happening this way.

But of course it is.

Eventually she switched off the water and dried herself, reveling in the scratchiness of the towel, the tingling sensation it left on her damp, now-pink skin.

Pink except for the purple bruise Ralph had left on her arm.

I could leave, she thought again. I could still leave. Wouldn't that be the sensible thing to do? I could still go back to New York, close up the cabin, tell Jeff and Susan not to come. I could get out of this nightmare.

And, she thought, reluctantly remembering Roy's words, I could try to sell the cabin after all. If people really are talking, if they think I'm a murderer . . .

But Nora's face kept swimming before her eyes, making Liz's throat catch with the pain in her deep blue eyes, the pain, the courage, and, lately, the mute appeal.

No, she admitted silently, realizing she'd known it anyway. I can't. I can't possibly leave her.

She shrugged into a clean white shirt and clean khaki

shorts, then packed her overnight bag with a dressy shirt and pants for the funeral, which she assumed would be soon, plus jeans, a sweater, a few changes of underwear, and a couple of t-shirts. After she threw the bag into the car she went down to the dock and sat there as the sun slowly dipped behind the opposite shore.

I should bring her here, she thought. She could heal here. She can't even begin to heal in that house with that awful man.

Maybe Dr. Herschwell will say he's crazy enough to be put away.

Would Nora leave then?

Would Nora sell the farm? She thought of Roy again. And then would she . . .

Liz shook herself. Stop it, kiddo. Stop it! She's too vulnerable, too needy, right now.

As the sunset darkened into twilight, Liz walked back to the car, stopping at the garden, admiring, briefly, Nora's unfinished handiwork. There were no weeds to speak of, and neat clumps of newly planted perennials, most of them divisions from Nora's own garden, dotted the cleanly mulched surface. "They'll grow," Nora had said when Liz complained that they seemed too far apart and that her mother's garden had been so full of flowers there'd been little room for weeds. "They'll fill in. It takes about three years for a perennial garden to establish itself. This may take less time, though, since there are some things already here."

Three years. Or less. Where would Nora be in three years? Where would she want to be?

Where do I want to be in three years, Liz mused, climbing into the car. They used to ask us that in college, to help us decide what we wanted to do.

Three years.

I'd like to be . . .

But I don't know. Not any more. One year ago I'd have said I wanted to be right there in New York, teaching at

Holden Academy, maybe moving up to department head, becoming an expert, maybe publishing something impressive, thinking about working toward a PhD — for she had considered that, dreamed of a university position, long ago.

One year ago I'd have imagined Megan by my side, she thought so unexpectedly that she pulled the car onto the road's grassy shoulder and sat there, staring blindly into the woods.

I'd have assumed she'd be there, that I'd want her there.

Pictures of Megan flashed before her eyes: Megan, in her yellow polo shirt and green jeans, laughing while they were hiking in New Hampshire a year ago — was it only a year ago? — when they'd come upon two squirrels arguing over a pile of acorns.

Megan, lying naked on cool white sheets, her body golden in sunlight, reaching up to Liz, pulling her down to her.

Megan, crying over the death of a dog in a movie, gripping Liz's arm when the truck struck it, shaking her head inconsolably when Liz whispered, "It's only a story; they didn't kill a real dog, honey."

But Janey was consoling Megan now, was caressing her golden body, loving her delicious laugh.

Liz thought then of Ralph, of his gentleness with Corinne, of the apparent depth or at least the violence of his grief, and she was momentarily filled with compassion for him, and unexpected respect despite his tragic — the word came unbidden to her — his tragic madness.

And she thought of Nora as she'd first seen her, and Nora learning to swim and to drive, and Nora teaching her how to garden, and Nora patting Thomas, and stoking the stove and bathing and feeding and tending her parents, and listening to Liz talk about her own parents, understanding Liz's long pent-up pain, accepting it — and Nora early that morning, lying in Liz's arms, her face relaxed for a time while she slept.

After the shaking had stopped and she'd slept for a while, Liz had awakened and leaned over, watching Nora's eyes move under their lids, listening to her breathe, and her throat caught now, remembering a wave of tenderness stronger than anything she'd felt for Megan.

Megan had been sentimental but not truly vulnerable or open to Liz, and Liz had not let herself show Megan her own vulnerability. They had been brittle together, laughing and making love and playing.

When Liz's mother died, Megan had done all the right things, helped Liz with the announcements and the arrangements, cleared out the hospital room, held Liz and soothed her, said "It's all right to cry" (but Liz had not cried), sat next to her in the family pew at the funeral, accompanied her to the graveyard, greeted the relatives.

Remotely.

She'd also rummaged in her pocketbook while the minister prayed, and she'd whistled and giggled while clearing out the hospital room, changed the radio station to the news while holding Liz and urging her to cry.

Withheld herself from me, Liz realized, as I withheld myself from her.

Skimming the surface; skimming the surface of love.

But it's so much easier that way! So very much easier. So very much safer.

Making love with Megan . . .

It was good, good enough, anyway; they knew each other's bodies well, knew what worked and what didn't.

"But there was no connection," Liz whispered out loud. "No connection. The deepest part of me and the deepest part of you; we never met. Never, Megan. Never."

"And that," she realized with an unexpected and tremendous sense of relief, "is why I left you."

And that also — God help me; it's so much harder! — because we *do* meet, is why I love Nora.

* * * * *

220

The Hastingses' car was in front of the farmhouse when Liz drove up, and Charles and Marie were in the kitchen with Nora and Ralph. Nora, Liz saw, had put on a fresh dress and brushed her hair; Ralph, too, was in fresh clothes and looked sleepy rather than belligerent, even when he turned around and obviously saw her. The pills, Liz thought, thank you, Dr. Herschwell!

"We were just making a list," Nora said, smiling bravely when Liz walked in, "of people to notify. And working out funeral plans."

Liz nodded. "I'll just . . ." she began awkwardly, but she wasn't sure where she could go in order to leave them alone.

Nora interrupted quickly. "No, please stay. It's all right." She patted the chair next to her and introduced Liz.

"How do you do?" Liz said formally, sitting down, ignoring Ralph, who was beginning to glower after all.

Charles Hastings nodded and said, "Good to meet you."

"Nora was telling us about her cousins," said Marie, "and we called information and actually found a number for one of them."

"For Andrew," Nora explained to Liz. "The one I told you about."

Ralph grunted. "Little limb of Satan, that boy," he growled.

"Yes, but Father, he's grown up now. They all are."

"We don't have room to have them all here. Too much noise and fuss anyway. Too expensive, too. All that food."

"Now, Ralph," said Marie, patting his arm, "you want to do things right, don't you? For Corinne's sake."

"Corinne," said Ralph, his eyes filling with tears. "I saw her last night, you know. Standing right by my bed. She was beckoning to me."

Liz saw Nora shiver; she touched Nora's foot with her own under the table.

"Maybe she was waving, Ralph," said Charles calmly. "To

tell you she's all right. She's with God now, Ralph. No more pain or suffering for her."

"But plenty for me." Ralph stared at Liz, as if pretending he'd just noticed her. "Why is she here? This is just for family, Nora." His voice was rising dangerously. "She shouldn't be here. She should be in jail, she . . ."

"She's my close friend, Father," Nora said, keeping Liz, who had started to get up, from standing. "I want her here. I need her here."

"But she killed my Corinne!" he shouted, shaking off Charles's hand. "She's a murderer! Murderer!" he shouted, his eyes snapping.

"I'll go outside," Liz said quickly to Nora. "There's no point in upsetting him. I'll be out by the garden."

It was another hour or more before Nora joined her. Clouds had covered the moon, and Liz had moved to the stoop, half dozing, half listening to the drone of voices from the kitchen. Thomas had rubbed against her legs when she'd first sat and she'd picked him up, rubbing her face against his soft hair. "We're exiles, Tom," she'd said to him. "Exiles."

When Nora came out, Thomas jumped off Liz's lap and mewed; Nora gave him an absent-minded pat and then sat next to Liz. "Hi," she said, leaning her head on Liz's shoulder.

Liz willed herself not to move. "Hi. How are you?"

"Okay, I think." Nora put her hand up to Liz's cheek. "You've been so wonderful. I don't think I could've gotten through any of this without you."

"Yes, you could have. You're stronger than you think, Nora."

Nora sighed. "I don't know. I never had to do anything like this before. I just wish you hadn't been involved."

"What do you mean?"

"You know. Father's stupid accusation."

"Oh, that," Liz said, deliberately casual. "It's annoying, but I guess the autopsy will clear it up."

"Yes. But that'll take a while."

"Will it? But all they have to do is . . . Nora, you can't want to talk about this!"

"It's okay. I thought that, too, that all they'd have to do would be look in her stomach. But they have to take tissue samples, the medical examiner told me. And blood, I think. All that has to go to a lab to be examined. It could be as late as next week, he said. Or later, but he said they'd try to hurry it up."

"Next week," Liz said. "My brother's coming then. At the end of the week. The weekend."

Nora lifted her head, then kissed Liz lightly on the cheek. "I'm glad," she said. "He'll distract you from all this."

Liz allowed herself to take Nora's hand. "Maybe I don't want to be distracted."

"Surely you do!"

"From all the fuss, yes. But from you, no. In fact," she said, marveling at her own certainty, "the way I feel right now, I don't want to be distracted from you ever again."

Nora was silent, but Liz could see her smiling in the little light that came from the cloudy moon. "Last night," Nora said finally, "or really this morning, when you were holding me? I didn't want to ever leave your arms. And sometimes when we've been talking, I've wondered how I used to manage just talking to Thomas or the Hastingses, or Mrs. Brice and Patty and Sarah."

"You've been more lonely than you know." Liz kissed her swiftly and then stood up. "But don't jump to conclusions, please. You've been having such an awful time with all this. You can't . . ."

"Think clearly?" Nora stood also, facing Liz. "I think I can, Liz. I think I can think clearly enough to know that I don't want to stop being with you, that I don't want this to end when you go back to New York."

223

"Neither do I," Liz admitted. "But . . ."

"Let's just see where it goes, where we go. Meanwhile . . ." Nora put her arms around Liz's neck and drew her close.

THIRTY-TWO

They slept in each other's arms again that night, still chastely, or Nora slept; Liz alternated between staring wakefully into the darkness and gazing at Nora, noticing the moonlight playing on the curve of her cheek, the way the short ends of her hair curled damply at her temples.

They spent the next few days making funeral arrangements and sorting Corinne's clothes and other belongings; Liz had been afraid that would be too painful for Nora to do so soon, but Nora had insisted. "I'm numb now," she kept saying. "It's really not hard. I'm surprised that it isn't, but it isn't."

But after another sleepless night in Nora's narrow bed, Liz reluctantly told Nora she thought she should go back to Piney Haven to sleep.

"Oh, no," Nora protested. "Please don't. Please stay."

"I want to stay," Liz said, taking her hands. "But if I don't get some sleep, Nora, I won't be any use to you."

"Well — maybe you could sleep in the parlor? On the sofa? I don't think it's terribly lumpy. I'll miss feeling you next to me," she added shyly. "But it is a bit crowded, I know."

"I'll miss feeling you next to me, too," Liz said stiffly, wanting to say more, but telling herself she shouldn't, that this was not the time.

Nora slid her hands up Liz's arms to her shoulders, then wrapped her own arms around Liz's body. "I do want to be with you, Liz," she whispered. "It's just — I'm so . . ."

"Shh." Liz moved back enough to put two fingers against Nora's lips. "Shh. I know. It's all right, Nora. It really is."

Is it, she wondered later, alone in the parlor, staring out the window at the thick darkness. Did she really understand what we were talking about, what I was talking about, anyway?

Am I going to lose her?

Don't be an idiot, she admonished herself, turning briskly to the sofa and snapping a sheet over it. You can't lose what you don't have.

And you're being a selfish bitch to think the way you've been thinking when she's so upset and sad.

Saturday morning before Ralph was awake, they took their coffee outside and sat in the rapidly warming sunlight, sipping slowly, silently, until Ralph's voice boomed out from the house. It is going to be an impossible day, Liz thought, wishing it over, and Nora thought, This is the day of my

226

mother's funeral, thought it carefully, deliberately, as if testing her reaction.

But she couldn't measure that, couldn't imagine how she was going to react.

Louise Brice, in a neat dark gray suit with a silver and amethyst pin on the left lapel, settled next to her husband in a pew in the exact center of the church. "Look, Henry," she said, poking him, "there she is. That Hardy woman." She pointed to Liz, who was walking with Nora to the front pew in which Ralph had just been deposited by Sarah Cassidy and Patty Monahan, both rather weepy-looking; together, after settling Ralph, they moved to several pews back from the front. "Disgraceful," Louise murmured. "That Hardy woman sitting with family. And I certainly don't think a woman should wear pants to a funeral. And who's that, I wonder? I didn't know the Tillots had any relatives left. Oh, wait, maybe it's one of those cousins who moved away all those years ago. My goodness, look, Henry, there are at least five of them!"

Two dark-suited men, one with a great shock of blond hair and the other, older, with a neatly trimmed goatee, took their places in the pew behind Nora and Liz. With them were two women, presumably their wives, the older one large and matronly, wearing a dark green dress in which she looked uncomfortably hot. The other, arm-in-arm with the blond man, tossed her head as she approached the pew, sending her mane of no-color straight hair cascading over her back; she leaned over and squeezed Nora's shoulder and then Ralph's. Behind the foursome came an elderly man, very solemn and stout, in a dark blue three-piece suit. He leaned over the back of the front pew to say something to Ralph, who, as Louise later said, "seemed too lost in grief or thought to respond."

"How he can stand having that woman in the same pew

227

is beyond me," Louise whispered to Henry. "The gall of her even coming!"

"Louise, let me get this straight," Henry whispered back; he was already feeling hot and out of sorts and he wished, as he leaned toward his wife, that he hadn't let her talk him into wearing a vest. "What you've actually heard is that Ralph accused Miss Hardy of poisoning Corinne. Right?"

"Exactly." Louise snapped open her black leather handbag and removed a delicately scented handkerchief.

"Not," Henry continued, surreptitiously loosening his tie a little, "that she's actually been formally charged?"

"Well, no, not yet. But" — Louise mopped her damp forehead, releasing a faint trace of lilac cologne from her handkerchief — "I don't think they've finished the autopsy report on poor Corinne. I imagine they're waiting till after the funeral." Louise nodded to Helen Whipple and her husband, who had just arrived, and then craned her head around to smile at the Davises, coming in with Roy Stark and Georgia Foley. The Davises sat humbly toward the back, but Roy and Georgia marched confidently down the aisle and sat in the third pew from the front.

"Who on earth is that?" Louise whispered, watching Roy. "He seems to be with Georgia Foley. But why?"

Her husband looked amused. "Someone you don't know, dear? But how can that be?" Discretely, he opened his vest.

"I wonder what Georgia's doing here; I don't think she had anything to do with the Tillots. I hope she's not going to pester poor Nora about selling the place, although I daresay it would be a good idea. Look how fussily Georgia's dressed; who would wear a blouse with a fichu to a funeral?"

"Why, I don't know, dear," Henry said mildly, stifling a laugh; what in hell was a fichu? Sounded like a sneeze.

"Look how that man with Georgia is talking to the Hardy woman. I wonder if he's a friend of hers. She doesn't look very pleased to see him, I must say!"

Henry sighed and patted his wife's hand. "Perhaps he's

228

just a nice sympathetic fellow or some young relative of the Davises. He and Georgia came in with them, didn't they? The Hardys probably used to get their produce from the Davises, since the farm's so close to the lake. Don't speculate so, Louise, for heavens' sake!"

The church was, in the end, only about a quarter full. The group at the cemetery (for even though the report on the blood and tissue samples had yet to be released, the body itself had been released for burial) was even smaller: Nora and Liz and Ralph; Sarah and Patty, both of whom were still teary; the cousins and the elderly man, who was a brother of Corinne's; the Brices; the Cantors; Charles Hastings, who'd led the service, and his wife. The two Neds, who had come to the church out of mingled curiosity and politeness, lingered for a while on the church lawn, but did not go to the cemetery. The Whipples, the Lorens, Roy and Georgia, and a few others did, but they stayed in the background during the short burial service.

Once the casket had been put into the ground, and the closest relatives and friends had left, a little cluster of people remained around Helen Whipple.

"I feel so sorry," Helen said, tugging at the hem of her black suit jacket and smoothing it over her ample hips, "for poor Liz Hardy, dragged into this whole sad business."

"Well, I don't know about being dragged in," said Maryann Loren. "She certainly has gone on spending a lot of time at the farm. You'd think since she's a suspect, or was, that she'd want to steer clear."

"Honestly, Maryann," Helen snapped, "I really do think that was a ridiculous accusation. Probably something Ralph made up in his demented state."

"That's possible I suppose," Maryann admitted. "But one does still wonder."

"What's possible?" asked Roy, coming up to the group hand-in-hand with Georgia Foley.

"Oh," said Helen, while Louise Brice studied Roy with mingled hostility and curiosity, "we were just guessing" — she looked sternly at Maryann — "about poor Mr. Tillot's role in that silly accusation against Liz Hardy. Hello, Georgia!"

Georgia nodded, dropping Roy's hand.

Roy looked very serious. "Maybe it's not so silly," he said slowly. "She does seem a bit odd, don't you think? And I saw her at the Tillots' the very morning after Mrs. Tillot died. You'd think she'd have wanted to stay away, given what people were saying."

"Oh, come on!" Helen said angrily. "You can't be serious. Why, I've known that girl since she was a child, far better than you, if you don't mind my saying, and she's not a bit odd."

Roy bowed slightly. "You may be right," he said. "I don't know, of course. I like Liz Hardy, actually. I certainly hope you *are* right." He inclined his head politely, saying, "Ladies . . ." and he walked away smiling cryptically, his arm linked in Georgia's.

"Who is that unpleasant man?" Louise asked. "Some new flame of Georgia Foley's?"

"I hope not," Helen answered, looking after him with undisguised distaste. "He's been around for a few months, filled in part time at the high school after that math teacher left, and lives out at the old Kincaid place. He's too slick for me; I never did like him, even back when he first came into the post office. It's him I'd keep an eye on, not Liz Hardy. I certainly don't put any stock in what he said."

"Yes, but as I said before," Maryann reminded them pointedly, "if the Tillots do have money . . ."

"Oh, honestly, Maryann," Helen retorted, "just what are you suggesting?"

"Motive, of course," Louise Brice said, nodding at Maryann.

"It's a horrible thought, I know." Maryann appeared to shudder. "But Liz Hardy has been very friendly to poor Nora, who's bound to inherit."

Helen Whipple tossed her head. "I will not," she said, turning sharply toward the cemetery gate where her husband had been waiting patiently along with Louise's and Maryann's, "honor that idea with any kind of reply."

THIRTY-THREE

"All right?" Liz whispered to Nora later, arranging plates of sandwiches to take from the kitchen to the carefully cleaned and aired parlor and adjoining dining room. Ralph was enthroned in a large wing chair in the parlor amid the relatives who'd been at the graveside service.

"I think so," Nora said, her face flushed from bending over the stove, heating more water for coffee and tea.

"Shouldn't you go in and socialize? I've got the knack of how things work. I can take over."

"No, it's okay. I think I'd rather be in here."

"Nora, there you are!" came a loud male voice, and the blond cousin burst in, waving a wine glass. Ignoring Liz, he put an arm around Nora and led her to the table.

"Andrew!" Nora protested, squirming in his grip. "Please! I've got to get the coffee."

"People can live for a few more minutes without coffee," Andrew said as Liz poured hot water into the pot. "And see? They won't even have to, thanks to your friend Miss Hardy."

"Liz, please," said Liz, though she wasn't sure what to make of this rather blustery take-charge man out of Nora's past; she wasn't sure if he could be trusted. But trusted with what, she wondered, watching him covertly as she poured.

"Now Nora," Andrew said, "Gail and I insist that you and Ralph come and live with us. Sell this old dump — it really must be awful living here with no electricity or anything — and come share our space. We have got," he said, his face breaking into a jovial smile, "a house with five bedrooms, can you imagine? And almost as many bathrooms, and extra rooms like a family room and a couple of studies."

"Why?" Nora asked.

"Why?"

"Why such a big house?"

"Well, partly for the kids, who in any case are gone most of the time now, but also as an investment, except we've decided not to sell it for a while. If we hold onto it and wait till we're doddering, we'll get a better tax break. It's our first home, you see; we had an apartment till Kevin was born."

"Oh," said Nora. But Liz could tell she had no idea what he was talking about.

"Anyway," said Andrew, "we want you and Ralph to come and stay for as long as you like. Permanently would be fine."

Nora shook her head. "No, I — we don't want to move. And Father is . . ."

"But you must move, Nora dear," interrupted the woman with the long hair who had sat next to Andrew in church; she had just come in and was standing near the table. She must be Gail, Andrew's wife, Liz reasoned, when she glanced up from separating sandwiches into neat piles.

"You can't possibly stay here," Gail went on. "Why, it

would be downright criminal! How you've managed to take care of two old people in these terrible primitive conditions . . ."

"People lived this way not so long ago," Nora said sweetly and wearily, as Liz knew she would. "It's not hard when you're used to it."

"But," said Gail, "there's simply no need for you to be used to it any more, is there, Andy?"

"Absolutely none. So that's settled then. As soon as things die down here, we'll put this old place on the market and move you and Ralph out to . . ."

Nora stood up, shaking off Andrew's hand. For a moment she glanced wildly at Liz, and Liz stepped forward; Nora's eyes looked trapped. But then they blazed and she said calmly, "Thank you very much. I know you're being kind. But Father would never leave, and I don't want to either. This is my home. This is where I grew up and where my mother lived, and I won't leave it."

You go, girl, Liz said to herself, feeling an admiring smile creep over her features. But admiration gave way to alarm as she picked up the sandwich plates and after nodding supportively to Nora as she passed, she wondered, Does she truly mean she'll never leave?

"What do you really want to do?" Liz asked Nora much later when everyone had left and after Ralph, who had become maudlin and belligerent again, had been given his evening pill and was finally sleeping.

Nora let herself tiredly down into her chair at the kitchen table and wrapped her hands gratefully around the cup of tea Liz had brewed for her. "Do?"

"You know," Liz said, trying to sound casual, sitting down and sipping her own tea just as gratefully. "About the future?"

Nora closed her eyes. "Nothing," she said after a long

234

pause. "Right now I just want to sleep. I want to wake up and have Mama still be here and I want to give Father his bath and Mama hers and make them breakfast and put Mama back in bed and Father in his chair. And then I want to have a quiet cup of tea alone with Thomas. I want to weed the garden or bake bread or pick berries or make jam. And I want to work on my poetry and do some proofreading and make lunch. I want everything to be the same." She smiled wistfully at Liz.

Liz tried to ignore the tightness in her throat and in her stomach, and concentrated on her firm belief that aside from what she herself hoped for the future, it would be dangerous for Nora to remain with Ralph. "I guess all that could happen," she said slowly, "except for the parts about your mother, assuming your father can be controlled by the new pills. Is that what you really want?"

"Right now, yes, I think so." Nora regarded Liz for a moment and then reached for her hand. "Liz, dear Liz, have I hurt you? Should I be adding that I want to go to your cabin and work in your garden and sit at your table and look out at the lake and — and lie next to you for a little while?"

Liz forced a smile. "I suppose that is what I wanted you to say, yes. But I also . . ." Abruptly, decisively, she stood. "Oh, hell, Nora, I'm worried about you, about what will happen to you when I go back to New York if you're here alone with that crazy old man. I know he's your father and I know on some level you love him, but you heard Dr. Herschwell say he thinks he's seriously ill. I know they're going to do some sort of evaluation of him, but suppose some night before that the pills don't work or he refuses to take them and he — I don't know."

"Turns on me?" Nora asked evenly. "Accuses me of poisoning him? Tries to poison me?" She shrugged. "Any of those things could happen. But I'm stronger than he is, I think, and I do the cooking, and I . . ."

"That's just it!" Liz exploded. "You do everything! You have virtually no life except drudgery. " She stopped, seeing Nora's eyes flash, realizing she'd gone too far.

"You too?" Nora said accusingly. "You too? I thought you understood. I thought you knew." She turned away, her shoulders slumping.

Cautiously, Liz went to her, stood behind her without touching. "I know that you love the farm," she said, "and your garden, and your quiet life. And I'm very, very aware that I've disrupted it." She paused, then found herself almost pleading, and hoped she was pleading as much for Nora's sake as for her own. "But there's — oh, Nora, there's so much out there in the world outside the farm, outside Clarkston, so much that you're missing!"

"Did it ever occur to you," asked Nora without turning, "that right now I might not be interested in what's outside?" She turned. "Is a nun interested in what's outside?"

"No," Liz said, startled. "But you're not . . ."

"That's right, I'm not a nun. But you don't have to be a nun to like solitude, to need it, to crave it. "

"I know that, Nora, but . . ."

"It comforts me, sustains me," Nora whispered. "It always has. And now . . ."

"Then," Liz interrupted stiffly, "I guess you won't need me, Nora, will you?"

Silence.

"Will you?"

When there was still no answer, Liz gathered up the sweater she'd brought in case the evening was chilly, felt in her pants pocket for her keys, picked up her overnight bag, and went out the door.

"I'm sorry," Nora moaned, covering her face with her hands. "Oh, God, Liz, I'm sorry! It's all changed so fast, my life, my world, my — myself. I didn't mean . . ."

But Liz was already in her car.

THIRTY-FOUR

Fighting tears, Liz drove back to Piney Haven, one hand on the steering wheel, the other occasionally dabbing at her eyes. She tried not to think, and when that proved impossible, she tried to tell herself Nora was upset, that she'd feel differently tomorrow.

But I don't know that, she realized. And I really don't know Nora either.

I don't know her at all, maybe. Maybe I've been wrong about her, about how she feels.

Maybe I was wrong about Megan, too. And myself.

Maybe no one knows anyone.

She pulled the car into its parking place in front of the cabin and sat there motionless in the dark, thinking, I'll leave tomorrow. Or, damnit, as soon as the police are sure I didn't kill Corinne — for Detective Morris had suggested, looking embarrassed, that "it might be a good idea" for her to stay in Clarkston till then, even though there was no real evidence against her. I'll drive back to New York, stay with someone till the sublet's up. I'll forget Nora and this whole summer; I'll sell the cabin, if Jeff agrees. Maybe Nora was just an interlude, a summer romance.

An almost romance; it never really . . .

In the distance, the telephone cut into her thoughts.

Thinking it might be Nora, could be Nora, must be Nora, Liz clambered out of the car and ran into the cabin, snatching up the receiver and barking, "Hello?" breathlessly, desperately into it.

"Well, hi, sis! Did you ever think about getting a machine for the cabin? I've been trying to get you all day and half the night. You okay?"

"Jeff. I — it's a long story. What's up?"

"Up? Nothing. Just wanted to confirm next weekend. We'll be leaving early in the morning so we can do a little New England tour *before* we see you as well as afterward. I wanted to make sure it was still okay with you for us to come."

"Come?" Liz asked stupidly, momentarily bewildered. Then she remembered and, groaning inwardly, said, "Oh, right. Um, sure. Yeah, sure. It's fine." Of course it is, she told herself; Nora's not going to be in the picture, so why wouldn't it be? Except that means I can't go back to New York till later.

"Great." Jeff paused a moment, then asked again, "You okay?"

Liz felt her eyes fill with tears. "Yes," she said. "No."

"Want to talk?"

"No." She felt her voice falter and realized she was about

to sob. "No, Jeff, I — I've got to go. See you next weekend. Goodbye." Quickly, before he could reply, she hung up.

Almost immediately the phone rang again.

"Listen," Jeff said, "I don't believe you're okay and I'm worried. What's going on? Girl trouble?"

"Right," Liz said tiredly, her tears abruptly staunched.

"Anything I can do? Advice? Tirades about the fickleness of women? Poisoned chocolates? Anything?"

Liz winced at "poisoned chocolates," then had an absurd desire to laugh. "You're a sweetheart," she said. "But no. I'll be okay."

"Any gay bars in Clarkston?"

"I don't think so."

"You could always go into Providence. Find yourself a nice easy cutie, h'm?"

Liz laughed weakly. "Jeffie, how often do I have to tell you it doesn't work that way for dykes? At least not for this dyke. Not enough testosterone or something."

"That's probably just as well. Wouldn't work for this guy either. Sis, I'm sorry. I'm glad we'll be there in a few days to distract you. Wait'll you see Gus. He's talking a blue streak now, and he's all excited about seeing you."

"Oh, come on, he hardly knows me! He can't possibly remember me."

"But he does. We've been talking you up. He wants to swim and go out in a boat and have breakfast outside and listen to frogs, all the stuff we used to do, remember? I didn't tell him he'd have to pick blueberries, though."

Liz leaned her head against the wall. "Good," she said wearily. "But maybe he'd like picking them even though we didn't."

"Yeah, maybe. You're right. I bet he might want to." He paused. "Better?"

"Um-hm. Thanks."

"Anytime, babe, anytime. See you soon, okay?"

"Okay. You need me to pick you up at the airport?" She found that now she was reluctant to hang up, to face the dark cabin alone.

"Nope. We're renting a car."

"Oh, that's right. You're doing a New England tour first. That's why you're leaving tomorrow. Sorry. Momentary lapse."

"No problem. Hey, want to come along? If you're fancy free, why not, huh?"

Liz smiled bitterly. What would he think, she wondered, if she told him she didn't feel she should till the police cleared her of murder? She hesitated, longing to tell him, to tell him everything, in fact. But then he'd probably get on a plane tonight without Susan and Gus, ready to do battle.

And there still was Nora.

Maybe. Was there?

"No, Jeff, that's okay, Thanks, though. You guys should have your own vacation, *en famille.*"

"You're part of our *famille.*"

"I know, Jeffie, but just no, okay?"

"Okay, but think about it. You can always change your mind."

"Thanks."

"Well — g'night, sis. Have a drink and go to bed. The sun'll rise again tomorrow, you know?"

"Yeah, I know. Jeff, I . . ."

"You what?"

"I love you."

"And well you should. I love you, too, babe. 'Bye."

" 'Bye."

Thank God for him, she thought, hanging up and climbing the stairs to her room. At least he's always there.

Mechanically, Liz brushed her teeth, changed into the t-shirt she slept in, and crawled into bed. But she couldn't sleep, so she went out to the dock and sat on its edge, watching the stars.

And Nora, sleepless at the farm, sat out by the garden, Thomas on her lap, staring up at the sky till dawn.

THIRTY-FIVE

Stiffly, Nora stood, tipping Thomas, who mewed reproachfully, off her lap. She stretched and limped — her leg was cramped from sitting all night — into the house, where she put on her muslin apron and began heating water for the bath ritual. Her eyes felt gritty, her mouth dry and sour. Mechanically, she got out the bath things and, when the water was ready, carried them as usual into Ralph's room.

"Good morning, Father." She set down the basin and kissed his damp forehead; though she seldom did that, she felt this morning they both needed it. "Did you sleep?"

"No." His voice was edged with pain and she saw that his eyes were red. She put a hand on his pillow; it was wet. Had he been weeping, then, all night? Shouldn't the new pills have prevented that?

She knelt by his bedside, caressed his cheek. "I miss her, too," she whispered. "I loved her, too. Can't we mourn together?"

He pulled away from her. "You let that woman into our house," he bellowed. "A viper in our midst. You let her influence you, take you away from me, from your mother, from your duty. You let her disrupt our schedule, our home. You let her destroy your mother. You know she . . ."

"Father," Nora said sharply, standing, her throat aching with the tears she couldn't shed in front of him, "listen to me. Liz Hardy did not poison Mama. Nothing could be further from her mind or her heart. She liked Mama. She tried to understand you. And she helped me, helped me enormously. She's my friend, Father, or she was, before I foolishly turned her away. I wish . . ."

"Good! Good girl for turning her away. Not foolish at all," Ralph said. "She's evil, Nora, I could see that. She's too interested in you. Why? Wants to get her hands on this place, you wait and see. But she can't have it, because we won't let her. Will we?"

"Oh, Father! Liz has no interest in 'this place' as you call it. Why would she? Why would anyone? The house is run down, there's no electricity, no water . . .."

"The land, Nora, the land." Ralph pushed himself to a sitting position. "I can see now that I made a mistake. Thought keeping the house the old way would protect the land, too. But it won't. People want land now, not houses. I see that in those newspapers you get."

Nora stared at him, aghast. "You mean — you mean you wouldn't have electricity and water and — and everything because you thought that would protect the farm, keep it for youself? But you always said . . ."

His eyes gleamed. "Oh, it's true I don't hold with those

243

newfangled things. But your old father has more tricks than that up his sleeve. I knew no one would ever want to buy a house that's like this one; people want modern things. I knew you couldn't sell it."

Nora sat abruptly on the edge of his bed. "What?" she whispered. "You mean you kept the house like this to keep me from selling it?" she whispered. "Not because of its history the way Grandfather did? Not because of not wanting to pay more taxes? Just to keep me here?"

He seized her hand. "Oh, honey," he moaned. "I knew I'd need you, that Mama would need you. We were already middle-aged when you were born. I had to think of the future. I knew we couldn't face the end of life, growing old and sick, alone. And I was right, Nora, look what happened to Mama, to me!"

"You didn't let me have friends, you didn't let me go to the movies with my friends," Nora said, her voice flat and emotionless. "You didn't let me learn to drive. You've made me . . ." She got up, ignoring the bath-basin, ignoring his grasping hands, and ran out of his room ignoring his shouts, then his moans, ran through the kitchen, out of the house and blindly to the barn, where she flung herself into the Ford, thrust the key in the ignition, and spun the car around, scattering Thomas who'd been stalking a bird; she roared down the farm's dirt road.

She slowed when she got to the main road. I will not, she told herself, go to Liz; I will not do that. I will not go running to her as if she's some kind of saviour and I'm weak and helpless and God knows what.

But she drove to the lake anyway, to the plot of vacant land across from Liz's cabin, and she sat on a rock near the shore, looking toward where Piney Haven was hidden by trees and smiling in spite of herself as she remembered Liz teaching her to swim and herself teaching Liz about the plants in her garden.

* * * * *

When Nora got back to the house, she spotted the Hastingses' car and groaned.

"Mr. and Mrs. Hastings!" she said gaily, forcing a spring to her step when she went in the front door and strode into the kitchen. "What a nice surprise!"

Marie stood and took Nora's hands. "Oh, my dear," she said, "your father was so worried about you. If we hadn't stopped in . . ."

"That's water under the dam." Swiftly, Charles pulled out a chair and seated Nora. "We've got him settled now. I'll just go in and tell him you're all right." He patted her hand and left the room.

"Nora, dear," said Marie, bending closer, her eyes fixing firmly on Nora's, "your cousin, that nice Andrew Parker, came to see us last night and we had such a good talk with him. It's so wonderful that he and his wife have offered to take you and your father in. He told us all about their huge house, which will be empty soon since their children are almost grown and anyway are away at school or college most of the time, and he said there are hospitals nearby in case your father should get sick, even a mental hospital, and they'd just love . . ."

"No," Nora said automatically. But now it almost tempted her. If Father could go there, just Father . . .

"Nora, dear, listen to me. Your father's not getting any younger. His mind is clearly going, what with that ridiculous accusation. Miss Hardy may be interfering, but she certainly isn't a murderess. What will you do if he really has a psychotic episode, which Dr Cantor says is quite possible, and goes after you? Dr. Cantor says he's to have an evaluation to find the right medication and other treatment, too, perhaps, but what if none of that works? You can't risk being alone with him, Nora; you need protection and so does he. If the doctors think

245

he can remain out of a hospital, it would be better for both of you to be with other people, don't you see that? Naturally we'd be sorry to lose you, but . . ."

Nora tuned her out, watching the sun's patterns on the floor. She drank the tea Marie brewed and handed her, but as Marie droned on, she silently recited Emily Dickinson and Shakespeare and Yeats, and wondered if she were losing her mind as rapidly as her father seemed to be losing his. For he was, of course; Mrs. Hastings was right; Dr. Herschwell had as much as said so. And the evaluation — Nora had forgotten about that!

". . . So you see it will be easy to make the move and of course we'll help. Charles will take care of explaining to your father; he's already started. I'm sure Georgia Foley will be able to find a buyer for the farm. And Ralph . . ."

"No!" Nora almost shouted the word, surprising herself. Thoughts came in weary fragments: not Andrew, but Father? The farm — solitude. But — a prison, too. Thomas. Liz . . .

She shook herself, actually shook her shoulders, snapping herself back into reason, into politeness. "You're being very kind, Mrs. Hastings, everyone is, but I don't know yet what we're going to do. I don't know if we're going to do anything. I can't think yet. Please!"

Marie patted Nora's hand. "Oh, I know, dear, I know. It's all terribly hard, and I don't mean to rush you. It's just that your cousin has to go back soon, and, well, of course, I know it's hard to go into someone else's home when you've been running your own, but your cousin said they could even fix up part of their house as a little apartment, with a kitchen and everything, so you wouldn't have to share. Two women in a kitchen is, I agree, a blueprint for trouble."

Nora thought of Liz moving smoothly with her around her kitchen and smiled.

"Good," said Marie. "I'm glad you . . ."

"But I don't, Mrs. Hastings," Nora said quickly. "Please."

She looked at Charles as he came back into the room. "Please. I'm very tired. Thank you for caring so much, but . . ."

The telephone rang; its sound still startled Nora, but she was glad for the interruption. Charles gave a little wave and turned to go as Nora reached for it, but his wife hesitated.

It was Detective Morris. "I knew you'd want to know as soon as possible, Miss Tillot," he said, "though I also know how difficult all this is. Forgive me for sounding clinical. The tests are in on the blood and tissue samples taken from your mother's body; they're all negative. I was off duty when they came in. I'm sorry for the delay in getting back to you, especially since the results came in so quickly."

Nora put her hand to her head; Marie immediately went to her and took her arm. Annoyed, Nora turned away slightly, but Marie still held on and Charles pushed a chair over to her. "What does that mean?" Nora asked, refusing the chair.

"It means that there's no basis for the accusation that your mother was poisoned. She died solely of a brain hemorrhage, a stroke, as we suspected."

"So there's no — no question at all? My friend Liz Hardy is . . ."

The Hastingses looked at each other anxiously.

"Ms. Hardy is no longer under any suspicion. Actually, she never really was, but we had to make sure. Now may I speak to your father, please? He needs to be told the news."

"I'll tell him."

"I think," said Detective Morris gently, "it might be better if I did. Begging your pardon, but he might not believe you, since he seems to have a, shall we say, a suspicious turn of mind."

"You're right," Nora said. "I'll get him. It may take a few minutes."

"I'll wait."

"Thank you."

Nora laid the receiver on the counter and turned to the

247

Hastingses. "That was Detective Morris," she explained. "There was no trace of poison. I've got to get Father so he can tell him. Then I'd like to call my friend Liz and tell her. I'm sorry, but . . ."

"But we should leave." Charles took his wife's elbow. "We'll check in with you later. Are you sure you're all right for now?"

"Yes, I'm sure," Nora said, her heart leaping with the knowledge that she now had an excuse to call Liz. Would I have called her anyway, she wondered, hoping she would have, to apologize, but doubting it. "Thank you."

She stood silently in the kitchen while the Hastingses left; then she went into Ralph's room.

He was sitting by the window, looking morosely out. "Charles Hastings was here again," he said reproachfully. "And his wife. I don't want you to see them any more, Nora. We don't need them. They interfere."

"Father," Nora said, "Detective Morris is on the phone. He wants to talk to you."

Ralph turned his head; his eyes were still red and the skin around them was puffy. In spite of herself, Nora again felt sympathy — or maybe, she thought, it's only pity — for him.

Had he really loved Corinne? Or had he just loved what Corinne had done for him till she'd gotten sick, cleaned and cooked and washed and solaced and obeyed? Yes, thought Nora, that's it: obeyed. Made him king. King in his castle, and Mama and I — me, anyway — belonged in the servants' quarters, "best girls" only as long as we stayed in our place.

"I don't want to talk to him."

"You have to, Father. He has important news."

For a moment Ralph's eyes gleamed. "About that woman? Did he find the poison?"

"No," said Nora, relishing it in spite of trying not to. "No, he didn't. There was no trace of poison. But he wants you to hear it from him."

The gleam left Ralph's eyes, or changed. Yes, that's it,

248

Nora thought; it's changed. For the light in his eyes showed cleverness now, craftiness, a look that said "you and I know the truth, even if no one else does," and aloud he said, "She bribed him, then, I bet. They all do that, you know, Nora. Bribes. Tricks. But I won't be tricked. I know and" — he snatched Nora's hand, pulling her to him awkwardly, till she almost toppled into his lap — "you won't be tricked either."

Roughly, she wrenched herself away. "He wants to talk to you," she repeated. "You need to hear the truth from him." She pulled the walker toward him and put her arms around him to pull him up.

He pushed her away, hard. "No! I will not talk to liars. And if you insist on believing him, I will not talk to you either. Go away."

Unconsciously compressing her lips into a thin, tense line, Nora wheeled and silently left the room.

THIRTY-SIX

Her mouth still tense, Nora went back to the phone. "I'm sorry," she said to Detective Morris. "He won't talk to you. Maybe you could write him a letter. I told him, but he won't believe it."

There was sympathy in the detective's voice. "Very well. We could get him a copy of the medical examiner's report."

"Thank you," Nora said wearily. "And maybe you could get one to Miss Hardy as well? I think she'd like to know, officially, I mean."

"Yes, certainly." There was a pause. "Ms. Tillot? I'm very sorry for your loss. And for all this unnecessary trouble."

"Thank you. Thank you for calling."

"You're welcome. If there's anything . . ."

"Thank you." Nora paused for a second, then said, "Goodbye."

"Goodbye."

For a moment after she'd hung up, she stood there. Slowly she realized that her hand was sore from where Ralph had grabbed it and pulled, and that Thomas was mewing and rubbing against her legs. Nora bent to pat him, then picked him up and cradled him against her cheek. "What should we do, Tom?" she whispered. "I don't think we can go on like this. Can we?" She held the cat out at arm's length, looking into his green eyes. He blinked, but didn't struggle, swinging slightly as she held him under his front legs. "He's crazy, Thomas. Even without that evaluation, we know that, don't we? Liz knows it, too, and the Hastingses and everyone. He's really, really crazy. Maybe, after all, Andrew . . ."

Thomas curled his body into a C, pulling his back legs up, and Nora, seeing he was uncomfortable, put him gently down. But she couldn't ask Andrew, couldn't accept his offer. It wouldn't be fair to bring a crazy man into his household. Surely Andrew didn't understand how sick Ralph was; she'd have to write and tell him. "A nice letter," that's what Corinne would have called it. "Write Aunt Sally a nice letter, dear," Mama would say the day after Christmas, the day after a birthday, or when someone had done a kindness, like the time the teacher had sent work home when Nora had measles. "A nice letter. That does so much, always remember that, Nora."

"Mama," Nora said softly. "Mama."

A nice letter, she thought dully. I should write a nice letter to Liz, too, to thank her, to thank her for . . .

No!

Not a nice letter. This isn't a nice-letter matter. Not a matter for a letter. A letter for a matter. Oh, God, I *must* be going batty!

Thinking of Liz had made heat and color rise in her

cheeks, made her heart pound harder and her breath come faster, and filled her with energy, as if life, she thought, trying to put words to it, as if life is coming back to me.

Decisively, Nora picked up the phone again and dialed, not Liz — for she knew she had to see Liz, though she had no idea what she would say or do when she did, aside from telling her about the autopsy report — but Patty. And yes, Patty could come but not for another hour, so Nora, trying to expel all thought from her mind and trying to use the sudden strength and energy she felt, filled a bucket with warm soapy water and, on her hands and knees, scrubbed the clean kitchen floor.

But expelling thoughts didn't work; she kept replaying the scene in her father's room over and over, hearing him say, "She's evil, Nora — wants to get her hands on this place — I thought keeping the house the old way would protect the land, too — no one would ever want to buy it — your old father has more tricks — you couldn't sell it — I knew I'd need you." What did work, though, for only the second time in her life, was ignoring Ralph, who called from the bedroom, pleaded, moaned. "I'm busy, Father," Nora finally shouted. "You can wait."

"No, no! Nora, I need you," he cried, sobbing now. "I'm dizzy, I'm so dizzy, I feel sick."

She heard the bed squeak, the thump of the walker, and deliberately turned her back as he emerged from his room, his pajama top unbuttoned, his bathrobe loosely tied below his hairy belly, one slipper half off.

"Nora, I'm so sick. You'd better go for the doctor. I'm dizzy." He swiveled the walker awkwardly, positioning it in front of Nora, but then slipped and tumbled, a dead weight, against Nora, forcing them both to the wet floor.

For a moment, Nora couldn't move or speak. She could barely breathe; he had landed across her chest. Then pain seared through her shoulder and traveled down into her arm, and she realized her arm was pinned under her, backwards, stretching over her head; something had come apart inside.

The pain was unbearable and she felt herself fighting for breath.

"Father, please move," she gasped. "Please! Can you roll off me?"

Ralph moaned. "Help me," he said. "Help me."

With her good arm, Nora pushed him away as hard as she could.

"Don't, Nora," he sobbed. "Don't leave me. Don't ever leave your old father. You're a good girl, Nora; I . . ."

"Father, are you hurt?" she asked coldly, struggling to a sitting position and gasping again as pain shot through her arm, which now, as she sat, dangled by her side. It was not, she discovered, possible to move it without excruciating pain in her shoulder.

"Yes, I . . . My leg," he moaned.

Nora tried to bend forward to examine his leg but the pain made her cry out in agony. She reached her hand up and tenderly felt her shoulder. There seemed to be a lump where there shouldn't be. Holding her breath, she pushed against it and felt something snap, popping back into place. Instantly the pain eased, receding to a dull ache.

Ralph moaned again and Nora, on her knees now, leaned forward to look at his leg. There was a red mark on the shin, as if he'd hit the walker with his leg, but nothing else seemed wrong. "Can you move it?" she asked.

Ralph nodded, and demonstrated.

She touched the red mark.

"Ouch!"

"I think you bumped it," she said, standing up cautiously, cradling her arm. "On the walker. But I think it's all right."

"Help me up." Ralph writhed on the wet floor. Like a fish, Nora thought, like a huge fish that's been caught.

"I don't think I can, Father," she said. "I've hurt my arm. My shoulder."

"Use the other one," he growled.

"I'm not strong enough to get you up with one arm. I'm

not sure I'd be strong enough with two. Patty should be here very soon. She'll help me."

"What the hell am I supposed to do till then?" he snarled. "Just lie here?"

"Yes," Nora said, trying not to smile. "Just lie there. I'm sorry, but there's nothing else I can do."

"Thankless child," Ralph muttered.

"Thankless parent," Nora retorted. But she sat down on the floor next to him anyway, and got him to sing "Down by the Old Mill Stream" and "Alice Blue Gown" — though that one made them both cry — till Patty arrived.

THIRTY-SEVEN

It was hard with only one smoothly working arm, but somehow Nora managed, after she and Patty had settled Ralph in bed, to back the Ford out of the barn and drive to Liz's cabin. "Shouldn't you get an X-ray?" Patty had asked anxiously. "My boyfriend hurt his arm once and didn't get one and it turned out it was, like, cracked and it still really bothers him sometimes." Nora had replied, "Maybe. But there's something I've got to do first," and she explained to Patty about the medical examiner's report.

But when she got to Liz's, she stopped the car a few yards from the cabin and sat there indecisively. Afraid, that's what it is, she said to herself: I'm afraid to face her.

She was about to try to turn the car around again and leave — perhaps, she thought, if I drive around a little — when Liz emerged from the cabin in her bathing suit, a towel around her neck.

For a moment Liz stood staring at the car. Then, with a look halfway between joy and anger, she strode to it, around to the driver's side. Nora rolled down the window, reaching across her body to do it, for it was her left shoulder that was hurt; throbbing now, again, too.

"What's with your arm?" was the first thing Liz said, which later struck them both as funny, considering.

"Father fell on me. I was washing the floor and he slipped. That's not important. Detective Morris called. The tissue samples and stuff were negative. You're cleared."

Liz smiled tentatively. "Thank you. Thank you for telling me."

Nora's eyes filled with tears. "Liz, I don't know what to do. I'm sorry, I'm sorry for the things I said."

Liz reached into the car and touched Nora's good shoulder awkwardly. "What things? About the farm? About solitude? But that's how you feel, you can't help that."

"Yes, I can," Nora sobbed. "I didn't mean I couldn't ever be with you. I just needed time, time alone. It's all happened so fast. I wanted it not to have changed so quickly: Mama, the farm, father. And you, you're — oh, I don't know." Nora sniffed loudly. "I'm not making any sense, am I?"

"No." Liz opened the car door. "Will you at least get out and come inside? Please?"

Nora climbed out. "You were going to have a swim."

"Yes, I was. But I can have a swim any time." Liz steadied her as she swayed a little; Nora gasped sharply in pain. Liz put a hand on each of Nora's arms, holding her still. "Wait," she said. "Wait. You're really hurt, aren't you?"

Nora nodded. "I think I might be, yes. Except I'm so glad to see you I almost don't care."

"That's flattering, but I care. First things first. Let's get you to a doctor."

Two hours later, Nora, with her arm in a sling (a minor dislocation, the doctor said, perfectly in place again but sprained), was sitting on the sofa in Liz's living room sipping red wine. Liz was sitting beside her, her own wine untouched on the table in front of them. Nora had just called Patty and asked her to give Ralph a meal and stay till she and Liz both got to the farm.

"The options," Liz was saying. "Let's list them."

Nora felt a wave of giddiness; the pain and the shock, she supposed, not to mention the wine on top of the aspirin she'd taken. "Write them down, you mean, like a pro and con thing?"

"Well, maybe not quite like that. But it might help."

"It might," Nora said more seriously. "Okay. Father and I could go live with Andrew. But I don't want to live with Andrew. Father could go live with Andrew and I could stay in the house. But Andrew doesn't know how crazy Father probably is."

"True. But maybe he does or maybe when he does he'll still be willing, if the doctors can find the right medication. So another alternative could be that your father could go live with Andrew and you could sell the house and come back to New York with me. But you don't want to sell the house, and New York's no place for anyone who likes solitude, quiet solitude, anyway. And gardening. And who has an outdoor cat. Maybe actually living with me wouldn't be good for you either. So in that case maybe your father could go live with Andrew and you could stay in the house and I could get a job here and stay in the cabin."

Nora looked at Liz in astonishment. "In the *winter*?"

257

"I could have the cabin insulated. There might be time, just, before it gets cold."

"You'd do that?" Nora asked. "You'd leave your job and New York and everything to move here?"

Liz nodded. "I think so," she said slowly. "I'd been thinking about it, anyway, but then it looked as if we — you know."

Nora took Liz's hand. "Or," she said softly, "you could come and live in the farmhouse with me. We could fix it up. Plumbing, electricity. What would be the good of you living here and me living there if the point is for us to be together?"

"What indeed?" Liz said. "But you want to be alone."

Impatiently, Nora shook her head. "Not every minute. You could come and live in the house even if Father didn't go to Andrew's, maybe."

"I don't think so. I think that would really make him crazy. Nora" — she leaned forward — "Nora, do you think maybe he should be in a nursing home or a mental hospital instead of living with you or with Andrew? I know most places like that are awful, but they aren't all awful, and I don't know about the money end of it, but — Nora, I don't think it's safe for you to be around him, for anyone to be, and it's probably not safe for him either. We don't know what that evaluation will find, but . . ."

"I know," Nora said softly. "I know it's not safe. Not any more. I think there might be enough money, especially if we sold the farm. But I don't know what a nursing home or a mental hospital would cost either. Or what insurance would cover. Medicare. He doesn't have anything else. And he'd hate it so, being in an institution!"

"Do you think he's really happy where he is now?"

"No, but . . ."

"If he were in a nursing home or a mental hospital, a good one, he could get constant professional attention for his problems."

"He hates doctors. He doesn't even really trust Dr. Cantor, and he's known him forever." Nora shook her head, dropped

258

Liz's hand, and rubbed her eyes. "I know you're right. I know I'm being foolish."

Liz took a sip of wine. "No," she said, "not foolish. Just stressed. You don't have to decide now. Let's see what the evaluation says; that's the first step, I think. But while we're waiting for that, Nora — Nora, forgive me, I know people have said it and said it, and I know you hate hearing it, but please consider yourself, too. You can't go on throwing your life away! Whether or not I'm in your life, you can't do that. Just keep in mind that as time goes on, if he stays with you, you're going to have to be more and more at his beck and call. All that free time you love so much, it'll diminish. He's going to be more demanding now that your mother's gone."

"Yes." Nora's eyes filled with tears. "He is. But . . ."

"But you love him." Liz hesitated a moment, then moved closer to Nora, holding her gently. "I know."

"Thank you for understanding that." She paused, then said, "You must think I'm weird. Weak and indecisive and — and . . ."

"No," Liz interrupted, "I think you're wonderful. And" — the words slipped out before Liz could weigh the wisdom of saying them at this moment — "and I love you very much."

But Nora surprised her. "I love you, too," she said, twisting around and looking into Liz's face, her own expression mirroring Liz's surprise. "Oh, my God!" she exclaimed. "Liz — oh, Liz, I never thought I'd say that to anyone!"

"And I never thought I'd say it to anyone again, or mean it so much. I never even knew it could mean so much. But there we are."

"Yes." Nora closed her eyes and put her head on Liz's shoulder. "There we are."

For a moment they sat there silently. Liz could feel Nora's heart beating rapidly — or is it mine, she wondered.

"I want to kiss you," Nora whispered. "Really kiss you. I want you to really kiss me." She leaned back, tipping her face up to Liz, her eyes soft and shy and loving in the dim light.

"I want to be as close to you as one person can be to another. Show me, Liz. Please. Show me how."

Very gently Liz kissed her, holding her carefully, conscious of her hurt shoulder, then less conscious of it when she felt Nora's soft lips yielding, opening, and as Nora, her hand on Liz's back, pulled Liz closer.

"Shouldn't we lie down?" Nora whispered a few moments later, moving away a little and smiling up at Liz.

"Probably," Liz managed to answer, smiling back. She stood up, taking Nora's hand. "If you're still sure . . ."

"Oh, yes," Nora said, also standing. "I don't think I've ever been so sure of anything in my whole life."

Hand in hand, and more than a little dazed, they walked to the stairs.

THIRTY-EIGHT

"We'll just get him settled, Mrs. . . . ?"

"Miss," Nora nervously corrected the tall psychiatric nurse. "Nora Tillot. I'm not married."

It was a week later, the first day of Ralph's evaluation, and Nora, still dazed and reeling, was standing uncertainly with an equally dazed and reeling Liz in a dim, mustard-colored hospital corridor that stretched down to the room where hired ambulance men had just deposited her father. The sound of thin, wavery out-of-tune singing came from a much larger room near the nurses' station. She and Liz moved closer together as if for mutual protection in this alien place.

The nurse smiled professionally. "Miss Tillot. We'll just get him settled and then you can see him. But only briefly. We find it's best with evaluations for the patient not to have visitors for a while."

Nora glanced at Liz, who was looking down the hall to Ralph's room. Someone — a white-coated man with a clipboard — had just come out. He closed Ralph's door and strode briskly along the hall, passing them with a brief nod. Automatically, Nora nodded back. But she hated it already, the place, the people, the atmosphere.

"Oh?" Liz was saying pleasantly to the nurse. "Why is that? I should think visitors would be helpful."

"Many reasons." The nurse extended her arm toward their backs as if she were going to herd them to the opposite end of the hall like schoolchildren, which indeed she did, except without touching them. "The reasons vary from patient to patient. But in general we find we get a more complete picture that way."

"Some of the — his problems probably have to do with me," Nora said.

"Yes, that's likely in any family. And if so, you'll tell us about them, and so will he, in good time." The nurse led them past the room with the singing. Sunshine, Nora saw, peeking in, was coming through a wall of smudged windows; people, some of them pulling against or plucking at restraints of various kinds, were sitting around the room in wheelchairs, vinyl armchairs, metal folding chairs. A few of the more elderly ones were dribbling onto pastel-colored terrycloth bibs as they sang; others, not singing, both young and old, were staring vacantly into space. One agitated gray-haired woman was beating her hand, not in time to the music, against a highchair-like tray; another moaned "Nurse, nurse! I have to go!"

As the nurse shepherding them tried to hurry Nora and Liz past the open door, the gray-haired woman suddenly screeched, "I'll pee in my pants then, you goddamn bitch!"

Nora held back, staring angrily at a young nurse who sat serenely in a corner, as if no one were shouting or seeming

262

distressed. Another young woman, in everyday clothes, was thumping out the old song "Daisy, Daisy" at a scarred piano. "Come along, everyone, sing," she shouted above the general din, her own and everyone else's.

"Shouldn't someone help her?" Nora couldn't keep from asking their escort, who had stopped, too, as had Liz. Nora nodded toward the woman who had to go to the bathroom, and who was now crying.

"Help who? Oh, Mabel? No, it's part of her therapy."

"Part of her therapy not to be allowed to go to the bathroom?" Nora asked incredulously.

Liz put her hand on Nora's arm. "Easy," she said, so softly it was like a sigh.

"Miss Tillot," the nurse said, facing them both, "this is a psychiatric evaluation wing. Some patients need to learn that they can't have everything they demand. Some patients need to learn that we, not they, are in control before they'll let us help them. I know some of our practices may seem cruel at first. But we do know best. Now" — she bustled them farther along the hall and knocked on a closed door whose nameplate read "Ruth Farnum, Social Services" — "why don't you and your friend have a chat with Mrs. Farnum, and we'll call you when your father is ready for visitors?" She knocked again.

"Come!" someone called cheerfully from inside the office.

The nurse opened the door. "Ruth," she said, "this is Miss Tillot, Ralph Tillot's daughter, and her friend. Mr. Tillot's the new admission in 107."

A small, neatly suited and coiffed woman came toward them, edging around a desk awash with manilla folders and a pile of loose papers held down by a large orange. "How do you do?" she said, holding out her hand — weathered, leathery skin, Liz noticed, liking her. "I'm Ruth Farnum, the social worker assigned to Mr. Tillot's case. Come in, sit down. Thank you, Doreen," she said as the nurse left; then she indicated two chairs in front of her desk, and closed the door. "Now," she said, sitting back down, "which of you is which?"

"I hate this!" Nora whispered to Liz later when they were on their way to Ralph's room after Mrs. Farnum had commiserated with Nora about her hurt shoulder and explained, pleasantly enough, but as if it was the most normal thing in the world, that Ralph would be given various psychological and medical tests over the next several weeks, would be seen many times by his psychiatrist, and would be closely observed by psychiatric nurses, "activities leaders," and other personnel. "We'll be watching him all the time, actually," Mrs. Farnum had said, "and after today, we must ask you not to visit him for a week. You may telephone and talk to his nurse, and you may send him brief messages through her. And of course you may call me at any time, and of course the psychiatrist will share some of his findings with you, but you must remember, and I know this is hard, that he is your *father's* psychiatrist, and much of what passes between them must remain confidential." She'd stood up then, obviously dismissing them. "I know this is very difficult," she'd said with, Nora was sure, genuine kindness. But then why do I hate her, she'd wondered. "And I want you to know I'm here for you. Any questions, any complaints, any concerns, please feel absolutely free to bring to me. Ah, what timing!" she had exclaimed when the nurse named Doreen had knocked and then opened the door. "Is Mr. Tillot ready for his family?"

"Ready," Doreen had said, "whenever you are. Turn right," she'd added unnecessarily as Nora and Liz had stepped out into the hall. "Room 107," she'd reminded them, and disappeared.

"I know you hate it," Liz whispered now that they were outside Ralph's room. "I hate it, too. But it's got to be, Nora, and it's best for him. You know that. Just keep telling yourself that."

"I feel like a monster." Nora's face crumpled, and for a moment she leaned her head on Liz's shoulder.

"Courage," Liz whispered into Nora's hair. "Courage." She gave her a little push toward the door. "I'll wait out here."

"No! No, Liz, please come in."

"Not a good idea," Liz said lightly. "I'm a murderer, remember? I'll just explore a bit, shall I? See what's going on in the big room, the day room, I think they called it. Reminds me of *One Flew Over the Cuckoo's Nest.*"

Nora managed to laugh a little. "Oh, God, you're right. It all does, doesn't it?"

"Atta girl." Liz patted her shoulder. "Yes, it all does. Go. Then let's go out to lunch or something. Someplace wonderful, yes?"

Nora quickly established that the hall was empty; she stretched up and kissed Liz's cheek. "Yes." Then she took a deep breath and went into the room.

The blinds were drawn and there was no light on. The room was bare except for the hospital bed in which Ralph lay, a small fake mahogany nightstand, a more or less matching fake mahogany dresser, and a large vinyl armchair. Ralph's small suitcase was on the wide windowsill. Flowers, Nora thought, approaching the bed; surely they'll let me send him flowers!

"Father?" she said. "Hi, it's me."

Ralph stared blankly at her, then turned away.

"Father?" She went closer, took his hand — but it was limp in hers.

"It's Nora," she said, loudly, as if he were deaf. Wrong, she thought, forcing her voice back to a normal conversational level. "I've been talking to Mrs. Farnum, the social worker. She's very nice. She said you'll be seeing a doctor and having some tests. I think they'll keep you pretty busy."

Ralph ignored her.

"I heard singing coming from that big room they have, the day room, they call it. It's bright and sunny."

Ralph lay motionless, his hand still inert in hers, his eyes fixed on the wall opposite where Nora was standing.

Nora blinked back tears. "I'll just open the blinds, shall I? It's a lovely day."

"No."

His sudden response startled her. But at least it was a response. "What? Why not? It's so dark in here, depressing."

"Get out."

"Father!"

"You and that woman, Dr. Cantor, that other doctor, you're all against me. I'm going to kill myself. I am. You'll be sorry. You'll have done it. I'm not crazy. You are. You're all crazy."

"Father, listen, listen, please." Nora lifted his hand, moving it up and down as if using it to punctuate her words. "You've had a terrible shock. Mama's death, that's been awful for you. No wonder you're depressed, sad, mixed up. The doctors here are going to try to help you. They'll find some pills that'll make you feel better. It's not a pretty place, here, I know, and I know you'd rather be at home, but I don't know how to help you any more, Father. I'm sorry, but I don't."

Ralph turned to her brusquely, his eyes both wild and cold. "Get me out of here!" he thundered. "That's how you can help me, goddamnit! Get me out of here. I'll die here, I'll kill myself here."

"You can't, Father. Stop saying that." Nora wiped her eyes. Oh, God, she thought, that's probably the wrong thing to say; now he'll look for something. Surreptitiously, she opened the nightstand drawer and removed a pencil, dropping it into her purse.

"What are you doing? What's in there? Let me see!"

"Some paper," Nora said, "a plastic glass, a toothbrush and hairbrush. Hospital issue, I guess; your own ones are in your suitcase. Why don't I unpack it?" she said brightly, closing the drawer and opening the suitcase. "I'll let you know which drawers I put things in so you can find them. "

"Give me my belt," he said.

She picked up his trousers from where they were draped over the back of the chair.

No belt.

"It's not here," she said, puzzled. Then it hit her why it was gone. So were his shoelaces. She opened his dressing kit. So was his razor.

"Where the hell is my belt? Let me see! Let me see my own things!" Ralph sat up, dangling his feet over the side of the bed.

Alarmed, she went to him; where was the walker? Had they taken that away, too?

"Wait, Father, I should get someone. I don't think I can help you without the walker."

"Well, get the goddamn walker then!"

"It doesn't seem to be here. I'll just go ask. You stay put."

Nora fled into the hall, but no one was in sight except for a small wizened woman in a pink bathrobe, creeping along the wall. She grabbed Nora's arm. "Sally," she said breathlessly, fixing Nora with watery blue eyes. "Sally Ann! Now where is Mother? I can't find her anywhere!"

"I don't know," Nora said, feeling as if she would scream if she had to stay another minute. Where was Liz? Where were the nurses? Where was Mrs. Farnum?

Ralph lurched into the doorway and Nora ran to him, holding him back. The old woman tottered up to them, grinning toothlessly, and tried to put her arms around Ralph. "Timothy," she said. "Where is Mother? I want Mother!"

"Nurse!" Nora shouted, feeling embarrassed and foolish to be yelling like that, as if she were crazy, too. But what else could she do? She supposed her father had a call button, but there was no way she could let go of him to get it. "Help! Someone, please help!"

Liz came running down the hall, followed a moment later

by two male nurses. One of them grabbed the woman (the Pink Lady, Nora called her later, describing the first part of the scene to Liz), and the other grabbed Ralph. "Hey, now, fellah," that one said, not unkindly, "Don't want to go AWOL, do we? Best you get back to your quarters, sir. That's it," he said, supporting a suddenly docile Ralph and steering him back into the room. "That's the stuff. Best you come back another day, ma'am," he said politely over his shoulder to Nora. "Or ask the nurse. New admission, isn't he?"

"Yes," Nora said.

"Well, then it'll be a few days. They'll let you know. This your daughter, sir?" he asked Ralph. "Mighty fine-looking woman."

"No," Ralph said, glowering. "I don't have a daughter. That's two murderers there." He raised his voice, making the words echo down the hall. "Two murderers!"

THIRTY-NINE

Liz pointed to a table at the back of the small restaurant; they'd driven into Providence to a quiet place she'd remembered from the last couple of summers at the cabin. The waiter nodded and led them to it, handing them menus and leaving quickly.

But Liz called him back and ordered a half bottle of white wine.

Nora had cried most of the way into town and now she looked rigid, closed.

"Can you talk about it?" Liz asked gently after they'd settled.

"No daughter," Nora whispered. "Murderers."

"He's sick, Nora. Mentally ill. It's all surfaced because of your mother's death. He doesn't really mean he has no daughter, I'm sure. He's just mad at you now, because of the hospital."

"He does mean it," Nora said. "He hates me."

"And you?" Liz asked. "You don't hate him?"

The waiter arrived with the wine, holding the bottle out to Liz. She nodded, and watched Nora, not the waiter, while he poured.

"Yes," Nora said when he'd left. "Yes, sort of. I do sort of hate him. So we're even, is that it? A mutual hatred society?"

"That's not exactly what I meant," Liz said carefully. "But it'll do. People say that hate," she said, after taking a sip of wine, "is very close to love. I don't think you can hate someone you don't love."

"Oh, sure you can," Nora said. "What about, I don't know, Hitler, mass murderers, people who abuse animals or children?"

"I don't think it's the same. It's hate, I guess, but it's abstract hate, impersonal, not as deep or as painful as when it's someone you love or once loved. Someone who's betrayed you."

"As I've betrayed my father."

"Nora, you really haven't betrayed him! You're helping him. He thinks you've betrayed him, but you're doing the only possible thing anyone can do for him."

Nora sighed and took a long swallow. "I know. You're right. Of course you're right. But it's awful anyway. And it feels like betrayal."

"That," Liz said, opening a menu and handing it to Nora, "is exactly how he wants it to feel."

"Just the ladies I want to see," Roy said outside the post office when Nora and Liz pulled up after their very long and, it turned out, very liquid, lunch. "I can't believe my luck." He made great show of opening the passenger door; Liz, amused, noticed the skillful way Nora avoided the hand he offered to help her out.

"This is no place," he said, when Liz had come around from the driver's side, "to talk business, but Georgia and I — you know Georgia, Liz; she was handling your property, and Nora, you must know her, everyone in town seems to. Georgia and I would love it if you'd join us for dinner sometime soon."

"That's nice of you, Roy," Liz said evenly, "but . . ."

"I'd love to," Nora said.

Liz stared at her, mystified.

"Good, wonderful!" Roy beamed at her. "Liz?"

"I — well, yes, on second thought, sure," she sputtered.

"Great! How about tomorrow night?"

"Fine," Nora said defiantly. "Is that okay with you, Liz?"

Numbly, Liz nodded. "What on earth," she said when Roy, giving them a thumbs-up sign, had climbed into his car and driven off, "was all that about? I thought you hated his guts, just like I do."

"I do hate his guts," Nora said. "But, Liz" — Nora looked straight at her, her eyes swimming with tears — "if Father has to stay in some kind of — of psychiatric nursing home or something, and I think I have to face that he will, I'm going to have to pay for it. And I don't know how I'm going to do that unless I sell the farm. I called around a little and asked a couple of nursing homes how much they cost. It's more than I thought. There's only enough money for around a year, probably, after Medicare runs out; they only pay for a while, Dr. Herschwell said. So if Roy wants to buy the place, and I can't think of any other reason he'd ask us to dinner with Georgia, that could be the solution for him and — and my" — her eyes softened and she squeezed Liz's hand — "my ticket to you. Permanently."

Liz squeezed her hand back. "Are you sure?" she asked when she could trust herself to speak. "You love that farm, Nora, the outdoors, the quiet."

"I don't think," Nora said softly, "that I want to live on the farm any more. Too many bad things have happened there. Besides, I looked at it this morning with fresh eyes, sort of. I pretended I was you, seeing it for the first time. What did you see, then?"

"I saw an old, falling-down house," Liz said after casting her mind back to her first real visit. "I saw shabby rooms, and old, worn-out furniture. I saw a kitchen that created work instead of saving it. I also," she added, her voice dropping, "saw the most extraordinary human being it has ever been my privilege to meet. And if we don't get out of here soon, I'm going to kiss that human being in the middle of the post office parking lot."

"Let's hurry up and get our mail, then," Nora said, light coming back into her eyes. "And then let's — I don't know. What shall we do?"

"How about a swim? Unless we're too drunk. Or your arm . . ."

"Drunk? I'm not drunk. And my arm's better. Water's good for injuries. I can swim one-armed anyway. And do, um, other things. Are you drunk?"

"No. Not on wine anyway," Liz said. "Not on wine. Come on, let's get the mail."

Liz, waiting for Nora, rubbed her fingers over the dock's rough surface — the dock, near which she'd learned to swim, to which she'd tied her first boat, from which she'd caught her first fish. Could I do it, too, she wondered. Could I do what Nora's doing, sell the cabin, sell the land, if that's what Roy wants?

It must be, she mused, as Nora came toward her in the borrowed bathing suit Liz had come to think of as Nora's own. It must be what he wants. Why else would he invite both of us, and why with Georgia? After all, she remembered, watching Nora walk, the graceful way she carried her head, swung her good arm, and kept her hurt one close to her body, he *was* that interested buyer Georgia mentioned when I first met her.

"Last one in," Nora shouted, breaking into a run, "is a rotten egg!" She ran past Liz to the end of the dock and jumped in, splashing Liz, who jumped in after her, swam to her quickly, dunked her, then hugged her.

Nora clung to her, her body molded to Liz's as much as possible given her sprain, her hair streaming water onto Liz's shoulders.

"You seem better," Liz said. "Do you feel better?"

Nora nodded and stretched out her good arm, holding Liz by the shoulder. "I do. I feel — it's strange, but I feel lighter, somehow. As if I've — oh, it's an awful cliché, but I really do feel as if I've put down a burden. Or as if I'm in the process of putting one down, anyway."

"That," said Liz, kissing the end of her nose, "my brave one, is because you are in that very process."

"And you?" Nora asked, her head on one side in the pose Liz loved. "How do you feel?"

Liz hesitated. "I'm not sure," she said. "Happy for you. Proud of you. Very much in love with you. Grateful. But a little tentative, I guess, otherwise." She ducked out from under Nora's arm and flipped onto her back, floating.

Nora stood beside her, holding Liz lightly in place. "About?"

"About this place. About what I'll do with it. About . . ."

"About me? About how you feel about me?"

Liz folded into a sitting position, then touched bottom with her toes and stood. "No, Nora. Not about you. I know exactly how I feel about you."

"And I know exactly how I feel about you." Nora moved closer to Liz and wrapped her arm around her, twining one leg around Liz's, nuzzling her neck. "Can one make love in the water?" she whispered. "One-armed?"

"Yes," Liz whispered back, trying to hide her surprise,

"but it's better at night when there aren't any motorboats or fisherman around to interrupt." She felt for Nora's hand and grasped it, then kissed her. "Let's go inside. If you really feel all right now?"

Nora kissed her back, softly, then long and deep.

"Yes," she murmured. "Yes, I do. Let's."

IV

FORTY

Now it's sleeting, Nora said to herself sleepily, spooning closer to Liz and displacing Thomas, who mewed and re-curled himself against her legs.

Liz grunted and pushed against Nora, her rear tight against Nora's belly; Nora smiled, waking more fully, and draped her arm across Liz's chest, right hand cupping Liz's left breast. But then Brinna whined softly and thumped her tail. Nora, sighing, turned over and sat on the edge of the bed, thrusting her already sock-clad feet into slippers, and padded down to the kitchen of the old apartment attached to the Davises' farmhouse, where she and Liz had been living for four months, since October; she let Brinna out onto the frost-whitened grass. The sky was gray and lightening; there was an orange-red streak just visible at the edge of the woods, over the vegetable stand's roof.

A light went on in the main house, where Clara still lived with Harry who, in the months that had passed, had become a docile, nearly mindless shell.

Nora went back inside.

"Farmer's hours again?" Liz came into the kitchen and hugged Nora from behind.

Nora turned, kissing her and nuzzling her neck. "Still. Besides, there's a lot to do today."

Liz groaned and opened the fridge, removing a half-full can of coffee; Nora inserted a filter into the plastic basket; Liz spooned coffee into it; Nora pushed the basket onto its track, switching the machine on as if she'd been using appliances all her life and sat down at the small oilcloth-covered kitchen table. Liz let Brinna in when she whined and poured the coffee when it was done; by then, Nora was buttering toast.

"Clara's up," Nora observed, "at least I saw her light go on when I let the dog out."

"I wish she'd let herself sleep late. Is Sarah Cassidy coming today?"

Nora nodded. "It's Harry's bath day."

"I'm thankful every bath day that it's not you doing it any more."

"Harry's easy, compared to Father. And only twice a week is nothing. But that reminds me, I've got to take more of that lotion to the nursing home for Father. His skin's breaking down again, and the stuff they use isn't very good."

"Can't anything be done about that? I mean beyond the lotion?"

Nora shrugged. "They try. They turn him and try to get him up, and they bathe him. Old people's skin breaks down. I don't think there's any more they can do since he refuses to get out of bed." There was a defensive edge to her voice.

Liz reached across the table and took her hand. "Hey," she said, "no guilt, remember? You had to do it."

"I know."

It was true. Ralph had grown increasingly paranoid and belligerent during his evaluation, had attacked a nurse, grabbing her arm and twisting it, then done the same to the activities director, and had been generally disruptive. By October, a while after the psychiatrists had finally settled on the right combination and dose of drugs, it was clear that Ralph couldn't go home, and they'd moved him to Hillside Manor, a nursing home with a specialized psychiatric wing. But the memory was still raw in Nora's mind. Ralph had moaned and cried and pleaded at first when Dr. Cantor, Dr. Herschwell, and Charles Hastings had explained to him that Nora couldn't look after him at home any more and that Hillside Manor was really a fine place. "Award-winning," Charles Hastings had said, and Louise Brice had explained to Nora that her own mother had lived there for five years before she'd died. "Of course Mother wasn't in the psychiatric section," Louise made a point of saying, "but she came to like being at Hillside more than she liked visiting me and Henry." Despite the fact that Ralph had finally agreed to go to Hillside on the grounds that Nora was "refusing" to care for him, he had cried and clung to Nora when the ambulance people wheeled him into his new private room, which Nora and Liz had filled with flowers and pictures. They'd also hung his clothes in the closet and tuned his new TV set to a football game.

It was the football game, oddly enough, that had calmed him down. The TV had been Liz's idea and a stroke of genius; it had fascinated him and he had stopped his complaints about it as soon as they'd turned it on.

Nora stood now, shaking off the memory. "I'd better get dressed. I've got to finish that galley proof before we go to that party of Roy's."

"You okay?"

Am I, she wondered. The guilt and the sadness still came in waves. But, increasingly, so did the joy. *"O Joy, take care!"* What was that from?

279

Nora bent and kissed Liz. "Yes," she said. "Thanks. Are you?"

Liz nodded and kissed her back, then, when Nora had left, poured herself more coffee. It would be a busy day, first helping Clara clean, for that was part of the agreement; Liz and Nora were exchanging household help and companionship for living temporarily in the Davises' apartment. Then they had to visit Ralph, and after that, see the lawyer about one or two final papers for both the house and the cabin, and afterward, if there was still time before the party, Liz knew she should correct a few papers. She'd gotten a teaching job at a private school in the next town, after an awkward session with the headmaster and the trustees during which she'd explained about Ralph's accusation, news of which had spread more widely than she'd thought possible. But in the end they'd been very understanding, once they'd talked with Ralph's doctors and the police. They'd been almost as understanding when Liz told them she was gay, especially once they'd received the recommendation she'd had Holden Academy send to them.

I wonder, Liz thought, getting up and stretching before rinsing the cups and the toast plates, if Nora really wants to go to that party.

Nora did, and hummed cheerfully while they dressed, Liz in sleek black pants and a red velour top that set off her dark hair, and Nora in a bright blue and green dress that Liz had given her for Christmas, having discovered that Nora had long supressed a desire for colorful clothes. But when they drove up to the old farmhouse and Liz swung the car around to the yard in front of the barn, which was already packed with cars, Nora exclaimed, "Look at that! I still can't get used to seeing lights on."

"I know," Liz said. "It's weird, isn't it?"

280

"Its soul is gone," Nora said.

"Yes." Liz turned to look at her. "Are you sorry?"

"Only for the shattered illusion. Not" — she took Liz's hand — "not for anything else. Isn't it a rule that you can only get something wonderful by sacrificing something else?"

"Is it?"

"In literature it is, I think. In fantasy and fairytales, anyway. And" — Nora squeezed Liz's hand — "I got something wonderful. We've both had to sacrifice, after all. Let's get this over with."

"Right." Liz climbed out of the car and walked around to the front door beside Nora.

"Oh, good Lord." Nora pointed to a brass plaque beside the door.

"THE TILLOT HOMESTEAD," it read. "1782."

"Cheer up," Liz told her, forcing a smile. "That must mean he's not going to tear it down like he's going to tear down the cabin."

Georgia Foley, ostentatiously waving her left hand, from which shone a large diamond, greeted them at the door. "Oh, good!" she gushed, taking their coats. "You came after all. It is so good to see you, to see you *both*, I mean. It's special to have you here; Roy will be so pleased. He's been the teeniest bit worried," she confided *sotto voce*, leading them through what had once been Nora's dim front hall and was now brightly lit by a pewter reproduction of an eighteenth-century chandelier. "Roy and I are aware how difficult all this must have been for both of you and must still be. But we're so glad the lawyers were able to put the finishing touches on that really *stupendous* financial deal. Well, here we are! Look, everyone, here are Nora and Liz! Isn't it wonderful that they could come and celebrate with us?"

Several people in the crowd that filled the parlor ("My least favorite room, anyway," Nora whispered to Liz) looked up and one of them, Louise Brice, looking regal in a long green velvet skirt and cream-colored blouse, came forward, ignoring Liz but seizing Nora in a quick hug and kissing the air beside her cheek. "Nora, dear," she said, releasing her and looking keenly into her eyes. "Do you mind this very much?"

"No," Nora said politely. "Not very much. It's just a little odd, that's all. You know. The lights, especially."

"Come," said Georgia, linking her arm companionably through Nora's and hugging it against her body. "Come see the kitchen. We've got such wonderful new appliances, and Roy's decorator has been so clever at keeping the old-fashioned motif; you'll love it. Wait'll you see . . ."

Before Liz could object or follow, Georgia had whisked Nora off and Roy had sidled up to her.

"So," he said, holding out his hand, "no hard feelings? Now that we've actually settled it at last?"

"Right." Liz forced herself to shake his hand. But really, she scolded herself, he helped more than hindered, in the end. "I guess we have."

"Georgia and I are so glad you and Nora were able to buy the property across the lake from your old camp. You need any help finding contractors, you just let us know. I hope," he added, leering a little and winking, "that you and Nora will be as happy as Georgia and I. You should be pretty safe from harmful rumors about that, anyway — you know, your rela-tionship — since you'll be teaching outside of Clarkston. Small towns really do operate in the Dark Ages."

"Oh, really?" Liz said dryly, looking him right in the eye before she turned sharply and headed for the refreshments. "How interesting. Snake," she muttered when she was out of earshot. She felt thankful all over again that she'd been honest with her new headmaster.

"That Liz Hardy," Louise Brice said over the top of her champagne glass to Helen Whipple, "I don't care what anyone says, I think it's a terrible shame. It's just not right, not

282

normal, the two of them living together like a pair of old maids. I don't care about Miss Hardy, but a nice young girl like Nora . . ."

"She's not so young any more, Louise," said Helen, "and she's no fool either. If she wants to live with Liz, and she obviously does, why shouldn't she? It's high time Nora found some happiness, and I for one don't care how."

"Well, of course, no one wants more than I for Nora to be happy," Louise huffed, fingering the gold pendant she wore around her neck. "But I still think Liz Hardy's the kind of friend who'll be, well, possessive. If you take my meaning. For all we know she's a" — Louise dropped her voice — "you know. A lesbian."

"Oh, honestly, Louise!" Helen said irritably. "Nora's quite old enough to take care of herself. And last I heard, lesbians are people, too. If Liz even is one. Either way it's none of our business and I for one . . ." She stopped when Charles Hastings, his round face looking a little flushed above his clerical collar, came up to them.

"Hello, ladies," he said heartily. "Wonderful party, isn't it? And Roy and Georgia have certainly done a fine job with the house. Now let's hope they do as well at developing the land. When's the ground breaking for the first new house? Anyone know?"

"Early spring, I heard," said Helen Whipple, welcoming the change of subject, pleased with herself, too, for she had been in a position weeks ago to figure out at last what Roy and Georgia were up to — not that she entirely approved, although it would, she supposed, be good for the town to widen the tax base. And of course a growing population would keep the post office open; the Postal Service had already begun to hint that they might close it down. But that would be unlikely now, with two new housing developments, the one here and the other out at Yellowfin Lake, expanding the town. "Roy Stark's already set up a post office box for that corporation he and Georgia formed, and I think they're going to start

283

clearing the land right away. Is that right, Roy?" she asked, turning as Roy joined them.

"That's right, folks." Roy put one arm briefly around Helen and the other around Louise. "We're going to start clearing some of the woods here at Tillot Farm Estates, and we'll continue as long as weather permits, but we're going to wait till spring for Piney Haven."

"You'll be leaving some trees there, surely?" said Marie Hastings, resplendent in scarlet chiffon and her long-dead mother's garnet earrings.

"Oh, yes, absolutely. Here, too, but more at Piney Haven. That'll be the resort, after all. Boat house, tennis courts, restaurant, beach, small tourist cabins among the trees, but you town folks'll be able to use it by day, too. I expect all of you to come to sun yourselves and relax as soon as we open. Target date," Roy added, beckoning to a waitress bearing a tray of full champagne flutes, "is a year from July. Right, honey?" he added as Georgia appeared and snuggled under his arm.

"Right, darling," she said.

"And when," asked Helen, with a hint of sarcasm in her voice, "is the happy day for you two?"

"This coming June," Roy said, beaming, "isn't it, Reverend?"

"Yes, indeed." Charles nodded to Dr. and Mrs. Cantor, who were passing in earnest conversation with Nora and Liz.

"Congratulations, my dear," Dr. Cantor was saying, his thin, solemn mouth almost smiling; he gently held Nora's hands. "I know everyone has been saying how hard all this must be, but I imagine you're glad to put it all behind you, for this wasn't a happy place for you, especially toward the end. And you're doing a service to the town. You, too, Miss Hardy. "

"Liz, please," Liz murmured, wondering if she dared take Nora's arm in public.

"Yes," he said gravely; "thank you, *Liz* — a service to the town, broadening the tax base, bringing in much-needed money."

"It's sad about the land, though," Nora said. "I'm sorry to see that go. Especially Liz's. But it was the only solution to Father's nursing home bills."

"I can see why you sold the farm, Nora," said Mrs. Cantor, a small, capable-looking woman, surprisingly cheerful, Liz thought, in comparison to her husband. "But" — she turned to Liz — "why the old cabin? If I'm not prying . . ."

You are a little, Liz thought, amused. Aloud, smoothly, she said, "Too many memories. At first we wanted to keep it, my brother and I, but in the end it was too hard for both of us."

And that had turned out to be true, Liz thought, for when Jeff and Susan and Gus had visited, and she and Jeff had sat for most of one night down by the dock, Jeff had said, "I can't do it; it's like forcing me back into the past to be here," and Liz had realized then that she felt the same way after all, and that she wanted to move forward into her new life with Nora and toward the new, more honest self she'd found with her.

"Mmm," Mrs. Cantor was saying. "Yes, I can see that. Why I remember," she said with a little silvery laugh, "a few years after my father died . . ."

Predictions, thought Liz much later that night, shivering with Nora on the land across from Piney Haven that they'd bought jointly and where they planned to build their house; I'm so bad at them! But perhaps this will work; I think at least we'll try to be careful. Careful, honest, brave, trusting — not remote, not guarded . . .

A new life, thought Nora, standing as close to Liz as she could, is such a thing really possible? She thought of the lines she'd written soon after her mother's death: "*a new person, whole but forged from fragments.*" Can I really do that, emerge from my solitude enough to be with Liz closely and still be me? Can we both heal enough to be together, and help each other go on healing?

"I promise," Liz whispered softly into Nora's hair as if they'd both spoken out loud, "to try."

"So do I," Nora answered, kissing her. "So do I."

About the Author

Nancy Garden is the author of around 30 books for children and teens, a number of which feature gay and lesbian characters and issues. Her young adult novel, *Good Moon Rising*, was a Lambda Book Award winner and her highly acclaimed *Annie on My Mind*, burned, banned, and tried in Kansas, is listed by the American Library Association as one of the 100 Best of the Best Books for Young Adults.

A former editor and pre-Stonewall activist, in addition to working on her own books, Nancy today teaches writing and speaks around the country to librarians, teachers, and lay people against censorship and in support of GLBT youth. She and her partner of 33 years divide their time between Massachusetts and Maine.

Publications from
BELLA BOOKS, INC.
The best in contemporary lesbian fiction

P.O. Box 10543, Tallahassee, FL 32302
Phone: 800-729-4992
www.bellabooks.com

SUBSTITUTE FOR LOVE by Karin Kallmaker. One look and a deep kiss... Holly is hopelessly in lust. Can there be anything more?   ISBN 1-931513-62-7 $12.95

MAKING UP FOR LOST TIME by Karin Kallmaker. 240 pp. When three love-starved lesbians decide to make up for lost time, the recipe is romance. ISBN 1-931513-61-9 $12.95

NEVER SAY NEVER by Linda Hill. 224 pp. A classic love story... where rules aren't the only things broken.   ISBN 1-931513-67-8 $12.95

PAINTED MOON by Karin Kallmaker. 214 pp. A snowbound weekend in a cabin brings Jackie and Leah together... or does it tear them apart?   ISBN 1-931513-53-8 $12.95

THE WAY LIFE SHOULD BE by Diana Tremain Braund. 173 pp. With which woman will Jennifer find the true meaning of love?   ISBN 1-931513-66-X $12.95

GULF BREEZE by Gerri Hill. Could Carly really be the woman Pat has always been searching for?   ISBN 1-931513-97-X $12.95

THE TOMSTOWN INCIDENT by Penny Hayes. 184 pp. Caught between two worlds, Eloise must make a decision that will change her life forever. ISBN 1-931513-56-2 $12.95

BACK TO BASICS: A BUTCH/FEMME EROTIC JOURNEY edited by Therese Szymanski—from Bella After Dark. 324 pp.   ISBN 1-931513-35-X $12.95

SURVIVAL OF LOVE by Frankie J. Jones. 236 pp. What will Jody do when she falls in love with her best friend's daughter?   ISBN 1-931513-55-4 $12.95

DEATH BY DEATH by Claire McNab. 167 pp. 5th Denise Cleever Thriller.
      ISBN 1-931513-34-1 $12.95

CAUGHT IN THE NET by Jessica Thomas. 188 pp. A wickedly observant story of mystery, danger, and love in Provincetown.   ISBN 1-931513-54-6 $12.95

DREAMS FOUND by Lyn Denison. Australian Riley embarks on a journey to meet her birth mother . . . and gains not just a family, but the love of her life.   ISBN 1-931513-58-9 $12.95

A MOMENT'S INDISCRETION by Peggy J. Herring. 154 pp. Jackie is torn between her better judgment and the overwhelming attraction she feels for Valerie.
      ISBN 1-931513-59-7 $12.95

IN EVERY PORT by Karin Kallmaker. 224 pp. Jessica's sexy, adventuresome travels.
ISBN 1-931513-36-8 $12.95

TOUCHWOOD by Karin Kallmaker. 240 pp. Loving May/December romance.
ISBN 1-931513-37-6 $12.95

WATERMARK by Karin Kallmaker. 248 pp. One burning question . . . how to lead her back to love? ISBN 1-931513-38-4 $12.95

EMBRACE IN MOTION by Karin Kallmaker. 240 pp. A whirlwind love affair.
ISBN 1-931513-39-2 $12.95

ONE DEGREE OF SEPARATION by Karin Kallmaker. 232 pp. Can an Iowa City librarian find love and passion when a California girl surfs into the close-knit dyke capital of the Midwest? ISBN 1-931513-30-9 $12.95

CRY HAVOC A Detective Franco Mystery by Baxter Clare. 240 pp. A dead hustler with a headless rooster in his lap sends Lt. L.A. Franco headfirst against Mother Love.
ISBN 1-931513931-7 $12.95

DISTANT THUNDER by Peggy J. Herring. 294 pp. Bankrobbing drifter Cordy awakens strange new feelings in Leo in this romantic tale set in the Old West.
ISBN 1-931513-28-7 $12.95

COP OUT by Claire McNab. 216 pp. 4th Detective Inspector Carol Ashton Mystery. ISBN 1-931513-29-5 $12.95

BLOOD LINK by Claire McNab. 159 pp. 15th Detective Inspector Carol Ashton Mystery. Is Carol unwittingly playing into a deadly plan? ISBN 1-931513-27-9 $12.95

TALK OF THE TOWN by Saxon Bennett. 239 pp. With enough beer, barbecue and B.S., anything is possible! ISBN 1-931513-18-X $12.95

MAYBE NEXT TIME by Karin Kallmaker. 256 pp. Sabrina Starling has it all: fame, money, women—and pain. Nothing hurts like the one that got away. ISBN 1-931513-26-0 $12.95

WHEN GOOD GIRLS GO BAD: A Motor City Thriller by Therese Szymanski. 230 pp. Brett, Randi, and Allie join forces to stop a serial killer. ISBN 1-931513-11-2 $12.95

A DAY TOO LONG: A Helen Black Mystery by Pat Welch. 328 pp. This time Helen's fate is in her own hands. ISBN 1-931513-22-8 $12.95

THE RED LINE OF YARMALD by Diana Rivers. 256 pp. The Hadra's only hope lies in a magical red line . . . climactic sequel to *Clouds of War*. ISBN 1-931513-23-6 $12.95

OUTSIDE THE FLOCK by Jackie Calhoun. 224 pp. Jo embraces her new love and life.
ISBN 1-931513-13-9 $12.95

LEGACY OF LOVE by Marianne K. Martin. 224 pp. Read the whole Sage Bristo story.
ISBN 1-931513-15-5 $12.95

STREET RULES: A Detective Franco Mystery by Baxter Clare. 304 pp. Gritty, fast-paced mystery with compelling Detective L.A. Franco ISBN 1-931513-14-7 $12.95

RECOGNITION FACTOR: 4th Denise Cleever Thriller by Claire McNab. 176 pp. Denise Cleever tracks a notorious terrorist to America. ISBN 1-931513-24-4 $12.95

NORA AND LIZ by Nancy Garden. 296 pp. Lesbian romance by the author of *Annie on My Mind*. ISBN 1931513-20-1 $12.95

MIDAS TOUCH by Frankie J. Jones. 208 pp. Sandra had everything but love.
ISBN 1-931513-21-X $12.95

BEYOND ALL REASON by Peggy J. Herring. 240 pp. A romance hotter than Texas.
ISBN 1-9513-25-2 $12.95

ACCIDENTAL MURDER: 14th Detective Inspector Carol Ashton Mystery by Claire McNab. 208 pp. Carol Ashton tracks an elusive killer.
ISBN 1-931513-16-3 $12.95

SEEDS OF FIRE: Tunnel of Light Trilogy, Book 2 by Karin Kallmaker writing as Laura Adams. 274 pp. Intriguing sequel to *Sleight of Hand*.
ISBN 1-931513-19-8 $12.95

DRIFTING AT THE BOTTOM OF THE WORLD by Auden Bailey. 288 pp. Beautifully written first novel set in Antarctica.
ISBN 1-931513-17-1 $12.95

CLOUDS OF WAR by Diana Rivers. 288 pp. Women unite to defend Zelindar!
ISBN 1-931513-12-0 $12.95

DEATHS OF JOCASTA: 2nd Micky Knight Mystery by J.M. Redmann. 408 pp. Sexy and intriguing Lambda Literary Award-nominated mystery.
ISBN 1-931513-10-4 $12.95

LOVE IN THE BALANCE by Marianne K. Martin. 256 pp. The classic lesbian love story, back in print!
ISBN 1-931513-08-2 $12.95

THE COMFORT OF STRANGERS by Peggy J. Herring. 272 pp. Lela's work was her passion . . . until now.
ISBN 1-931513-09-0 $12.95

CHICKEN by Paula Martinac. 208 pp. Lynn finds that the only thing harder than being in a lesbian relationship is ending one.
ISBN 1-931513-07-4 $11.95

TAMARACK CREEK by Jackie Calhoun. 208 pp. An intriguing story of love and danger.
ISBN 1-931513-06-6 $11.95

DEATH BY THE RIVERSIDE: 1st Micky Knight Mystery by J.M. Redmann. 320 pp. Finally back in print, the book that launched the Lambda Literary Award–winning Micky Knight mystery series.
ISBN 1-931513-05-8 $11.95

EIGHTH DAY: A Cassidy James Mystery by Kate Calloway. 272 pp. In the eighth install-ment of the Cassidy James mystery series, Cassidy goes undercover at a camp for troubled teens.
ISBN 1-931513-04-X $11.95

MIRRORS by Marianne K. Martin. 208 pp. Jean Carson and Shayna Bradley fight for a future together.
ISBN 1-931513-02-3 $11.95

THE ULTIMATE EXIT STRATEGY: A Virginia Kelly Mystery by Nikki Baker. 240 pp. The long-awaited return of the wickedly observant Virginia Kelly.
ISBN 1-931513-03-1 $11.95

FOREVER AND THE NIGHT by Laura DeHart Young. 224 pp. Desire and passion ignite the frozen Arctic in this exciting sequel to the classic romantic adventure *Love on the Line*.
ISBN 0-931513-00-7 $11.95

WINGED ISIS by Jean Stewart. 240 pp. The long-awaited sequel to *Warriors of Isis* and the fourth in the exciting Isis series.
ISBN 1-931513-01-5 $11.95

ROOM FOR LOVE by Frankie J. Jones. 192 pp. Jo and Beth must overcome the past in order to have a future together.
ISBN 0-9677753-9-6 $11.95